TO KILL A LAWYER

LANCE MCMILLIAN

TO KILL A LAWYER

To My Son James—The Best Buddy
A Guy Could Ever Have

I have a secret passion for mercy.
But justice is what keeps happening to people.

—Lew Archer, *The Goodbye Look*

1

The clock reads three minutes before midnight. I study it with fervent concentration, wondering whether I want it to slow down or speed up. Clocks like this one—classic-style with the long hand, the short hand, twelve numbers in a circle, the works—were a fixture in the school days of my youth. Back then, I was of one mind, wishing time to hurry forward, for the final bell to sound, for the rest of my life to become mine and mine alone. Now I'm not so sure.

Tick. Tick. Tick. Each second chimes in persistent rhythm. The noise clangs a discordant note in the uneasy silence of the small room. The unhappy strangers—two dozen by my count—nurse their own thoughts. Tissues dab at quiet tears on a few of the faces. An empty gurney stares at us through a one-way window. One minute before midnight.

Danny Davis raped and killed Olivia Montez in an abandoned southeast Atlanta tenement nearly a decade ago. I prosecuted Davis for the crime. Blood, semen, and Olivia's DNA under Danny's fingernails made the case a cinch. When I asked for the death penalty, the jury readily obliged. Tonight, the bill comes due.

Executions always happen shortly after midnight—reflecting the strong impetus to get the deed done on the scheduled date before the courts change their minds. Justice delayed is justice denied. Or something like that.

I didn't eat much dinner. Watching a man die doesn't do much for the appetite. No law says I have to be here, but a sense of moral duty compels me to attend all the same. I went before the good citizens of Fulton County and asked them to take the life of this man. The least I can do is see the thing through. For years, explaining my compulsive need to attend the executions of men I prosecuted proved a challenge.

Then I watched the first episode of *Game of Thrones* in some random hotel somewhere and found the missing wisdom in the words of Ned Stark: "The man who passes the sentence should swing the sword. If you would take a man's life, you owe it to him to look into his eyes and hear his final words. And if you cannot bear to do that, then perhaps the man does not deserve to die."

Exactly. The death penalty is final. If I'm going to wield it, I've got to be resolute enough to stomach what my actions have wrought.

The mother of the condemned man sits on the far side of the room, close to the glass partition. Her sobs are muted but loud enough in the quiet interval between the beats of the clock. Sympathetic family members form a human shield to separate her from the hostile forces sharing the same space—me mostly. Like the other two executions I've attended, harsh glares of accusation land on me from the family about to lose one of their number. I don't take the acrimony personally. I did lead the charge to kill a mother's son.

I sit on the back row next to Julia Montez—mom of the deceased. She doesn't hold a tissue, and her face is free of tears. But burning anger bubbles just below the surface. A decade later, the pain of losing Olivia, only nineteen at the time, still rubs like a grater on her skin. I doubt a dead Danny Davis will bring Julia much closure, but a damaged heart hunts for solace wherever it might be found. Now after midnight, the room retains its eerie quiet. Cell phones aren't allowed in here, and the forced inactivity—so foreign to the modern age where a handheld distraction is always within reach—contributes to the feeling of agitation in the air.

The door to the execution chamber opens. A shackled Danny shuffles to his death bed—the guards remaining close to him, because that's what guards do, even when a man has nowhere else to run. The formerly-muted sobs on the other side of the room now graduate into wails. The reaction on my side is more subdued. I take a peek at Julia next to me. The lines on her face tighten as she sees the face of Olivia's killer in the flesh for the first time in years. As for me, I just feel sick.

My taste for the death penalty waned about a year ago when I prosecuted the wrong man for murder and lost faith in myself as an instrument of justice. In the aftermath, I fled to the woods for some alone time—a lifetime's worth being the plan. Except I ended up getting married instead. But before my new wife came along, I used the downtime to do some reading, including Neil Gaiman's *American Gods*. As the hitchhiking college student Samantha Black Crow explains to the protagonist Shadow, "I believe … that while all human life is sacred there's nothing wrong with the death penalty if you can trust the legal system implicitly, and that no one but a moron would ever trust the legal system."

For the longest time, I was that moron—at least when it came to trusting my own role in the deployment of public retribution. Now I have a more modest view of my abilities. I returned to playing the justice game but have no more room for the death penalty in my heart. A doubting Thomas makes a poor executioner.

* * *

Danny Davis looks small through the glass partition. I remember him as appearing fierce in court—defiant and contemptuous to the bitter end. But strapped onto the gurney with bounded arms stretched out almost like Jesus on the Cross, the docile prisoner shows no reaction to the technicians inspecting his body for the appropriate vein in which to inject the poison.

A couple of minutes later, the needle that will deliver a fatal dose of pentobarbital rests securely in the inmate's arm. Before the magic button is pushed, the warden allows the condemned man to speak some last words. The message is brief.

"I love you, Mama."

More tear-filled wails reverberate within the observation room. Another glimpse at Julia Montez and I see the tightest of tight smiles on her face. Revenge is a helluva drug. I return my attention to the prisoner and question whether I should attend these things in the future. Ned Stark be damned.

Six minutes and thirty-nine seconds later, Danny Davis departs from the land of the living.

* * *

Back in the car, my cell phone rings before I can even shut the door. The caller ID confirms my hunch—Scott Moore, my best friend, one of the best detectives in the state. He doesn't waste time on any pleasantries.

"Davis dead?"

"Yeah."

"Good. He was a nasty piece of work."

Scott has no compunction about the death penalty, especially for Danny Davis. While working homicide with the Atlanta Police Department, Scott handled the Montez case from the start, including experiencing in living color the sights and smells of the grisly murder scene. The knife wounds across Olivia's body numbered in the dozens, including all over her face. I've seen more than my fair share of crime scene photos, and these were among the hardest to digest. Perfect for convincing the jury that the punishment for the horrible act should be death.

He asks, "Did Davis whimper at the end? Please tell me he suffered."

"Not really. Honestly felt like he was dead already."

"Too bad. What about Julia? How did she take it?"

"She might've been smiling."

"Well, she's earned the right. Anyway, not why I called. The Governor has been trying to reach you. Someone was killed tonight in Tuxedo Park. We have the case. First on the scene."

"How on earth do we have the case already?"

"The owner of the house where the murder occurred called the Governor instead of 911. I take it they are neighbors. I'm heading over now."

"If it's in Tuxedo Park, it's not a house. More like a mansion. Who's the victim?"

"Some lawyer named Jim Walker. Know him?"

"Don't think so."

"You missed your chance. The whole gang is on the way to the scene. You coming up?"

"A leader's got to lead."

4

A lawyer by trade, I now head an elite investigative unit with wide-ranging authority to investigate and prosecute crime all over the state of Georgia. Our team has an official name, but no one uses it. The local press quickly dubbed us the Atlanta Murder Squad, and that label stuck. After my last trial—the one that soured me on the death penalty—I walked away from chasing criminals forever. But events—and a hard push from the Governor—left my best laid plans in tatters. So having watched an execution in the dead of night in the middle of Nowheresville, Georgia, I now head north to Atlanta an hour away to investigate yet another killing in an ever-growing ledger. With clear eyes on the road, I flip on the sirens to make time, having no doubt about the unbending purpose that guides me.

Murder is my business.

2

There's rich, and then there's Tuxedo Park rich. The opulent world of *The Great Gatsby* comes to mind, and it's no coincidence that many of the grand estates that occupy the neighborhood were built during the excesses of the Roaring Twenties.

The GPS leads me to double gates made of iron—or maybe even silver. A police officer guards the entrance and blocks the way in case I doubt him. After I stop, he walks around to my window and snaps, "Who are you?"

"Chance Meridian."

The tough demeanor turns more respectful, but he does ask for proof of my claim. I flash the right credentials and get waved through. The meandering driveway belongs more to a country manor than a residence in the heart of a metropolis, but the normal rules don't apply to Tuxedo Park. I finally reach the house and spy a beehive of emergency lights.

I exit the car and shiver as the last gasps of winter whip around me. The cold jolts me awake at least. Sophie Applewhite—one of the detectives on my team—stands out front talking to a group of uniformed officers—all male—from the Atlanta Police Department. Sophie is a workout freak and has the figure to prove it, evident even when she's dressed for the weather. The men are practically drooling as she sends them on their way. I walk over to take the temperature of things. Sophie gives me a quick status update.

"I'm sending the uniforms out to search the grounds. Too cold and dry for footprints, but I told them to be careful all the same. The property is ten acres, so it'll probably take a while. No indication that the killer sneaked in from the outside, but we need to check it out to make sure. Scott thinks the murderer is still in the house. Talk to him yet?"

"Only briefly. Where did the murder happen?"

"The owner proudly calls it the 'Billiard Room.' You can guess why. The weapon of choice was a knife. We don't know the identity of the killer yet, but my money is on Colonel Mustard or Miss Scarlet."

I smile to be nice. Sophie is a big joker, but not all her comedic material lands. And at this hour of this particular night, I'm not in a laughing kind of mood. I say, "No, seriously. Where did the murder take place?"

"Seriously—in the Billiard Room. Take a right at the top of the grand staircase. You can't miss it. And the victim has a knife sticking out of his back."

I pause for a second to process the information before responding, "There's not really a Colonel Mustard or Miss Scarlet, is there?"

"No, but our cast of suspects is even more interesting. Wait until you see the butler."

With that weird prologue piquing my interest at least, I head to the house. The front door is wide open, and I enter a majestic foyer that gives me flashbacks to a long ago visit to the Palace of Versailles—spacious, opulent, expensive stuff adorning the walls. Despite knowing about Tuxedo Park most of my life, I realize I've never actually set foot in one of the homes until this moment, except for the Governor's Mansion—which doesn't really count and is nowhere near this nice. Heading up the curving staircase, I marvel at how the richest of the rich live.

The Billiard Room is exactly where Sophie said it would be, and Scott is talking to an evidence tech when I arrive at the crime scene. Other techs dust for prints and take photographs. The body of the victim occupies a prominent place in the room, splayed out flat on the longest pool table I've ever seen—almost twice the normal size by my reckoning.

Sophie was right about the knife in the back, too. A polished dagger of bright steel juts out from the dead man. An inscription—German from the look of it—decorates the blade, but the translation eludes me, my high school and college German being rusted beyond repair. The dagger's jet-black handle contains an emblem of some sort. I peer closer and see a Nazi-style eagle symbol, complete with its own swastika. What in the hell? The gargantuan pool table is another source of curiosity. Almost two dozen balls appear on the table, all without numbers, and the vast majority of them are the color red. The left hand of the deceased rests flat against the green felt. The wrist sports a watch—a Rolex. I inspect it hoping that the time stopped at the precise moment of death, just like in the movies.

Scott finishes with the tech and comes over. He asks, "See something interesting?"

"I was thinking that maybe the watch broke and would fix the time of death for us, but no such luck."

"The watch took a licking and kept on ticking."

"You're not funny, you know. What kind of pool table is this anyway?"

"Not pool. Snooker. And I am funny."

"What the hell is snooker?"

"No idea. Pool for rich guys with too much money, I guess. Bigger is better, right?"

I have my doubts. He brings me up to speed.

"Victim is Jim Walker, a partner at the firm of Cain & Cunningham. Fifty-two years of age. He was a guest tonight at a party hosted by Gustave Root—who apparently is a friend of the Governor's. Ten other people were in the mansion at the time, including über-famous actors Mark Romo and Jessica Allen. Even a hermit like you would've heard about them. They're all downstairs waiting for us to question them. You see the knife for yourself. No prints of which to speak. And, the cherry on top, the door to this room was bolted from the inside, meaning the only way for the murderer to escape after jamming the dagger in the victim was to leap from a twenty-foot balcony."

I make a face. Scott smiles in sympathy at my skepticism and concludes, "This is going to be a fun one. And I haven't even mentioned the butler."

"Sophie made a similar comment. What's the deal?"

"Some things you just have to see for yourself."

Moving to the other side of the snooker table, I bend down to get a better look at the dead man's face and realize that the night is going to be full of surprises. Scott picks up on my reaction and asks, "What?"

"I do know this guy."

"Yeah?"

"A long time ago when I was a baby lawyer, some city councilman was driving like a bat out of hell and killed a homeless guy who got in the way. I brought a manslaughter charge. Our friend here came to talk to me about the case—not as the actual defense counsel, but rather in some other undefined role—hoping to get me to be a little less aggressive."

"I guess he didn't know your reputation."

"Guess not. He didn't outright try to bribe me, but he dipped his toe in the water. I wasn't in the mood to be conciliatory and sent him on his way. He then went to my higher ups and found more fertile ground. I was ordered to plead the case down to a misdemeanor."

"Shocking."

And now Jim Walker lies dead on an ocean of green felt with a dagger sticking out of his back. I think again of Danny Davis being slowly poisoned to death and figure he had the better ending.

I check out the rest of the room. Various oddities decorate the walls—including a huge battle axe sharp enough to cut you simply by looking at it. A large television sits high on a fireplace mantle.

We walk out to a small, narrow Juliet balcony. Looking down, I see plenty of air between me and the ground. I also see a ladder leaning on the balcony's rails. A large swimming pool close to the back of the mansion completes the tableau.

I ask, "What's the deal with the ladder?"

"The party guests used it to climb up when Walker didn't answer their knocks, and they couldn't get the door to the room unlocked. So they got the ladder out of the garage and made their way up. It wasn't here when the murderer made his escape."

"By jumping off this balcony?"

"I share your incredulity."

"You think someone at the party killed him?"

"Stands to reason. Some stranger didn't just waltz in, commit a murder, and waltz back out. Has inside job written all over it."

"All the guests still here?"

"Yep. I was waiting for you before tackling them."

We study the scene for a few more moments, and I grow more doubtful about the balcony as an escape route by the second. My mind already starts working on a solution to the problem of the locked door. But first things first. It's time to interrogate the suspects.

Scott asks, "Ready to catch us a murderer?"

3

Scott picks a room downstairs—a study if judging by appearances—as the place to conduct the questioning. Like everything else about the house, the whole vibe screams money. Books and artwork line the walls, and antiquities apparently of great worth sit around like loose candy. The whole mansion could pass as a museum—except for the corpse decorating the snooker table one floor above us.

I ask, "Where are Marlon and J.D.?"

"Babysitting the suspects in the dining room."

Marlon Freeman and J.D. Hendrix are my other two detectives. Marlon is the team's grandfatherly sage of wisdom—one of the first African-Americans to make detective in the Atlanta Police Department and one of the best cops anywhere. His actual age is a closely-guarded secret. I could pull his personnel records to find the answer but don't want to dampen the air of mystery. A secret poll of the murder squad would confirm that Marlon is everyone's favorite person in the unit.

J.D. is young, fresh off a stint as a patrol officer. He was a witness in my last murder trial and took direction so well that I decided to work with him again. He's not much of a detective yet, but his instincts are sharp. His pale baby face is a marked contrast to Marlon's distinguished wrinkles.

I say, "Let's talk to Marlon before we start the questioning, see what he has learned just by sitting around them. With some luck, maybe he's solved the murder already."

"Wishful thinking. You just want to go home and sleep."

The thought does have some appeal.

* * *

Marlon bounces in like a spring chicken. Despite his age, he never appears tired—always being the first person into work and the last one to leave. Before joining the murder squad, his career was reduced to chasing truants around the county for the Board of Education. The Atlanta Police Department jettisoned him long ago for not playing nice with others—a euphemism for saying that he was an uppity black man who didn't know his place. Their loss is our gain.

I ask him, "Who did it?"

He strokes his chin, and for a moment, I think he might just tell me. But instead Marlon only offers a grim smile and a short shake of the head before answering.

"Quite the crew in there. Not a lot of talking going on. I don't know if that's because they're too tired, too stunned, or too smart. Answer probably depends on the person. But most of them are so tightly-wound at the moment that the slightest touch will make them pop like a balloon. I collected all their names and did a little probing. Here's a list for you. I think you should talk to them in this order, too."

He hands over a piece of paper that reads:

- Gustave Root—Host & Film Mogul

- Mark Romo—Actor

- Erica Cain—Big-Firm Lawyer

- Vivian Root—Gustave's Wife

- Celeste Wood—Painter, Jim Walker's Date

- Jessica Allen—Actress

- Leo Ivanov—Math Professor & Chess Grandmaster

- Oliver Twist—Magician

- Mr. Beale—Gustave's Servant

- Aaron Cain—Big-Firm Lawyer

I process the information. An eclectic assortment to be sure, but one name captures my attention above all the others. I ask Marlon about it.

"Oliver Twist? A magician? Really?"

"Sure. Never heard of him? He's the guy that made Stone Mountain disappear a few years ago."

A vague memory stored somewhere deep in my brain hints that I may have heard about the Stone Mountain stunt once upon a time. Or maybe not. With sleep looking unlikely before daybreak, I could use an injection of coffee to fire up my synapses.

Scott asks, "Why this order?"

"Gustave Root first because he's going to have the most background about the party, the layout of the house, the murder weapon, all of it. Mark Romo next—he's already three sheets to the wind, and you need to catch him while he's still conscious. Erica Cain was working on a laptop near the door to the Billiard Room. Maybe she saw something—I didn't ask her with everyone else in the room. Erica also keeps looking at Vivian Root in a funny way. Vivian next, presuming you get something to go on from Erica. Celeste Wood was Walker's date for the evening but doesn't act like she's experiencing much grief. She also was swimming out back in the heated pool while Walker was dead upstairs. If the murderer escaped from the balcony, she had to see him. Jessica Allen hasn't revealed anything interesting yet, but you have to talk with her sometime. Leo Ivanov keeps to himself, but he listens intently to every syllable uttered in that room. Oliver Twist was the first person up the ladder and into the Billiard Room. He discovered Walker dead. By all rights, he should be higher on the interview list. But he is a pompous ass and making him wait is liable to get under his skin. An agitated witness is a more talkative witness. And Mr. Beale, well—on him, I got nothing. I'm not even sure that he talks."

I jot notes besides each person on the sheet of paper. Noticing that Marlon neglected to mention the last name on the list, I ask, "What about Aaron Cain? Why is he last?"

"Wanted to talk with you about that. He's acting really out of it, having trouble staying awake with a glazed expression on his face. I've seen that look before. My guess is that he was drugged—maybe a roofie."

"The date rape drug?"

The question is rhetorical, and the seeds of an impending headache tiptoe behind my eye sockets. I lust again for some coffee. Marlon suggests having the paramedics on scene take a look at Aaron Cain. We agree.

I say to him, "You should sit in with us during the questioning. We could use your insight."

"Nah. You need me with the primates in the dining room to see what shakes out there. The tension figures to ratchet up a notch once you start calling people back one by one. Maybe their lips will loosen as each of them awaits their turn in the principal's office."

Makes sense. Before he leaves, Marlon—also the team's technology guru—sets up a camera that will record each of the interviews. Whatever anyone says can and will be used against them in a court of law. With the scene set, I issue the first summons.

"Tell J.D. to bring us Gustave Root."

4

Scott and I wait in the study for Gustave Root to arrive. To pass the time, I inspect a painting of a mountain range—maybe the Alps—hanging on the wall.

"Like it?"

The owner of the booming voice stands in the doorway—a sheaf of turbulent gray hair adorning the top of his end. The tinge of a European accent lingers in the echo of the words. I return my gaze to the painting, shrug my shoulders, and answer.

"I'm not big into art, but it looks fine enough to me."

"It's a genuine Hitler."

The bizarre statement fails to register much sense in my caffeine-deprived brain. I respond, "A what?"

"A Hitler. He painted it."

"*The* Hitler?"

"Is there any other one?"

"Adolph?"

"Yes, he was an artist, you know."

I give the picture closer scrutiny this time around. Sure enough, at the right bottom corner, the signature of the artist proclaims, "A. Hitler 1912." Turning back around, I see the man with the crazy hair smiling at me with large white teeth. At the periphery of my vision, Scott stares at him with judgmental eyes. In a neutral voice, I inquire, "And you have no problem displaying it on your wall?"

"It's a conversation piece."

Abandoning any pretense of neutrality, Scott chimes in, "The conversation being whether you're a Nazi or not?"

Gustave laughs and confidently strides further into the room. His height is medium, his build thick but waning. I figure his age as probably around sixty-five. Already I don't like him—I mean, the man has an Adolph Hitler painting on his wall.

He continues, "How does a sensitive artist with a reasonable degree of talent go on to become one of the world's great mass murderers? The psychology is fascinating."

That's one way of looking at it, and I must confess that standing so close to the literal handiwork of a genocidal maniac produces feelings of some indescribable character within me—nothing that I want to converse about, though. I counter, "We agree on the interesting psychology. But I'm more intrigued by the psychology of the man who would proudly display a painting by Hitler for all the world to see."

"The expectations of polite society bore me. I like the painting and the story behind it. Isn't that enough?"

"And there's the psychology I'm talking about."

He scoffs. I instruct him to take a seat in the designated chair so we can begin the questioning. He scoffs at that, too.

"I prefer to stand. I've already been held like a hostage in my own dining room for a couple of hours. I need to move my limbs."

Scott answers, "Sit down. A man has been murdered in your home. You called the Governor instead of the police—the result being we got fast-tracked on the case. And we're going to do the job right, which means recording each of the witness interviews. So put your ass in that seat and play nice."

Scott is as tough a cop as they come, and Gustave just got a taste. Let's call that a teaching moment.

Judging by the look on his face, Root only likes authoritarianism when he isn't on the receiving end of it. He swivels his head toward me in search of an ally but finds nothing for the trouble. With the lesson hopefully learned, he shuffles over to the chair and plops down, wearing a scowl of petulance every step of the way.

I say, "My notes say that you're some kind of entertainment mogul. Is that correct?"

"Don't be dense. You know who I am."

Actually, I don't. My free time is consumed with repairing classic

16

cars and not much more. I haven't set foot in a movie theater in years, and all my favorite movies were filmed before I was born. The rest of the planet may have moved on to the 21st century, but I'm still living in the past.

I respond, "Humor me. I don't get out much. You make movies or something?"

"Yes, I make movies. I own the largest independent movie studio in the world. Director, producer, done it all. Look over there—you can see my three Oscars on that shelf."

He motions to another part of the study. My line of sight tracks the movement of his hand and takes in the golden statues—made more golden by the special bright light arranged to shine on them alone. The Oscars are taller than I thought they would be, and all three lined up in a row do convey a powerful impression. Not bad for a Nazi.

*　*　*

Gustave proceeds to tell us about tonight's party. His company—Eagle Studios—has reached a production deal with the Chinese government. The announcement in Beijing was set to take place at midnight our time. The purpose of the gathering was to watch the press conference from the comfort of Root's movie theater in the mansion's basement.

Scott takes over the questioning and asks, "How did you settle on the guest list?"

"Mark Romo and Jessica Allen are two of my biggest stars. Jim Walker, Aaron Cain, and Erica Cain are my lawyers from the law firm of Cain & Cunningham. Oliver Twist is the one of the first acts I want to take to the Chinese market. Leo Ivanov makes good company and is nice enough not to beat me too badly in chess. Celeste Wood came with Jim."

"Any of the non-lawyers know Jim Walker before tonight?"

"Sure, everyone. Jim has—or had, I guess—a genius for making problems disappear. And all the guests at the party had occasion to make use of his talents at one point or another."

Walker's success in making that Atlanta city councilman's manslaughter charge go away rekindles in my memory. I ask, "What type of law did Walker actually practice? Criminal defense? Cain & Cunningham is a white shoe firm. I didn't know they muddied themselves in that type of work."

"Ha! You can shake any tree in town and have a defense lawyer fall out. Jim's worth was much more valuable than that. He was a 'fixer' and could arrange it so that one's troubles would vanish as if they had never even existed in the first place—without the pesky involvement of courts and judges. Or the media. I never knew him to actually practice law as you conceive it. His gifts transcended the courtroom. Have you ever heard of the saying 'I've never met a bad Jim'?"

I shake my head. The phrase is a new one for me. Scott approaches the question from a different angle and quips, "What about Jim Jones? All those people drank the Kool-Aid and died in Guyana."

Root narrows his eyes and purses his lips in disapproval. I decide to play along and add: "Jim Bakker, too. Fake Christian who defrauded a lot of folks out of their life savings."

Back to Scott: "Jimmy Hoffa. Does he count? Being a 'Jimmy' and all. I'm unclear on the rules."

And me again: "Jim Crow—although you might like that one, given your appreciation for the Third Reich."

Being bullied in his own study doesn't agree with the witness. After already narrowing his eyes and pursing his lips, Gustave is reduced to gritting his teeth to express his displeasure with us. He's running out of body parts. Good. Going straight to the Governor instead of the police like a normal person suggests a level of vanity deserving of a good bonfire. But we still need Root to talk and prod him to continue.

"Jim was a charmer. Everyone gravitated to him—the good Jim thing. Clever, too. Knew how to push the right buttons to get people to do what he wanted. Tough-as-nails negotiator when required. Could always be counted on to get things done, a skill impossible to teach and sorely lacking in the modern age."

I observe, "And yet Jim is now upstairs with a knife sticking out of his back."

"Yes, a pity."

"Who killed him?"

"No idea. I have a hard time believing it was anyone at the party."

Gustave tries to convey the sincerity of this opinion, but no one in the room is convinced. That some unknown person would hop the fence, traverse the large property, enter the mansion, run upstairs, kill Walker, leap off the balcony, and escape back out of the grounds again—all without being seen—is a fairy tale of the first order. You might as well pin the blame on Santa Claus at that point. And Christmas was a couple of months ago. I follow up on a point Root referenced earlier.

"What kind of problems exactly did Walker fix in the past for the guests tonight?"

"That information is not mine to divulge. You should ask each guest individually."

"Spill it. A murder investigation is not a time to keep secrets."

"No, I'm going to hold my tongue on this one. If someone is less than forthcoming with you, then we can revisit the topic."

We accept the answer for the moment. After more questioning, details of the night start to emerge. Dinner—prepared and served by Mr. Beale all by himself, meaning no other staff was in the house—started at nine and lasted for about an hour. Everyone ate together in the dining room except for Root's wife, Vivian, who begged off on account of illness and remained in her bedroom. The party then moved to the study for drinks and dessert. Gustave announced to all that he needed to talk with Jim Walker alone in the Billiard Room but only after checking on Vivian. He instructed the other guests to tour the mansion at their leisure and otherwise make themselves feel at home. Everyone would reconvene in the movie theater at midnight to watch the press conference in China. The partygoers then broke off from each other to do their own things.

Scott asks, "What time did everyone disperse?"

"10:45. I remember the chiming of the clock as I was heading out of the room."

"And who went where?"

"Jim headed up the stairs toward the Billiard Room. Aaron headed that way, too. He wasn't feeling well and went to lie down in the bedroom right next to the Billiard Room. I took the elevator to the third floor to see about Vivian. As to the other people, I cannot say."

I draw the beginnings of a mental map in my head of each person's whereabouts at the time of the murder. Marlon's information puts Celeste Wood outside in the swimming pool and Erica Cain on the second-floor hallway near the Billiard Room. Gustave places Walker and Aaron Cain in the same vicinity as Erica, with himself and Vivian one floor above that. Everyone else—to be determined. Root picks up the story.

"After checking on Vivian, I took the back stairs down to the kitchen for a quick glass of milk. Mr. Beale was cleaning dishes, and Leo Ivanov was playing chess on his phone. I then climbed the grand staircase in the front foyer and found the Billiard Room locked. Jim didn't answer my knocks, so I tried the key in the knob. The door still wouldn't open, which meant it had to be latched from the deadbolt inside. I banged on the door harder. Mark Romo was nearby, and he tried helping me. Put his shoulder into the door even. Nothing. The noise drew a lot of attention by this point. I ordered Mr. Beale to get a ladder from the garage so we could try getting into the room from the balcony. Oliver Twist offered to climb the ladder. Mark volunteered, as well. I told Erica she should try to find Celeste because it appeared that something had happened to Jim."

He pauses, and I picture a chaotic scene as the partygoers reacted to what was happening. Remembering Aaron Cain in the bedroom next to the Billiard Room, I ask, "Did Aaron come out of his room in light of the racket y'all were making?"

"Not that I saw."

Gustave finishes the rest of it. He waited outside the door while Twist and Romo used the ladder to get to Walker. Romo shrieked in a panic before unlocking the deadbolt, heightening Root's impending sense of dread.

He explains, "Strange that the first thing I noticed upon entering the room was Jim's Rolex—the light hit the gold in a way that created this noticeable glare, and he clutched a red snooker ball in his watch hand. Only then did I process that he was lying prone with a dagger sticking out of his back."

Root shivers a little—the first inkling that he is actually disturbed that a murder took place under his roof earlier in the evening.

I ask, "Did you recognize the murder weapon?"

"Yes. It is part of my collection—the *SS-Ehrendolch*, a Nazi Honor Dagger, quite rare, commissioned by Heinrich Himmler himself. He ordered SS officers to deploy the dagger immediately against anyone found disrespecting the honor of the SS. The weapon is one of my finest pieces."

"I noticed an inscription on it."

"Yes, *Meine Ehre Heist Treue*. 'My Honor is Loyalty.'"

A hint of admiration twinkles in Root's dark eyes. More than any other person, Himmler was responsible for carrying out the horrors of the Holocaust. I shudder on the inside. Hitler's artwork is one thing. Giving Gustave the extreme benefit of the doubt, it's at least art. But pride in a Nazi torture tool suggests something even more sinister. The night keeps getting weirder and weirder.

I ask, "Where did you keep it?"

"In this room. Right over there."

He points to a shelf, and the absence of the dagger from its proper place is noticeable. Judging from the rest of the mansion, Root apparently is not one to leave shelf space empty. He adds, "And before you ask—no, I didn't see anyone hovering near that shelf tonight. Never noticed the dagger missing, either."

According to Gustave, everyone—except Vivian in her bedroom—was here in in the study just before Walker made his way upstairs to the Billiard Room.

21

Scott says, "You mentioned needing to talk to Walker alone. What about?"

"Ah, yes. The United States government has a cache of Adolph Hitler paintings under lock and key, just sitting there, doing nothing. Walker had a line on how I might acquire those valuable historical artifacts."

"Legally?"

"Almost certainly not. That's why we needed to talk in private."

Scott glances at me to see if I have anything else, and I shake my head. He asks a final question.

"For the record, did you kill Jim Walker?"

"Of course not. I want those Hitlers."

5

Gustave stands to make way for the next suspect. But before leaving, he says, "I must insist that you refrain from asking any questions of my wife or Mr. Beale. Vivian is not well, and Mr. Beale is a mute who has had unpleasant experiences with authority in the past. Neither of them had any involvement with Jim's untimely demise. Don't fight me on this. I'll call Governor McReynolds if I have to."

That's the best joke I've heard in the past week. I answer.

"You're out of favors with the Governor, and we're going to question everyone in the house at the time of the murder, which includes your wife and this Mr. Beale. Now leave so we can get back to work."

He smiles and rubs a hand through his wild hair before answering.

"I don't think you realize how much money I've donated to the Governor over the years."

"And I doubt you realize that Minton McReynolds was my father's best friend and has known me since the day of my birth. I'm like the son he never had. So, for future reference, don't count on him taking your side over mine on matters related to my investigation."

The smile is gone, replaced by a sneer worthy of a stormtrooper. But with no weapons nearby, Gustave only spins around and marches his way out of the study. As he nears the door, Scott orders, "Wait!"

Root half-turns in response to the command. Scott asks, "What kind of unpleasant experiences has Mr. Beale had with authority?"

Another rub of the hand through his hair and Gustave answers, "Because of his uniqueness, Mr. Beale experienced a great deal of harassment at school and from the police while growing up in Europe. When I found him, he was working for a cruel circus ringmaster who mocked and abused him for being different. I bought out his contract for the circus from that sadistic man, and Mr. Beale has worked for me ever since. But I fear that being pushed around by you will trigger many bad memories for him."

"What does he do for you?"

"Everything. Mr. Beale is a man of many talents."

* * *

Mark Romo stumbles into the study. Marlon told us that the famous actor was three sheets to the wind, but I count four. Despite my cultural illiteracy, I recognize his face. Romo has reached that level of stardom where people know him even without trying. He plays some manner of superhero in big blockbuster films—one without a cape, I think. He plops down into the chair.

Scott asks his first question, "Long night?"

"You're telling me, man."

The words are slurred, the eyes dazed. A fuzzy beard—absent when he's off playing superhero—covers more real estate than is advisable. As for clothing, the guess is that he's wearing designer jeans, but I wouldn't know. Up top, a dark sports coat covers a white t-shirt—a well-thought-out wardrobe meant to convey the opposite impression. I'm only a few years older than him but the age gap feels like centuries. Scott continues.

"Wanna tell me about it?"

"I climbed the ladder, and Jim was laying on the pool table with a knife in his back. He looked like a ghost. Oliver Twist had checked his pulse and said he was dead. I yelled and ran over to the door to get the hell out of there."

"You unlocked the door on the way out?"

"Sure, man, yeah. The door was locked. I tried earlier from the other side when Gustave was trying to get in. It wouldn't budge. Even banged my shoulder into it. After seeing Jim with a knife in his back, I unlocked the door and high-tailed it downstairs to the bar as fast as I could."

Romo's eyes droop a little. He looks the part of a man living off the fumes of an ever-dwindling adrenaline rush. I wonder about his ability to navigate the ladder in his inebriated condition and ask, "Were you drunk when you made your way up the ladder?"

"No way. But I started hitting it hard afterwards."

"Did you recognize the murder weapon?"

We study his eye movement with great interest to see if it drifts to the spot on the shelf where Gustave kept his Nazi honor dagger. But Romo's gaze remains in place, and he stares at me in confusion as if I asked him to solve a differential calculus equation. I don't even bother pressing for an answer and broach another topic instead.

"What were you doing right before you made your way to help Gustave with the door?"

"I was pacing around talking to my agent on the phone about a role in a new movie."

"Where were you pacing?"

"Everywhere. That's what I do, man. Pace. I walked from one end of the house to the other and back again. Then I went to the second floor. When I hung up the phone, I heard Gustave raising a racket."

"See anybody on your walkabout?"

"Nah, man. I was trying to focus on what my agent was saying."

Scott asks for his phone, and Romo turns it over without any fuss. The recent calls show a fifteen-minute phone conversation beginning at 10:49 p.m. that confirms the story—giving Romo an alibi of sorts. I switch gears.

"You and Jim were friends?"

"Friends? I don't know about that. He's one of my lawyers. Expensive, too."

"Yeah, we understand he helped you out of a spot of trouble. Why don't you tell us about it?"

The question gives him pause. I can almost see the wheels in his head grinding in a desperate search for sobriety—some part of him instinctually realizing that this topic is one he shouldn't touch while drunk.

"Tell you what, man?"

"Your side of the story."

"Well, I wasn't drunk, if that's what you're thinking. I was driving home and that kid was standing in the road, wearing all black. I didn't even know he was there. Thought I hit a deer or something. That's why I drove away. When I saw the news about the dead boy, I did the right thing and told Gustave. He got Jim and me together. Jim took care of everything from there and made sure that the family got their money. Cost me a fortune, but Jim kept my name out of it at least."

"From the police, too?"

"Hell yeah. You're not going to tell them, are you?"

"Not as far as you know."

"Good, thanks."

Scott gives me a look of incredulity at the stupidity on display. But Romo doesn't notice. His head bobbles up and down as he fights a losing battle to stay awake. Time to move on to another witness.

I say, "For the record, I have to ask. Did you kill Jim Walker?"

A glazed stoner expression greets the question, and several seconds lapse as he searches for the mental fluidity to compose an answer. At last, he responds, "What, man? No way."

We help Romo out of the chair and send him on his way back to the dining room—if he can make it that far without falling down.

Scott complains, "A million-dollar face and a ten-cent brain."

"Welcome to America."

6

Taylor Diamond—the murder squad's office administrator who keeps the rest of us in line—arrives with coffee and donuts from Krispy Kreme. I tell her, "You just solidified your spot as Employee of the Month."

She acknowledges the praise with a graceful curtsy. Taylor and I went to high school together in the same small town. I left for the big city years ago. She recently arrived fresh off a divorce. Once here, she quickly succumbed to Scott's roguish charm, and they've been dating ever since. But I don't hold that against her.

Scott comes over and stuffs a donut into his mouth. The warm smell dancing off the frosting tempts my stomach, but I'm still not ready to eat after witnessing Danny Davis being put to death. Taylor gushes, "Have you seen this place? It's like a castle. I didn't know people really live like this."

After she bounds off to give the rest of the team their allotment of sugar and caffeine, I note to Scott, "Taylor has expensive taste. You might need to take a second job."

He flashes me his middle finger and plows through another donut. J.D. brings the next suspect to us.

* * *

Erica Cain exudes fierceness. Even after the longest of nights, she looks fresh enough to argue a case before the United States Supreme Court. The dark blue pantsuit that drapes her body is all business—obviously expensive, a natural accessory for a partner at one of Atlanta's biggest law firms. Her blondish hair has stray strands of gray but not much. She is fit for her age, which I peg around fifty. I'd bet a hundred dollars that Erica keeps a treadmill in her office.

She enters the study with a brown leather lawyer's briefcase at her side, the strap settled comfortably on her shoulder. After we all sit down, part of me anticipates that she intends to whip out her laptop to take notes. But instead she just crosses her legs and flashes us a look that says, "Get on with it." Scott obliges.

"Why do you suspect Vivian Root killed Jim Walker?"

I smile on the inside. Mozart was born to make music, Scott to be a detective. No doubt he pegged Erica Cain as a cool customer just as I did when she walked into the room. So he decided to knock her off-balance at the start, without so much as a prelude. Based on Marlon's insight that Erica kept staring at Vivian in a funny way, Scott played a hunch. The strategy works. A flutter of uncertainty worries Erica's handsome face. She stumbles for a few seconds before settling on an answer.

"I don't know what you're talking about."

"Mrs. Cain, you're smart enough to understand the stakes. Now tell us what you know."

"I certainly don't know that Vivian killed Jim."

"But you have suspicions. Why?"

She chews on her bottom lip for a few seconds. Gustave Root must be worth a whole bunch of billable hours for the law firm of Cain & Cunningham. Hard to throw the wife of such a man under the bus. But lying to the authorities ain't a walk in the park, either. She stalls.

"I really don't know who put such an idea into your head."

"You were in the hallway just down from the Billiard Room. What did you see?"

"Nothing. I was sitting on a chair in the hall working on my laptop. My husband Aaron didn't feel well and had gone to lie down in one of the bedrooms. I checked on him. When I came back out in the hallway, Vivian was standing outside the Billiard Room with her ear to the door. That's all."

She tries to play it off, but the admission is significant. From Gustave's telling, I came away with the impression that Vivian stayed in her bedroom the whole night. Now she's as thick in the bushes as anybody. Scott presses on.

28

"How long did she stay there?"

"Not long. Gustave came up, and they had a short conversation. She then headed upstairs. Back to her bedroom, I suppose."

This scene between husband and wife was missing from Root's description of the night's events. And not by accident.

"See anybody else in the vicinity around this time?"

"Not until Mark Romo showed up and tried to help Gustave with the door. But I was busy working on my laptop and not really paying attention."

"What happened after that?"

"We started worrying about Jim, thinking he had a heart attack or stroke. People started running in all directions to find a ladder to get into the room from the outside. Gustave instructed me to find Celeste Wood—that's Jim's girlfriend—and tell her that something was wrong with Jim."

"Did you find her?"

"Yes, she was swimming. We watched Oliver Twist and Mark Romo climb up the ladder and then heard Mark yelling from inside. We rushed up ourselves back through the house and saw Jim with that knife sticking out of him."

By my count, that makes five people so far who were in the Billiard Room right after the murder—Root, Mark Romo, Oliver Twist, Erica Cain, and Celeste Wood. If we find their fingerprints in the room, proving that they were left there before the murder will be a challenge. Vivian's prints, too, since she lives here.

I ask, "Recognize the murder weapon?"

"Did I recognize the murder weapon? Why would I recognize a knife?"

We ignore her questions, but I do credit her response as a denial. I note, too, that she never moves her eyes toward the dagger's shelf.

"I understand that Jim Walker had an aptitude for making embarrassing problems disappear, that he was a kind of 'fixer' or something."

The witness is in no hurry to answer. My take is that Walker skirted the bounds of legality and that he did so under the banner of Cain & Cunningham. Too much candor could get Erica's firm in trouble.

She says, "Jim knew a lot of people and leveraged those contacts whenever possible on behalf of our clients."

"Like paying off Mark Romo's hit-and-run victim to hide his identity from the police?"

Erica swallows hard. The knowledge I just spilled is not information she wants to see running loose in the public domain. Anything happening to Romo is big news—hush money payouts to mask his involvement in killing a kid the biggest of all.

"I'm not going to discuss client business."

That's fair. Attorney-client privilege is a good get-out-of-jail card for her in a pinch. But that reprieve is only temporary. I turn my attention to matters closer to home.

"Did he ever fix anything for you or your husband?"

The concern she flashes is momentary, but enough. The question disagrees with her, and she hurries to be done with it.

"Of course not."

"Nothing?"

"Absolutely not."

"Is that your final answer?"

The only response is a hostile glare. No matter. She showed her hand—her body language putting the lie to the words coming out of her mouth. Scott and I slowly turn our heads to look at each other, wearing sarcastic smiles of disbelief. Our theatrics convey the blunt message that we don't believe what she is peddling, which hopefully is bad for her morale.

She huffs, "Are we almost done here? I would like to check on my husband."

"What's wrong with him anyway?"

"He's dizzy, confused, and so lethargic he can barely function. Don't even dream of trying to talk to him tonight. As his lawyer, I forbid it."

Scott makes a noise next to me. His disdain for lawyers is the stuff of legends, and I intuit his judgmental stare at Erica Cain, Attorney at Law, without even looking at him. But prudence mandates that we let this one pass. Last thing I want is to videotape our badgering a possibly-drugged witness who lacks his wits. That kind of conduct is a ticket to trouble—first with a judge, then with the press.

I say, "My understanding is that Aaron went to the second floor at the same time Walker headed upstairs to the Billiard Room."

"What of it?"

"Where were you?"

"I needed to work. Gustave suggested a chair and side table in the hall just outside the bedroom where Aaron was going to lie down. But first I went to the kitchen to get my husband a Coke. Is that a crime?"

"How long did that take?"

"Not long, and my husband was tucked under the covers when I went up there, if that's what you're getting at. And I stayed with him until I went back into the hall and saw Vivian Root outside the Billiard Room."

"Was he awake?"

"Not really."

"So you're his alibi, but he's unable to be yours."

The implication isn't exactly subtle, and she stares hard at me in the wake of the unspoken accusation. I bet she is mean as hell when the occasion calls for it.

I ask, "Did he ever drink that Coke?"

"You're going to have to ask him that."

Realizing that Erica Cain is likely a dried turnip at this point, we send her on her way. As she exits the room, I decide to leave one last impression.

"And Mrs. Cain?"

"Yes?"

I let the silence linger for a tense spell, two legal gunslingers facing off in the early dawn. She stands her ground, and I admire the tough pose, all the while trying to take a sledgehammer to her practiced equanimity. I deliver the parting shot.

"We're going to find out what you're hiding."

She spins around and leaves us, her heels clicking on the marble in the hall with every step.

Scott mutters, "Somebody killed the wrong lawyer."

7

The first thing I notice about Vivian Root is that she's black. The surprise on my part is genuine. Gustave Root's enthusiasm for the traffickers of Aryan superiority would seem to preclude a marriage with a woman of the wrong skin tone. Maybe love does conquer all. The next thing I notice about Vivian is that she's beautiful. Much younger than her husband—maybe by as much as forty years—Mrs. Root's allure is a classic type, almost Egyptian in aura, even as she wears a thick maroon bathrobe.

Her eyes are puffy and rimmed with redness—a recent crying spell the likely culprit.

Scott asks, "How are you feeling?"

"Okay."

"Up for answering some questions?"

She nods her head in a submissive gesture, avoiding all eye contact. It ain't much, but we at least have it on record that that Vivian is both able and willing to answer our questions—just in case Root wants to get cute later.

"How long have you and Gustave been married?"

In contrast to Erica Cain, Scott starts soft with this witness. The goal with Erica was to make her squirm as quickly as possible—to breach her walls with a Perry Mason-type quick strike, to get her talking out of surprise if nothing else. But one glance at Vivian is enough to realize that she needs a lighter touch. Easing her into a comfortable conversation—a more Columbo-like approach—is a better way to mine for truth.

She answers, "Seven years."

"That hardly seems possible. How old are you?"

"I was nineteen when we got married."

The answer depresses all of us. Gustave would've been in his late fifties at that point. Ugh. An older rich guy seeking youth and pleasure through a nubile trophy wife—the story is all too real. Bible scholars estimate that King David—a man after God's own heart—was three decades older than Bathsheba when he summoned her from a neighboring roof. Some things never change.

"How did the two of you meet?"

A sad, mirthless half-laugh drips in a trickle from Vivian's lips. She meets our eyes for a second but looks past us before responding.

"I was trapped in an awful situation surrounded by horrible people who didn't have my best interest at heart. Gustave offered me an escape hatch. I took it. Now I get to live in this big house. I'm a lucky woman."

"What kind of bad situation?"

"I'd prefer not to say."

Scott honors her request for the time being. But he does let the residue of the response rest in the air for a bit. It gives off a bad fragrance. A young woman making a hard bargain to seek a better life is an old story, too. Scott shifts to the events earlier in the evening and asks why she didn't attend the party.

"I was a little under the weather. Gustave felt it best if I stayed in my room."

The wording suggests that Vivian doesn't agree with her husband's assessment. Her manner, too. She comes across as a hostage reading from a script, one who doesn't really believe her lines.

"Do you always do what Gustave says?"

"His house, his rules."

She bites her lip—or maybe her tongue. I don't believe that last answer was part of the script. She stares at the floor again, likely hoping we didn't notice the Freudian slip.

"Did you come downstairs at any time?"

That's the $64,000 question, and I hope for her sake that she gives it to us straight. I'm not optimistic. Her eyes move up, down, left, and right as she formulates an answer to what should be a simple question.

"Well, I'm down here now."

"Before the murder?"

She takes another pause and fiddles with her hands, still working over-time to avoid looking us at directly—maybe believing that if she doesn't see us, we won't see her. But we see her all too well. I try to show compassion on my face, but I'm out of practice and unsure if the effort takes.

Scott says, "You need to be honest with us."

"I don't want to get in trouble."

"Who don't you want to get in trouble with? Us or your husband?"

"All of the above."

"Did you kill Jim Walker?"

"No!"

"Then as long as you tell the truth, nothing you say will get you in trouble with us."

"That still leaves Gustave."

So much for love conquering all. But another off-script detour is a good sign. Her growing comfort in giving us a glimpse behind the tarnished curtain of her marriage suggests we might get some truth out of her, after all.

Ignoring her comment, Scott says, "Tell us about when you came downstairs."

The subtle shift in phrasing is another pressure point. No longer a question—a statement. *We know you came downstairs.*

Vivian sighs—a mournful sound too old to be coming from her young body. But I figure she's lived that kind of life. The signs are there.

"I went down to the second floor and stood outside the Billiard Room."

"Why would you do that?"

"Gustave told me he was going to have a talk with Jim alone. I was trying to hear what was being said."

"Did you hear anything?"

"Nothing. Gustave wasn't in the room yet. He found me lurking outside the door and told me to go back to bed. I went back to bed."

Scott lets the moment breathe a little before asking the obvious next question. Vivian takes a sip of water. She is opening up on cue, but we still want to avoid pushing her too far too fast.

"Why did you want to hear the conversation between your husband and Jim Walker?"

"Is this confidential?"

"We're investigating a murder. Nothing is confidential. But we're not in the business of spilling secrets just for the hell of it."

She absorbs Scott's words in silence. Concern doesn't exactly line her face—the skin is too perfect for that. But a prick of agitation is clearly still poking her in parts unseen, and she remains mute as the seconds pass. Apart from the introductions, I haven't said a word during the interview because ganging up on her is the wrong play. I sense, though, that now is the time to wade into the stream and carry her that last little distance to the other side. Leaning forward, I give her a gentle prod.

"Vivian, you've come too far down the path to turn back now. We're here for you, but you need to tell us the truth."

For a second, I'm unsure if she even hears me. She appears transfixed on something behind us but gives up the stare in due time, opting instead for a deep breath to find her courage. With that out of the way, she takes the final step.

"Jim and I were lovers."

And boom goes the dynamite. Her back sits straighter in the chair, and she meets my gaze now without any trepidation—becoming stronger right before my eyes in the wake of the confession. An insight grabs me—she wanted to tell us about her affair. The thought becomes a hard one to shake off. Not that I believe her hesitancy was a ruse up to this point. I don't—she was nervous and scared. Still is. But just the telling has lifted an almost physical weight off her shoulders.

"Did Gustave know?"

"I'm not sure. That's why I was listening."

"But you had suspicions that he knew?"

"Gustave knows everything."

The tone is ominous. I can almost smell her fear. But her willingness to talk out of school points to an even stronger motivation pushing

35

her forward—desperation. Vivian wants out of the marriage with her husband, and she just crossed the Rubicon by publicly admitting her adultery.

"How did your relationship with Jim begin?"

"He came over one day a couple of months ago to talk with Gustave. But Gustave was late—some filming crisis on the set. Mr. Beale was off somewhere, too. Maybe the doctor, I think. We were alone, and it happened. Jim was always a big charmer. After that day, we would sneak around whenever we could. Gustave keeps me on a short leash, but Jim could be creative in arranging meetings."

She sounds like a prisoner in her own home, and I wonder if she regrets whatever deal she made with Gustave to escape her former life. But that can wait until later. I instead steer the conversation to what happened earlier in the evening.

"Jim was going to be at the party, and that made me nervous. As I was applying my makeup, Gustave came in and told me that I didn't look well. Said I should probably stay in my bedroom, that it would be impolite to get our guests sick. My heart sank into the pit of my stomach. I thought that keeping me away from the party was his way of telling me that he knew about the affair. After dinner, he came up to check on me. He explained that he was about to meet with Jim alone in the Billiard Room to discuss something important. He had a gleam in his eye that unnerved me. That's why I went down to eavesdrop."

I explain what her husband told us about meeting privately with Walker to see about acquiring more Adolph Hitler paintings. Vivian mulls on the information for a moment and says, "Could be. Gustave loves Hitler."

She emits a laugh. Scott and I join her—the three of us marveling at Root's strange hobby. The built-up tension in the room dissipates a bit.

I ask, "How did you learn about Jim's death?"

"Gustave texted me that something terrible had happened and said to come to the Billiard Room. Everyone was in the room when I entered. A few people parted, and I saw Jim's body with that dagger in his back."

"Recognize the dagger?"

"One of Gustave's. Usually over there."

She inclines her head in the direction of the empty shelf.

"What did you think when you saw Jim dead?"

"I thought Gustave had killed him."

No one is laughing now. Vivian holds our gaze and doesn't back down. She adds, "Gustave announced to the room that he had phoned the Governor to have you guys assigned to the case. Must be nice to have friends in high places. That's how the Gustaves of the world get away with the things that they do."

Her eyes challenge us to tell her that she's wrong. I take her up on it.

"If that's his plan, he called the wrong Governor and the wrong investigators."

"Nice fairy tale. I long to believe it."

Another challenging look. Her tears are now dried, the redness in her eyes vanished. The timid creature that entered the room is long gone—and good for her. If Vivian is really intent on escaping her marriage to Gustave, she's going to need all the strength that she can muster.

I ask, "Do you need a place to stay? We can help if you want us to escort you from the house."

"Not yet. I'm not ready. One day I might take you up on that offer—if I think I can trust you."

"Fair enough. But we need to broach with Gustave whether he knew about your affair with Walker, except I don't want to do anything that might leave you with a black eye—or worse."

"Gustave wouldn't hurt me."

"You just told me you believe he stabbed a dagger into Jim Walker's back."

"That's different. Gustave worships his collectibles, and I'm the most desirable part of his collection."

The response is brutal in its honesty and another ugly insight into the state of the Root marriage.

With that, we send her on her way—back to the husband she thinks killed her lover. Scott asks, "Think she's going to be alright?"

"Probably for the first time in her life—if she can get away from him."

8

Celeste Wood has a swimmer's body—tall, toned, and tan. Her brunette hair is naturally curly but appears hastily dried after her late-night swim. The information we've received is that she was Jim Walker's girlfriend. If so, I don't detect a lot of grief. I wonder if she knows about Walker and Vivian.

Taking the lead, Scott says, "Ms. Wood, we understand that you were Jim Walker's girlfriend. We're sorry for your loss."

"Girlfriend is too strong. We dated some."

"How did the two of you meet?"

"He solved a problem for me."

She doesn't expound on the answer. We just sit there in response, content to stay silent for as long as necessary. Experience has taught me that most witnesses become uncomfortable with the quiet and will eventually fill the void. Talking takes the place of the silence that judges them. Celeste is no different.

"I got a DUI. Not a big deal in itself. But I had an upcoming exhibit at the High Museum, and the publicity could've scuttled the show. Jim made it all go away."

"How did he do that?"

"Front-row concert tickets, I think. The police chief was a Garth Brooks fan."

The flash of a memory hits me. In connection with that city councilman business, Walker offered me prime seats to the concert of my choice. I told him that Johnny Cash was dead.

She continues, "Jim said his work for me would be *pro bono* if I went on a date with him. Seemed like a good deal. We've been off-and-on ever since."

Scott asks, "Since you were his date tonight, I take it that recently you've been on."

"Hard to say. I had been mad at him."

"Why?"

I lean a bit forward in my chair, anticipating some complaint about Walker and Vivian. Once you start throwing love triangles into an investigation, possible motives for murder start sprouting like wildflowers in the spring.

"Jim sold some paintings that I had given him as gifts."

"Why would he do that?"

"He needed money."

"Didn't he make a boatload of money as a lawyer?"

"Tons. But he needed more."

"What on earth for?"

"He opened a bar—called it The Bar's Bar. Get it? A bar for lawyers. But things aren't going too well. Maybe lawyers like to get sloshed alone. Jim also drank too much of his profits."

"Did that bother you?"

"Not too much. I liked to drink his profits, too."

Any time I hear about an attorney opening a bar, I think of the movie *Casablanca*. A little-known cinematic fact is that Humphrey Bogart's character, Rick Blaine, was a lawyer in his past life. Except practicing law—and being dumped by Ingrid Bergman—made him so jaded that he fled to Morocco to peddle whiskey and good times. After my last trial, a similar feeling of ruin led me to turn my back on the world and do my own thing. But like Rick, the fight eventually came to me. And here I am.

Celeste adds, "Jim had somewhat of a gambling problem, too. He liked to bet on the Falcons."

"Well, that's stupid."

"Everybody has their blind spots."

The three of us ponder that universal truth for a few seconds. Life would run smoother for everyone if people could recognize their own blind spots. I pipe in and ask her, "What's your blind spot?"

"Men who drink and gamble too much."

She laughs. Beyond the absence of any discernable sign of mourning, her mood is a weird one to peg. I don't rush to any conclusions. People have their own peculiar reactions to tragedy, and she might be suffering from shock. But I have to ask her about it, at least.

"You don't seem too upset by the night's turn of events."

"Like I said, Jim angered me by selling the paintings I made just for him. Those were special gifts, and he treated them like commodities. He also pressured me into coming here tonight when I really didn't want to. Now he's gone and got himself killed, leaving me behind to be grilled by you guys. I'm not sure he was worth all this bother."

"Why didn't you want to come tonight? Had you met Gustave Root before this evening?"

"Everybody knows Gustave, but he really isn't my cup of tea. Do you know that he has a painting by Adolph Hitler on his wall over there?"

Celeste points at the picture, stares at it, and shakes her head in stern disapproval. I contemplate the painting again and wonder how I so quickly went from witnessing an execution in a state penitentiary to viewing the artwork of Adolph Hitler in a stately mansion. Life comes at you fast. I ask her opinion about the Führer as an artist.

"Soulless, unimaginative, pedestrian—no talent whatsoever at drawing humans. The inability to sketch people is a window into his hatred of humanity. He ultimately made a good career choice. He had much more skill as a homicidal maniac."

That analysis was certainly earnest. On the money, too, I reckon.

Scott asks, "Why did Walker pressure you so hard to come tonight?"

"Damned if I know. Said he had to have a date for tonight to keep up appearances, and that I was the only candidate sophisticated enough for this kind of crowd. Real romantic, right? He promised to buy back the paintings I gave him and return them to me if I agreed to come, which is why I now have the pleasure of your company."

She doesn't sound impressed. Scott follows up.

"Keep up what appearances?"

"Who knows? With Jim, everything had to always be first-rate—cars, clothes, the works. My guess is that showing up stag would've been a blow to his ego."

I think of Vivian and reach a different conclusion. Bringing Celeste as a decoy to the party was probably Jim's way of keeping Gustave Root off his scent.

"Did Jim date other people?"

"Probably. I never asked."

We change the focus to earlier events in the evening and inquire how she ended up in the swimming pool at the time of the murder.

"I like to swim and don't get to do it enough. The heated pool was another selling point in coming tonight with Jim. He said there would be some downtime and that Gustave wouldn't mind."

Scott says, "Didn't see anybody jump off the balcony outside the Billiard Room, did you?"

"No, I probably would've mentioned that before now if I had. But I was doing laps with my head down. Could've easily missed something like that."

"When did you realize something was wrong?"

"Erica Cain came running out waving her arms. We watched Oliver Twist and Mark Romo climb up to the balcony on the ladder. Then I heard someone yell—it sounded like Mark—and ran inside. Got to the Billiard Room and saw it."

"Did you recognize the murder weapon?"

"Didn't get close enough to be in a position to recognize it. I had no interest in staying in that room once I saw Jim splayed out like that."

Celeste doesn't steal a glance to the empty dagger shelf. Scott asks a final question.

"For the record, did you kill Jim?"

A hard laugh arises deep from her lungs.

"Yes! I confess! I killed him and then used the balcony as a high dive to make my getaway into the pool! And I would've gotten away with it, too, if it weren't for you meddling kids!"

I smile. Anyone who quotes Scooby-Doo is all right in my book.

9

I know Jessica Allen's name—and that she's an actress of some sort—but can't quite picture the face. But when she walks into the room, I recognize her on sight. She stars in those same superhero movies as Mark Romo. Don't know the character she plays, except that it does come with a cape. Once you get past the old standbys like Batman, Superman, Captain America, and Wonder Woman, I kinda get lost.

She's shorter than I would've figured. Age is late twenties. Her hair is blond but my guess is that the color doesn't come naturally—the same thing goes for her fake tan. The clothes reveal plenty of skin and pass for what I would take to be young and hip, which means they might not be young and hip at all. She looks better on screen than in person, but that's the norm. A mighty yawn bellows out of her when she sits down. A gesture of genuine fatigue or practiced indifference, I'm not sure. She tells us to call her Jess.

Scott decides to vary his routine and asks her right at the start, "Did you kill Jim Walker?"

The question acts as an electric shock to her manner. We got her attention at least.

"Of course not."

"Good. Tell me how you ended up here tonight. Doesn't feel like it would be your kind of scene."

"Glamorous, ain't it? Before Jim got murdered, the night was a real snoozefest. But Gustave writes the checks and wanted me to come. The China thing is supposed to be a big deal. Whatever."

"Well, thankfully someone killed Jim, so the night wasn't a total loss."

"You're funny. But the murder is the most interesting thing to happen to me all year. I even took a selfie with the body—you know, the whole pics or it didn't happen thing."

Classic millennial—and potentially important evidence as the closest in time depiction of the body after the murder. Scott sighs and rubs his hand over his face before growling out his next words, "Hand over your phone. I want to see this picture."

"Calm down, skippy. I was just messing with you. Never got the chance to be alone with him or I would've."

She giggles at us. Listening to her makes me feel older than I am. I turn forty in a week and, depending on whom you ask, might even be the oldest of the millennials. Personally, I identify as Generation X, if for no other reason than millennials are the worst. Scott begins again.

"Jim did work for you in the past, right?"

The giggle dies off, and she gives a little shrug of the shoulders. "Sure."

"Tell me about it."

"I'd rather not."

"And I'd rather not be missing my beauty rest to investigate the murder upstairs, but here we are."

"I can see why. You need all the beauty rest you can get."

Jessica smirks. And even I let out an easy chuckle. Scott smiles to show that he is a good sport. But the firmness in his face doesn't waver in its message to the witness—talk. She talks.

"The whole thing is stupid. In middle school, this girl I knew committed suicide. Her family claimed that it was because my friends and I had been bullying her. But, trust me, she had emotional problems before I ever set eyes on her. Anyway, I moved away and forgot about it. When I hit the big time, this family started making noises about going public. Extortion if you ask me. Jim met with these people and put the fear of God into them about how he'll sue their lot back into the Stone Age if they slandered my career like that. I threw some cash their way to shut them up for good and that was the end of it. Left a bad taste in my mouth."

Not a hint of concern about her role in the death of a young girl troubles her pretty face. I bet she made a fine middle-school bully.

Scott transitions into asking Jessica about the party, specifically how she occupied her time once everyone left the study after dinner.

"I went outside to smoke some weed. Gustave doesn't like the smell of it in the house."

"By yourself?"

"Sad, ain't it? Normally, Mark would be out there with me, but he's due to be drug-tested in a day or two. The insurance companies that insure his films require it of him."

"How close are you and Mark?"

"We Netflix and chill together from time to time, if that's what you're asking."

I think I get the meaning but will Google it later to be sure. Scott asks, "Smoke a lot of dope?"

"Oh sure."

Even though we're called the Atlanta Murder Squad, our legal jurisdiction is any crime in Georgia that scratches our interest. Part of me wants to arrest her for smoking marijuana just to mess with her—a kind of sacrificial offering to the memory of a long dead middle-school girl. But I fight the urge. Scott continues.

"Where outside were you toking up?"

"Toking up? Good lord! You sound like my dad!"

"Answer the question."

"The front porch."

"See anything?"

"Nothing except transcendental enlightenment."

Maybe I will arrest her, after all. She could find a bunch of enlightenment from the inside of a jail cell.

"How did you learn of the murder?"

"Heard a lot of noises and found Mark hyperventilating about a dead body. I went up to take a look. Poor Jim. Kinda cool otherwise, though. Even if I didn't get a chance to take a selfie."

Scott looks at me to see if I have any questions—or maybe to determine if I'm okay with him strangling the witness. I throw out, "Recognize the murder weapon?"

The muscles in my body freeze. Jessica stares right at the usual home of the Nazi dagger while she answers the question.

"Not really. But Gustave keeps a lot of weapons all over the place."

She squints and scratches her ear, then adds, "Strange. I remember seeing a knife on that shelf over there earlier tonight, but it's gone now."

We hold our tongues and watch. Her face looks like she's doing complicated arithmetic in her head. Finally, she says, "Was that—"

She doesn't finish the thought. With feigned disinterest, I ask, "When was this?"

"When we were all gathered in here after dinner."

"Didn't see anyone take it, did you?"

"No."

"Anyone hovering in the vicinity?"

"Not that I noticed."

When she leaves, I debate whether her revelation about the dagger was an authentic recounting of the facts or a planned performance. I can't tell but do know one thing.

Jessica Allen is an actress.

10

Leo Ivanov is Russian and looks the part. Short and stout like a tea-pot, he waddles into the interview with a heavy bearing—his beard a dense tangle of gray and black shrubbery. I check my notes. Marlon told us that Ivanov is a math professor who moonlights as a chess grandmaster—and that he listened like a hawk to all the conversations of the other party guests in the aftermath of the murder.

I ask, "You're a math professor?"

"*Da.*"

Even in that one syllable, the accent is pronounced. I asked him where he teaches.

"Georgia Tech."

No surprise there. Tech is famous for its three-semester calculus sequence required of all its students. I took one calculus class at UGA and that was enough. Like Ivanov, my professor had a challenging Eastern European drawl that made learning logarithmic derivatives even less fun than normal. The school still let me graduate, at least.

"You're also a chess grandmaster?"

"*Da.*"

"Any money in that?"

He roars with the laughter of a bear, and I smell the coffee on his breath in the ensuing wind gust. As the laughter dies down, he shakes his head vigorously.

"*Nyet. Nyet. Nyet.* Math pays the bills. But chess—chess is my passion."

Ivanov explains that he is the 77th ranked player in all of the world, but that only the top ten players or so can make a living solely off moving pieces around a chessboard. I played a lot of chess growing up with my dad and even today am apt to work chess puzzles in times of extreme boredom. But mastering chess is not something you can do casually on the side. And that's the problem. Devoting one's life to the most complex of games means navigating a tight cliff between sanity and fanaticism. Not everybody makes it. Bobby Fischer went crazy for a reason.

I continue, "How did you end up at a party to celebrate a film studio's partnership with the Chinese government?"

"Gustave invited me, and he always has the best cognac."

"How did you know Jim Walker?"

"My lawyer."

"We understand that he saved you from a tight spot. Why don't you tell us about it?"

His eyes narrow in suspicion and disappear behind his massive eyebrows, which remain—despite his age—black as the blackest crow. A few strokes of his beard later, he says, "I should not. Attorney-client privilege, correct?"

"*Nyet.* A murder case takes precedence."

That's not really true, but a person should never take legal advice from someone who carries a gun and a badge. After a thoughtful pause of some duration, Ivanov tells his tale.

"One of my students accidentally became pregnant with my child. Mr. Walker helped to arrange an abortion, among other things."

"Accidentally?"

He gives a roguish shrug.

I ask, "Why did you need a lawyer for something like that?"

"The student made overtures about reporting our liaison to the school. I spoke with Gustave, and he advised that I should employ Mr. Walker's services."

"Worried about losing your job?"

"For a consensual relationship with a student? *Nyet*—the protection of tenure. But still, too messy. Better this way."

"What all did Walker do?"

"Persuaded the student about the wisdom of aborting the child and also encouraged her to transfer to another school. Of course, the $100,000 I paid helped."

"That strikes me as a large payoff given the circumstances."

Another shrug. Maybe the student just drove a hard bargain. Ivanov adds, "Can you put a price tag on peace of mind?"

That's one way of looking at it.

"What's the name of this student?"

"*Nyet*. That name shall never pass my lips again."

"You could write it down for me."

He chuckles but remains firm: "*Nyet*."

I let the matter drop. We'll get the name one way or another. Scott asks Ivanov about his movements once the party guests started drifting out of the study.

"After taking a bathroom break, I strolled around until I found a quiet place, eventually settling in the kitchen for a cup of coffee. I then played a ten-minute blitz game of chess online."

"See anybody?"

"Mr. Beale was working in the kitchen and served me the coffee. I quite enjoy his company. He doesn't speak, allowing me to focus on the chess. Gustave arrived a little while later to drink a glass of milk before telling Mr. Beale that he was on his way to the Billiard Room to talk with Mr. Walker. He didn't want to be disturbed. That's it."

Only a partial alibi, if true. We're looking at a twenty-minute window in which the murder was committed, and Ivanov was on his own for the first part of that time.

"How did you learn that Jim had been killed?"

"I heard shouts and someone—not sure who—told Mr. Beale to retrieve a ladder. People seemed to be gathering at the back of the house. I joined them. Oliver Twist and Mark Romo climbed up the ladder into the Billiard Room. The rest of us who were gathered outside went back inside and took the stairs. By then, the door was open, and I could see that Jim was dead."

"Recognize the murder weapon?"

"*Da*. My grandfather fought for Russia in the Battle of Stalingrad. The Nazis have always been a particular scourge of mine. Gustave knows my family's history and made a point of showing the dagger to me on my first visit here. He wondered how many Russians had died at its hands."

Whatever the number, you can add one American to the dagger's resume. Root is probably giddy that one of his prized possessions lived to kill another day.

I note, "Gustave has some bizarre proclivities along those lines. I'm surprised you would get along with him."

Ivanov gives what is becoming his trademark shrug and answers, "Stalin had his own issues."

That's a hard response to argue with. Wrapping up, I ask, "Did you kill Jim Walker?"

"*Nyet.*"

"Any theories on who did?"

"You're asking the wrong question. Ask instead who can get out of a room that is locked from the inside. Solve that riddle, and you'll find your killer."

He makes a good point.

11

Oliver Twist is surprisingly alert given the lateness of the hour. He struts into the study wearing a black suit, black shirt, black tie, black socks, and black shoes. The hair, too, is an unnatural, shoe polish black. When he introduces himself to us, his mouth is the only part of his face that moves—an unnerving effect vaguely reminiscent of a ventriloquist's dummy. No doubt Twist has dropped serious money on a bunch of plastic surgery over the years. From where I sit, he should demand a refund.

I ask, "You're a magician?"

"Absolutely not. I'm an illusionist."

"What's the difference?"

"A magician does silly tricks. I bend the bounds of reality."

Scott grunts next to me. Probably rolls his eyes, too. Twist has no visible reaction to Scott's open disdain, but that might be the Botox. I continue.

"Speaking of bending reality, how would you go about getting into and out of a room that is locked from the inside?"

"Through the power of illusion, of course."

He actually moves his arm in a magician's wave as he delivers that non-answer. The peacock is strong in this one, but the presentation falls flat. I hope his performances in front of real audiences are better, or Gustave's plan to take Twist to China might get stalled in customs.

"Any suggestions more concrete than that?"

"I stand by my answer."

Of course he does. I ask him his real name.

"Oliver Twist. I legally changed it."

"Are you fan of Charles Dickens?"

"Not really. I just like calling myself Oliver Twist. Especially the

50

Twist part—a surprise ending, so to speak. Seemed a perfect moniker for an illusionist."

"And the name David Copperfield wasn't available."

"So pedantic. You think you're the first person to spout that line?"

"In my defense, the joke does write itself."

He tries to frown but the tightness in his face gets the best of him. I press him on his original name, and he coughs it up. Rupert Ramone. Scott laughs out loud. I don't think he and Rupert are going to be friends.

"Tell me about this evening."

"Hard to remember everything since it was so long ago now. You've kept me waiting an inordinate amount of time, but I will try to do my best."

Twist pauses almost as if he expects an apology on our part. If that is what he's hunting, I hope he's not holding his breath. Our expressions tell him to get on with it. He does.

"We enjoyed a gourmet caliber dinner, prepared by Mr. Beale, whose food is always divine. Afterwards, we retired to this very room to partake in dessert and drink—an exquisite chocolate soufflé and cognac for me. Gustave announced to the group that he needed to talk with Mr. Walker alone in the Billiard Room. The guests were left free to entertain ourselves until midnight. I grabbed a book of Shakespeare's sonnets off the shelf—I like to quote him in my act to show my erudition—and nestled myself in a chair over there by the window. Perhaps twenty minutes later, I heard the commotion upstairs and went out into the hall to investigate."

"Anybody in here with you?"

"Not a soul."

Figures. Hardly any of the suspects so far have a solid alibi—it's that kind of night. Twist picks up where he left off.

"Gustave called down from upstairs and explained the situation. I volunteered to climb into the Billiard Room from the outside balcony. Mr. Beale retrieved the ladder, and I ascended it with great haste. When I entered the room, Mr. Walker was face down on the snooker table with a shiny object of steel protruding out of him. I lifted up his left hand to check his pulse—the way you're supposed to do—and felt nothing. Everything was deathly quiet. The only sound was the thud of a red snooker ball he was holding as it fell onto to the green felt. The impact startled me. I dropped Mr. Walker's arm back down to the table immediately and stepped away. Mark Romo had joined me by that point, and I announced that Mr. Walker was dead. Romo shrieked like a hyena and ran out the door to the hall."

His smile indicates that he is incredibly pleased with himself—like he is somehow the hero of the tale he's telling. He'll probably work the story into his act somehow. My thoughts run in a different direction. Twist was alone with the victim for some period of time before Romo entered from the balcony. I understand enough about magic to know that a master of sleight of hand can do a lot of amazing things with the slimmest of openings.

Scott asks, "Did you recognize the murder weapon?"

I watch Twist like a hawk, but he fails to glance toward the spot of the vacated dagger. He proceeds to answer the question.

"Not really. I saw something in German inscribed on the blade. Probably part of Gustave's collection of Nazi paraphernalia. He's a connoisseur. But I couldn't swear that the dagger was his."

The answer doesn't give anything away. But the aura of fakeness that surrounds him makes me real curious about the secrets in his past. I decide to ask.

"You and Walker pals? We understand he got you out of trouble when you were in a tight spot. Be good to hear your side of it."

The blackness of his pupils turns a shade darker. Twist turns his stretched neck from me to Scott to the window and back to me. The neck could use a good oiling. The creaks are noticeable and make him sound like the Tin Man when he was still rusted. But Twist has bigger problems in the present. The question obviously staggers him, and he's not so eager to be talkative anymore. We wait him out.

"I don't see the relevance of that."

"Don't be silly. You're a suspect in a murder investigation. The victim knew secrets about you, secrets that you would prefer remain out of public view. You can go a long way toward clearing yourself by being as candid as possible right now."

"I'm not a murder suspect."

Turning to Scott, I say, "He's not a murder suspect." The response: "Could've fooled me." I swivel back to Twist and paint the picture for him—in crayons.

"Jim Walker was killed by someone at the party. You were at the party. Walker was killed in a locked room. You know people who are good at getting around locks of all sorts? Magicians. You're a magician. You just told us that nobody was with you at the time of the murder—meaning you have no alibi. You were also alone with Walker in the Billiard Room for some period of time before Mark Romo got there. What did you do in those seconds? And—let's not skip over your possible motive—Walker knew disreputable information about you. Add it all up, the math comes out the same. And it's not good for Oliver Twist."

"I'm not a magician."

He doesn't seem so cocksure on that point now, doesn't seem too certain about much of anything. Scott and I stay quiet, and let the silence do its work. At last, the witness relents, "What do you want to know?"

"How did Walker help you out of your jam?"

"My assistant, Missy, and I were practicing a variation of the Bullet Catch Illusion—where each of us would fire loaded guns at the other and catch the bullets in our teeth. Something went wrong, and I accidently shot her. She became paralyzed. Mr. Walker arranged a generous payoff to keep Missy silent and also ensured that no legal entanglements with the police would ensue. That's all. For an illusionist of my caliber, the incident was terribly embarrassing but certainly not so cataclysmic as to kill Mr. Walker over. It was years ago anyway."

The confession is a hard one for him to make, and he becomes smaller after making it.

But Jim Walker is of more interest to me now. The ledger of bad deeds from the party guests continues to accumulate, and I reflect that

Walker sure knew a lot of dirt about a lot of people. Celeste Wood's description of his money troubles makes me wonder if the dead man sought to capitalize on his peculiar brand of intellectual property. Blackmail is a powerful motive for murder.

We nibble around some more of Oliver Twist's edges, but our hearts aren't much in it. Scott tells him he can leave. As Twist slouches out, I call out a final question, more for sport than anything else.

"How did you make Stone Mountain disappear?"

By this point, he has shed a huge chunk of the vanity he came into the room with. In the wreckage, a semblance of an authentic human starts to seep out from the chiseled façade. He gives the question a decent bit of thought and delivers his answer in a non-stage voice.

"I separated people's perceptions of what they were seeing from the reality—therein, my dear sir, lies the power of illusion."

He disappears through the door.

12

Mr. Beale strides into the study, and I manage against all odds to maintain my poker face. For starters, he is the tallest human I've ever seen in my entire life—indeed, the tallest species of any type except for the giraffes at the zoo. But that's not the end of it. He is also both the whitest and thinnest human to ever grace my vision—a ghost with a frame so slender that he must be invisible from the side. Before this moment, I reckon I've never seen an albino in the flesh. But Mr. Beale qualifies. He is dressed in a snug-fitting tuxedo that I assume didn't come off the rack. His medium-length hair—the color of unadulterated snow—is perfectly in place.

When he reaches us, Mr. Beale extends a handshake to Scott, who accepts the offer. I watch Scott's hand disappear into the taller man's massive grip and even notice a hint of a grimace on my friend's face. Scott is a master of delivering handshakes that hurt when he wants, but the other man's surprise attack—a declaration of war if ever there was one—gets the better of him this time around. Mr. Beale's face, though, betrays no discernible reaction to the ad hoc contest of strength. Still wearing the countenance of a cipher, he rotates toward me and sticks out his hand for a seeming encore performance. After just witnessing the previous exchange, I shake my head and say, "No thank you. I'm good." He has no reaction to that, either.

The giant takes a seat, and all I can see are the pointy ends of his knees. I check the screen of the video camera, see little apart from his chest, and adjust the angle of the shot to capture the expressionless face. Scott—seething in a slow boiling kind of way—starts with the questions.

"Full name?"

The witness stares at Scott with all the emptiness of a black hole—except the hole is white.

"Do you talk? You can shake your head if the answer is no."

Mr. Beale remains frozen in place with creepy stillness. He could pass for a wax figure in Madame Tussauds. But I suppose that one of those Ripley's Believe It or Not museums would be a more appropriate home.

"Look, I know you understand English because you sat down in the chair when I told you. Stop playing games."

The eyes stay fixed on Scott. I peer into them to see if anything is inside but come up empty. The ocean-blue quality of the irises is unnerving, creating an almost unworldly feel when contrasted with the rest of him. I'm gawking pretty hard at this point, but he shows no clue that he realizes I'm even in the room. Could be he's in some kind of trance.

"Mr. Beale—huh? Any nicknames? Big-deal Beale, maybe? Lurch? Andre the Giant?"

If the thin man takes offense, he doesn't show it. Scott would take any reaction out of Mr. Beale at this point.

"Your boss told us you grew up in the circus? Is that so?"

Nothing.

"Maybe a clown and a contortionist had sex on a bed of nails, and you were the result?"

Nothing.

Scott swivels his head to me, but I've got no bright ideas of my own. He sighs and gives up on the ghost.

"All right, Beale. Well done. Run along and tell your boss—however the two of you communicate—to get his ass back in here."

With that, the stick figure returns to his feet and heads for the exit. When he's gone, Scott complains, "That guy gives me the creeps."

"Have some compassion. Man can't help how he looks."

"And I can't help that he gives me the creeps. But I promise you one thing. If that mutant tries to muscle a handshake on me again like that, he's going to be a one-handed albino when I get through with him."

* * *

J.D. Hendrix—a lieutenant by rank—escorts Gustave Root back to the study. Before leaving, J.D. motions us into the hall. We tell Root to take a seat and head out.

The youngest person on the murder squad shows no signs that he has been up the entire night—a fact I attribute to the glories of youth. He says, "Marlon thinks we should let Aaron and Erica Cain go home. Aaron might as well be in a coma. The wife is threatening to sue all of us if we keep them any longer."

I ask, "What did the paramedics say about Aaron?"

"Not much. Might have been drugged but that whatever's happening is not life-threatening. Marlon got some samples of Aaron's hair when you were talking with the wife. He's going to get them drug-tested. We'll know then."

Good old Marlon. If he pulled the hairs off of Aaron's sleeping head without consent, we might have an illegal search and seizure problem. But if the hairs drifted to the floor all by their lonesome and Marlon just happened to pick them up, then all's fair in love and war. But Marlon knows the score as well as anyone.

Scott says, "Except for Gustave in there, I'm comfortable letting the whole lot of them go at this point. We need everyone out to search the house properly anyway."

I don't disagree and tell J.D., "Hold Vivian and Mr. Beale until we're done with Root. Release everybody else but explain we'll be speaking to all of them again soon."

J.D. nods and walks with purpose back to the dining room. He's a good kid.

* * *

Gustave looks worse for wear since we last spoke to him—especially his wild hair, which is ruffled in every direction possible. Puffing up his chest before we can even sit down, he barks, "This whole situation is intolerable. You harassed my wife and Mr. Beale after I explicitly told you not to. The Governor will be hearing from me."

Scott barks back, "Give me a break! Why did you order Beale not to talk to us? Do you want to solve this murder or not?"

"Have you ever heard of the right to remain silent?"

"That only applies when what you say might incriminate you. Did Beale kill Jim Walker?"

"Don't be preposterous. Mr. Beale is a gentle soul."

"Did *you* kill him?"

The two of them trade hostile looks. Gustave keeps his mouth shut, and I watch with fading interest. Most of my thoughts are focused on sleep. But feeling a need to break the impasse, I interject, "What kind of trouble did Walker help the Cains escape? Erica didn't want to share."

Gustave breaks eye contact with Scott and turns his attention my way. He messes with his hair as he considers whether to answer the question. I give him a little extra push.

"Mark Romo told us about the hit-and-run. Celeste Wood—the DUI. Jessica Allen didn't quite admit to being a middle-school bully but told us about her predicament all the same. Leo Ivanov confessed to getting a student in the family way, albeit accidentally, and Oliver Twist acknowledged paralyzing his assistant. You told us to ask your guests about their troubles first before you would break their confidences. We did, but Erica didn't play ball. Now it's your turn to spill what you know about the Cains."

He nods and says, "Sylvia Pinker."

"And?"

"That's all I'm going to say. Find the rest for yourself."

Fine. I think to myself that Marlon will crack that mystery before dawn, but a quick peek out the window informs me that dawn is already here.

"One of the guests mentioned that Jim Walker may have had a thing for Vivian. Know anything about that?"

My phrasing is designed to protect Vivian—both as the source of the information and from any claim that she reciprocated Walker's interest in her. Gustave twitches for a fatal half-second but tries to cover up his displeasure with a laugh about as authentic as a plastic pink flamingo.

"Who spread that nonsense?"

"Why? Does it bother you?"

"Ha! I've never been one to adhere to bourgeoisie notions of morality. Vivian can do what she wants. But no—Vivian had no interest in Jim. I will say, though, that if it had meant getting those Hitler paintings, not only would I bless a sexual union between Jim and Vivian, I'd even film it for posterity."

And people say that romance is dead. Vivian will no doubt be surprised to hear that she has the freedom to sleep with whomever she wants. But Gustave's answer strikes a wrong note for me in another way. I asked him about Walker's attraction to Vivian, not the other way around. Yet Gustave focused on Vivian's interest in Walker.

Scott says, "You failed to mention that Vivian was loitering outside the Billiard Room right when you came up. One might even say you lied. The question is why."

"Stop being insufferable. Vivian knew I was heading to the Billiard Room and wanted a word. Since I know she didn't kill Jim, involving her unnecessarily with the police struck me as a bad thing for a husband to do."

Call me old-fashioned, but filming your wife having sex with another man in exchange for Adolph Hitler paintings would also qualify as a bad thing for a husband to do. I ask, "How did you and Vivian meet anyway?"

"She needed a knight in shining armor, and I fit the bill."

He refuses to give more specifics, and I'm too tired to press him hard on it.

Before Gustave goes, I throw out a final question: "Does the house have any secret passages—any hidden way to get into the Billiard Room?"

"You're being fanciful now. That only happens in the movies."

Probably—but we'll check hard behind the bookcases all the same.

We send Root on his way and tell him everyone has to leave the property now until we finish with the crime scene. That gets his goat and earns us another threat about calling the Governor. I yawn.

When we're alone again, Scott says, "That guy reminds me of a James Bond villain, complete with his own exotic henchman and young sidepiece who really isn't into him."

The analogy makes a lot of sense after a night of no sleep.

13

Barbara Hsu, lead prosecutor for the murder squad, arrives bearing the gifts of signed search warrants for both Gustave's mansion and Jim Walker's home in Midtown. Barbara is one of the best trial lawyers in the city and earned the derogatory nickname "Dragon Lady" from all the criminals she has sent to prison over the years. But she embraces the label with pride as an acknowledgment that she is damn good at what she does. And—truth be told—having an intimidating brand isn't the worst thing in our line of work. The name adds to Barbara's scary aura.

The team gathers together in the study. We're now the only people in the house. I'm too tired to think and start the meeting off on that note.

"Am I the only one who needs sleep? Should we take a break and meet up again here in the afternoon to ensure that we do the search right? Patrol officers can keep any prying eyes away until we regroup."

The others nod their wearied heads in agreement. But before we split up, I want to hear the status of things. Sophie begins.

"Patrol officers searched the grounds and didn't find anybody hiding in the bushes, no indication of any intruders whatsoever. A tall, stone fence surrounds the perimeter of the estate—not the kind of wall one can simply hop over. I questioned the security guard who mans the front gate. Once all the guests arrived for the party, no one else entered the property. The gate can't open without the guard's say-so. Even if he wasn't paying the closest attention, we can still be confident that the rest of the world remained locked out from accessing the house. And we all know what that means. Someone at the party killed our victim."

That's what we figured, but it's nice to be sure. I say, "Marlon, that means you've been sitting in the same room as the murderer for hours now. Who did it?"

He laughs and gives a rundown on the goings-on in the dining room.

"No one confessed, if that's what you're looking for. But whatever you did certainly kicked the hornet's nest. Gustave returned in a foul temper, took out his phone, and immediately left a loud, angry voicemail with the Governor. He spent the rest of the time huddling close with Vivian and Mr. Beale—especially Vivian. He pounced on her when she came back after talking to you guys. Weird energy between the two of them. Mark Romo passed out drunk. Erica Cain was steaming mad and stayed that way. Celeste Wood kept to herself and appeared to resent being stuck with this group of people. She eventually took a nap. Jessica Allen started posting about being harassed by the cops on Instagram but giggled while she typed about it. Leo Ivanov kept his listening ears on the whole time, but maybe he's ex-KGB and it's a habit. Oliver Twist badgered people about how it went when they came back into the room. Everyone ignored him. Aaron Cain was barely conscious, and Mr. Beale just sat there with a blank face, never saying a word."

Scott asks, "How does Beale communicate with Gustave?"

Marlon answers, "Telepathy is the best guess at this point."

My cell buzzes in my pocket, and I work overtime to focus my eyes on the incoming text. The words don't register at first, or maybe I just don't want to understand them—the Governor wants me to swing over to the Governor's Mansion when I'm finished here.

And Jesus wept. I'll never sleep again at this rate.

The team makes plans to meet up in the afternoon. I hand out parting assignments, "Marlon—when you come back today, I want you on that door to the Billiard Room. Can the inside latch be turned from outside the room? Sophie and J.D.—you're in charge of searching Jim Walker's place. Send over a patrol car to keep an eye on it until you're ready. Taylor—do background checks and internet searches to find out everything you can about the people here tonight. Also, see what you can scare up about Sylvia Pinker. Gustave gave us her name in connection with the Cains. Some kind of trouble, but he wouldn't specify. Barbara—a number of the guests have had legal problems magically disappear through the help of Jim Walker. Scott will give you the details but see what you can root out about those situations. And everyone—for the love of God, get some sleep."

The meeting breaks up, but we all mill around together in the aftermath. Out of delirium, I suppose. Scott points to the Adolph Hitler painting on the wall and explains Gustave's fascination with all things Nazi.

Marlon mutters, "White people."

And with that, we call it a night.

14

When Georgia needed a new home for its governors in the 1960s, Tuxedo Park was the natural choice. Now, the massive Greek Revival structure—encircled by dozens of Doric columns on all sides—dominates the view from West Paces Ferry Road. I drive through the gates and stumble toward the front door on barely-functioning legs.

On the way, I see Susan Benson sneaking out to her car to leave before the sun gets too bright. She gives me a little wave and makes her getaway. Benson wears a bunch of different hats. For one, she is the Chief Justice of the Georgia Supreme Court and a living legend in the state's legal community. But her presence at the Mansion this morning is in a more unofficial capacity—as the Governor's lover, a fact more secret than the formula to Coca-Cola. The secrecy isn't because they're cheating on other people. Minton's wife, Ruth, died a few years ago, and Benson has never married. Rather, a romantic relationship between the state's governor and chief justice is dicey on ethical grounds. Separation of powers and all that. But I pretend not to notice. Not my circus, not my monkeys.

Closer to home, Benson remains a sore topic in my family because of her affair decades ago with my late father—the then-serving Lieutenant Governor. While ancient history in most quarters, knowledge of Daddy's extracurricular activities only recently reached me. The truth hurt at first, but I eventually forgave him just as Jesus has forgiven me. I even made peace with Susan Benson after an uneven start to our acquaintance. The rest of the Meridian clan, though, has yet to make that leap.

Governor Minton McReynolds looks like a governor—probably because his regal crown of white hair screams wisdom and gravitas. He gives me a warm hug at the entrance to the Mansion. The gesture is heartfelt. Minton held my newborn body in the hospital the day I was born and has been a guiding presence in my life ever since. Two years short of political retirement, he formed the murder squad a couple of months ago and appointed me to lead it as his lasting legacy to the state of Georgia—an untouchable group of lawyers and investigators dedicated to combatting crime and corruption at its source. "Restoring the public trust," he called it. Sounds nice on a postcard. As for Minton and Benson, if dating the former mistress of his lifelong best friend is awkward for him, he's never let on to me.

He leads me into the library and says, "What the hell is going on? Gustave Root keeps leaving me messages saying that you're a menace to democratic order. He's demanding that I relieve you of your duties posthaste."

The thought doesn't sound all that bad—if it meant that I could finally go to sleep. I emit a short chortle of derision before responding.

"Your friend Gustave is a Nazi."

"What the hell are you talking about?"

I give him the details of Root's Third Reich fetish and his unrequited itch for the federal government's stash of Hitler art. Minton's face reacts to the news as if he just encountered the foulest of smells—the stench of fascism still strong nearly a hundred years after the fact.

"That's not all. Your friend Gustave keeps throwing your name around like a meat cleaver, too. He is of the apparent belief that his past campaign contributions to you means that you're his puppet. Told me—and I quote: '*I don't think you realize how much money I've donated to the Governor over the years.*' Straight out of the horse's mouth."

"The hell you say?"

"No joke. You should block your friend Gustave's number if you want any peace and quiet for the rest of your life."

"Damn blasted, stop calling him my friend."

I smile honey at him, and Minton grumbles some more. He also removes his phone from his pocket and blocks Gustave's number, making a big production of the action for his audience of one. I needle him some more.

"Am I allowed to tell your ex-friend Gustave what you just did?"

"Please do. Any man who takes for granted that I can be bought deserves to be brought down a few pegs. Hell, worse than that—deserves to be thrown off the damn roof as far as I'm concerned. I don't suppose you solved the murder yet, have you?"

"I've already talked to the killer face-to-face."

"Really? Who?"

"Don't know. But it's definitely someone who was attending a party in the house at the time."

He scoffs at my sleight-of-hand. The realization hits me that I've yet to question Aaron Cain, meaning that I may have inadvertently told Minton a lie about talking to the murderer already. But I don't correct the record, figuring the odds are in my favor. I change the subject to make conversation.

"Does Susan just live here all the time now? She waved to me as she fled the scene."

"I wanted to talk to you about that."

"Yeah?"

"Susan is stepping down from the Supreme Court, and we're going to get married."

"Wow—congratulations."

"Many thanks. I have to ask a favor of you."

"Yeah?"

He hesitates—a hangdog manner overtakes him, and he looks down at his feet to avoid my eyes. I move my gaze to check out his shoes but fail to see anything of interest. He continues.

"We're going to announce the engagement to the world next week, and I am hoping that you could break the news to your mother before then."

That request wakes me up quick. Mom long ago forgave Daddy for his sexual indiscretion. But she has never extended a similar thought of mercy to the other party involved in her husband's infidelity. Minton wants me to undertake a kamikaze mission. I demur.

"You're the one who has been lifelong friends with her, and it's your news. Seems only fair that you be the one to deliver it."

"I'm scared of her."

"And I'm not?"

From one perspective, the scene is absurd. The most powerful man in the state quaking in fear right before my eyes. Except only people who haven't met my mother would be surprised at our playing hot potato to avoid being the bearer of bad news. Mom scares a lot of people. Her heart is as wide as the Mississippi River but so is her bite.

The Governor pleads, "Please, Chance. I already have another difficult conversation on my plate."

"Martha?"

He nods.

Martha Towns is Minton's long-time administrative assistant. She has no bite and is the nicest person I've yet to encounter in nearly four decades of wandering around the earth. She even bakes me cookies. By my recollection, I only remember her ever expressing harsh feelings toward one other person—Susan Benson. During our one conversation on the topic, Martha refused even to utter Benson's name, referring to her only as "that woman" and blaming her for leading my otherwise righteous father astray. I hope Minton's bombshell doesn't kill her—or that she doesn't kill him.

I say, "Minton, it's your bed. You should be the one to lie in it."

He begs and cajoles some more, showing no sign of letting up until he wears down my resistance. I envy him his energy and good night's sleep. When it becomes obvious that only my acquiescence will allow me to escape his clutches and go home, I relent. Driving off in search of a good pillow, I kick myself for allowing Minton to hoist his circus and monkeys onto to my shoulders. Mom figures to be livid and may very well devour the messenger in retaliation.

God help me.

* * *

I remove the key from the ignition of the car. Another five minutes and I would've fallen asleep behind the wheel, leaving my survival to the fates. On the way home, I made a detour to pick up a Chick-Fil-A chicken biscuit and fresh coffee for my wife Cate—a peace offering for never making it home last night. I grab the bag of God's chicken and head inside.

She stands in the bathroom brushing her dark auburn hair. Cate is the newest Justice on the Georgia Supreme Court, and today she will hear oral arguments. She once observed to me that the male justices can show up to court as sloppy as a pig, and no one cares. But the slightest blemish on a female justice brings out the freaks on social media. No surprise there. Weak men fear strong women.

When she sees me in the mirror bearing my gifts, she shakes her head with a wry smile and doesn't pull any punches.

"You look like absolute hell!"

Her frankness is one of her most appealing virtues. When the former Chief Justice of the Georgia Supreme Court—a vile man who needed a good killing and got one—propositioned Cate to join him in his hotel room during a state bar conference, she refused the offer on the grounds that she had no interest in his "limp, wrinkled dick." That told me right there that she was a keeper.

After warning me not to mess up her hair, she turns around to give me a long hug, saying, "That's the first night we've spent apart since getting married. I missed you."

The marriage is a couple of months old now. To the surprise of everyone, most of all ourselves, we bound ourselves to one another in matrimonial bliss less than two weeks after we first met. Each of us was broken in our own way—a cheating ex-husband on her side, the unsolved murder of my first wife and son on mine. But joined together, the hurts of the past don't sting as much, and the prospects for the future appear hopeful.

I answer, "You had the dogs to keep you company."

"Not the same and you know it."

We both are dog people. One of our first priorities as a married couple focused on adding to the family. Cate wanted to rescue a couple of mutts from the local pound, but I prevailed on her to go a different direction for defense purposes. A recent home invasion—in addition to the murder of my family three years ago—made me firm on this point. The result was the addition of two German Shepherd puppies that are being trained to be both loving and lethal. The next time an uninvited person sets foot in my house, death by canine is the intended result.

For reasons I have yet to fathom, Cate named the dogs Sweetheart and Bristol—branding not in keeping with the ferociousness that I was going for. But I made peace with her decision. In the words of Shakespeare's Juliet, "A rose by any other name would smell as sweet." The same principle works here. No matter what you call these new dogs of mine, their German Shepherd teeth remain just as sharp.

As she heads out the door, I say, "Got some news. Susan is stepping down from the Court. She and Minton are getting married. Announcement next week."

Shock fills her face. The retirement of one of Cate's colleagues is a big deal in itself. But the personal side is even more meaningful for her. She is one of the few people to know about the secret relationship, even to the point of spending a couple of nights with them at the Governor's Mansion a few months back. Both Minton and Benson took Cate under their wings during that time and have kept her there ever since.

"The Governor told you that?"

"Yeah. He wants me to break the news to Mom before then."

She holds a serious expression for a few seconds before bursting out in a laugh that shakes the foundation of the whole house. I grumble, "Take it easy or you'll mess up your hair."

Cate sticks out her tongue at me and heads to the carport.

With her hand on the door to leave, she turns back and says, "Before I forget, your fortieth birthday is coming up. What do you want?"

"For you to tell Mom about Minton and Susan Benson."

"I'd divorce you first. Next option?"

"Right now, all I want is sleep."

She laughs again and leaves me to it. I kick off my shoes but otherwise crash onto the bed fully clothed, setting the alarm for noon.

Sweetheart and Bristol join me and take up a disproportionate share of the real estate. No matter. I could fall asleep on a bed of nails at this point. I drift off to dream of clowns, contortionists, and eight-foot tall albinos.

15

Driving through the gates of Gustave Root's mansion for the second time that day, I reflect that I'm too old to be pulling all-nighters. The noon alarm sounded with distressing suddenness, and a quick shower did little to fire up my synapses. Lunch was Chick-Fil-A on the go. Maybe I'll have dinner at McDonald's for some variety. When I pull up to the house, the cars parked in front confirm that I'm the last of the team to arrive. But that's okay. I'm the boss.

I head straight to the Billiard Room. Marlon stands outside the door to the murder scene, a toolbox next to his feet. I ask, "Crack the code yet?"

"Nope. I've tried every which way possible and no dice. You can write it down in stone—the latch can only be locked from inside the room."

If Marlon writes it down in stone, it stays in stone. But I groan a little in my heart. Catching a murderer is hard enough in normal conditions. Now we have to deal with a Houdini who somehow engineered a magical escape. I probe Marlon's feelings on the matter.

"Got a solution to the problem for me? Did the killer jump off the balcony?"

"I'm not buying that."

"Me, either. But the possibilities are dwindling."

"No secret entrance to the room, either. I checked."

Scott and Barbara Hsu join us. Thinking out loud, I explain the dilemma for the benefit of the group.

"The killer locks the door from the inside. How then does he get away? First possibility—some trick exists to actually locking the door from outside the room. But Marlon has tried all the angles and ruled that out. Take that option off the board. Second—the killer locks the

70

door and makes a crazy leap from the balcony out back. Not to my liking, but it's possible. What else do we have?"

The four of us nurse the puzzle in silence for a spell. Marlon snaps his fingers and grabs our attention.

"Somebody stabs Walker out in the hall here. Walker rushes to get away, manages to slip into the Billiard Room, and locks the door to prevent a further attack."

We chew on the scenario. Barbara says, "No blood anywhere except the pool table, though. You'd think there'd be at least some droplets between here and there if he was walking that much."

Scott adds, "And would the knife have really stayed in his back that whole time?"

The group goes back to thinking. After a prolonged period of contemplation, Barbara asks, "What about the fireplace?"

I barely noticed the fireplace during my first visit to the Billiard Room. Now we all move in for a closer inspection. Barbara's thought is an interesting one. The fireplace is almost the size of a walk-in closet and even has a little space off to the side for a person to partially hide inside. I ask her, "How do you figure it?"

"The killer stabbed the victim and tried to make a getaway through the hall. But someone approached, and the killer locked the door in a panic, hoping for another chance to make a go at it. When that plan fell through, he hid in the fireplace and then sneaked out in the confusion once the body was discovered."

A neat theory, but probably only the diminutive Jessica Allen could pull off hiding in the chimney—big as it is—without attracting any notice. And I'm not sure someone would've had the opportunity to slip away in any commotion, either. After Twist and Romo climbed up the ladder, everyone else seemed to make their way to this room in pretty quick order. I suppose the murderer could've just popped out and tried to blend in with everyone on the fly. But I don't like those odds.

Scott ducks into the chimney to give Barbara's hypothesis a field test. He emerges looking like Dick Van Dyke in *Mary Poppins*. The soot covering his head gives the rest of us a good laugh. He goes off mumbling curses to find the nearest bathroom, and I strike off hiding in the chimney as a realistic possibility. Someone surely would've noticed if another guest was darkened with black powder.

Marlon suggests, "Suicide? Walker locks the door to ensure success."

He pretends to hold a knife and makes a motion bringing his hand over the top of his head to show how a person might go about stabbing himself in the back. But his heart really isn't into it. I remind him that the knife didn't have prints, and Walker wasn't wearing gloves.

Scott returns and announces, "I figured it out. The circus freak learned knife-throwing at an early age and hurled the dagger through an open window right into Walker's back."

Barbara—who has yet to meet the talented Mr. Beale—wears a confused look about the meaning of Scott's words. I leave it to the others to fill her in.

* * *

Three things from searching the house stand out. First, two other staircases—one at the side of the mansion and one at the back—provide access to the second floor and hence to the Billiard Room. The upshot is that all the suspects could've reached the scene of the murder without risking too much detection. Second, for being the lady of the house, Vivian's presence is barely noticeable. She has her own bedroom that is decidedly spartan compared to rest of the mansion and lacks anything that would suggest a personal touch. That's the extent of the evidence that she actually lives here. Third, Root's private closet features an autographed copy of *Mein Kampf* from Hitler himself and a framed swastika on the wall. I take multiple pictures of both to later give the Governor some more grief about his good friend Gustave.

Afterward, the team gathers again in the study to debrief. Taylor starts the ball rolling by sharing the results of her deep dive into each of the suspects.

"Not sure what level of detail you want from me. Most of these people are famous and generate a lot of internet chatter. But here are the highlights. I'll start with Mark Romo since he's the biggest name.

Mark has had a myriad of substance abuse problems—both booze and drugs. Starting to affect his career. Another high-profile slip up, and he may be toast."

A dead child after a hit-and-run would seem to qualify on that score. Taylor continues.

"Jessica Allen lives on social media and has already posted a ton about being harassed by the police last night. She can be mean, too. One time she got mad at a Twitter post critical of her and responded by unleashing an internet mob on the author of the tweet, giving out the person's address and everything. Except Allen named the wrong woman. Didn't stop her sycophants from harassing the poor lady, though. A lawsuit is ongoing."

Once a bully, always a bully. I'm surprised Allen didn't live-tweet our questioning of her.

"Next up—Gustave Root. The details are scant, but he may have been on Epstein Island with all those other pedophiles. No official interest in him from the authorities, but the rumors persist."

Taylor winces in disgust—and rightly so. Jeffrey Epstein's role as sex trafficker of underaged girls for the rich and powerful is revolting on too many fronts to count—Pedophile Island, the Lolita Express, all of it. Of course, Gustave would've been a guest there. How could it be any other way? Color me unsurprised. I have a robust theology about the depravity of men.

Vivian's words about how she ended up with her husband haunt me in the moment: "*I was trapped in an awful situation surrounded by horrible people who didn't have my best interest at heart. Gustave offered me an escape hatch. I took it.*" Hard not to put two and two together.

Before Taylor moves on to the next suspect, Scott mutters under his breath, "Epstein didn't kill himself." I reckon he's probably right on that one.

"Now about Oliver Twist. As a magician, he's no David Copperfield. Twist has never been quite able to break into the big time. But he recently signed a production deal with Gustave Root's entertainment company and is finally on the verge of his big break."

I'm skeptical. Setting aside the fact that he almost killed his assistant in a trick gone bad, Twist's faker-than-fake stage presence is about as fresh as three-day old fish. But what do I know about putting on a magic show?

"Not much on everybody else. Aaron and Erica Cain are high-powered lawyers who don't seem to have much of a life otherwise. Celeste Wood's artwork is pretty awesome, but I didn't learn anything personal about her except that she was on the swim team in college. Leo Ivanov—everything was either about chess or math. Nothing interesting there. Finally, we come to Vivian Root and Mr. Beale. Strangest thing—couldn't find a solitary scrap about either of them. Both are digital ghosts. Find me their real names, and I can search again. But as of right now, no indications are out there that either of them even exists."

I start to connect the dots. If Gustave Root found Mr. Beale in Europe and took Vivian away from Epstein Island, then a meaningful possibility exists that neither is in the country legally—a fact that Gustave would not hesitate to hold over their heads if push came to shove.

Scott asks, "What about Sylvia Pinker? The woman Gustave indicated was mixed up with the Cains."

"Oh yeah, her. She's a lawyer in town and easy to find. Formerly worked for the firm of Cain & Cunningham. I called her up and asked about her relationship with the Cains. But she refused to talk and even cited some kind of non-disclosure agreement. When I explained that I was calling in connection with Jim Walker's murder, she hung up on me."

* * *

The charge to Barbara was to uncover more details about Mark Romo's hit-and-run, Celeste Wood's DUI, and Oliver Twist's accidental shooting of his assistant. Holding a long yellow legal pad—the best friend to lawyers everywhere—she summarizes her findings.

"I'll start with Twist. Paramedics rushed his assistant, Missy Howard, to the hospital for emergency surgery related to a gunshot wound. Any kind of shooting, the ER calls the police. The cops pressed Twist pretty hard and were thinking about at least a reckless endangerment charge but wanted to wait until they could talk to Missy first. By the time she was conscious again, the district attorney had already decided the shooting was a tragic accident and nothing more. The word was that some connected lawyer had pulled the right strings on Twist's behalf. I got this intel from a friend on the force."

Barbara shakes her head in stern disapproval at the unequal distribution of justice. Too bad Jim Walker never had occasion to try buttering up the Dragon Lady to drop the charges against one of his clients. I would've paid good money to see the resulting bloodbath.

Scott asks, "So Twist is a jerk and no great shakes as a magician. But this information actually makes it less likely that he killed Walker, right? Too many people already know about Twist's dirty little secret for Walker to hold it over his head."

"Unless he has other secrets," Marlon observes.

We all ponder what other mysteries may be stashed away in Oliver Twist's closet as Barbara continues with Celeste Wood.

"Arrested for DUI and nothing ever happened after that. The initial citation still exists in paper form, but nowhere else. Can't even find her mug shot. Doubt the prosecutors ever knew about the charge. That kind of thing happens a lot with misdemeanors if the you know the right people."

Or if the police chief is a Garth Brooks fan. But I doubt Celeste's DUI played any role in Walker's murder. If she killed her date to Gustave's party, the reasons were more personal.

And that leaves Mark Romo. Still nothing on that front. The police never learned about his involvement in the hit-and-run that killed the kid, meaning Barbara has to make her own list of unsolved accidents in the area with similar facts until we can find the dead child we're looking for.

* * *

Sophie and J.D. begin by describing their search of Jim Walker's home. Sophie starts.

"Nice place. All masculine—not a hint of a woman's touch anywhere. But not a slobfest like a normal guy. No offense intended to present company."

She glances around at the men in the room with an expression that suggests she did intend some offense. But none of us take her up on the offer. Some of the men here are slobs, but I won't name names. She continues.

"Expensive furnishings everywhere. I was afraid to touch anything but then figured that Walker was dead and had bigger problems on his plate. Just one example, but he probably had $50,000 in watches in a case right on his nightstand—a Rolex, couple of Omegas, and other brands I've never heard of."

The one Rolex on him when he died was not enough, apparently. I study my own nice-looking $100 watch and sit mystified as to what extra value a timepiece that costs thousands of dollars brings.

Sophie goes on, "So we're searching but not learning anything insightful except that dead guy Jim had a sweet tooth for the finer things. But then J.D. stumbles into Walker's home office, and things start to get interesting. I'll let him tell it."

"Bills. A lot of bills. The victim owed a lot of people a lot of money, mostly in connection with The Bar's Bar. That thing must be bleeding cash. Looked to me like Walker personally guaranteed a number of loans on that place, and the collectors are banging on his door. Why does a big-time lawyer feel the need to open a bar anyway? He's already rich."

Metaphysical questions like that are above my pay grade. But emptiness can make a person seek meaning in all kinds of strange ways—even opening a pub.

J.D. adds, "Found some bankruptcy pleadings on his desk, too. Doesn't appear to me that they've been filed yet. But any way you cut it, Walker appears to be in financial hock, despite his new contract with Cain & Cunningham."

I ask, "What's this about a new contract?"

"Part of his papers. A new contract doubling up Walker's pay to a cool $1.5 million a year with a lot of other legal mumbo jumbo in it. Aaron Cain signed it, too, as managing partner of Cain & Cunningham. Two weeks ago based on the date."

He pulls a copy of the document out from a satchel and says, "Here it is if the lawyers in the room want to look at it."

Barbara sticks her hand out and retreats to a corner to pour over her new reading material.

A buzz sounds, and all of us check our phones for an incoming message. But only Marlon finds success. After a moment, he announces, "Just got word about the hair sample from Aaron Cain that I sent to the lab. Testing confirms that he had Rohypnol in his system—a roofie, the date rape drug."

A confused silence lingers in the room. Marlon's news would've made a bigger impact—if any of us only knew what to do with it.

16

The last experiment of the day involves the balcony to the Billiard Room. While most of the team gathers next to the pool, Sophie and J.D. perch themselves on the murderer's possible escape route and look down at the rest of us.

I yell, "So the question is—could someone escape by means of jumping off that balcony? Thoughts?"

Marlon points out, "There's another possibility. The balcony to the bedroom Aaron Cain was resting in is right over there—fifteen feet away. We need to rule that jump out, too."

"Impossible," Scott contends.

The railings for both balconies preclude a would-be jumper from getting a running start, and a standing leap of that length strikes me as a bridge too far—especially for a late middle-aged lawyer with Rohypnol in his system. But Marlon's right that we need to eliminate it as a possibility. After some discussion on the feasibility of a balcony-to-balcony means of escape—including a debate as to whether Mr. Beale's legs could reach that far—we all agree to rule that option out as a working hypothesis.

And that leaves jumping down. J.D. peeks over the balcony to the ground below and doesn't like what he sees. He declares, "Ain't nobody jumping this!" He backs away from the edge for good measure. Sophie brushes past him and says, "Get out of the way."

He gets out of the way.

Sophie peers down to the ground below. Without any hesitation, she whips her legs over the metal rails of the balcony, providing a worrisome shock to the rest of us. She then carefully maneuvers her hands to the bottom of the rails before letting her feet dangle between the balcony and the ground. Holding the position as she studies the ground below her—an impressive feat of strength in itself—she starts to swing her legs for the dismount. She then flies through the air and endures a hard landing for her trouble. One grimace and a shake of her ankle later, she flashes an uncertain smile and says, "Harder than it looks."

I don't know whether to applaud or yell at her. From up top, J.D. looks like he might vomit. Everyone else starts to breathe again.

Scott asks, "Could any of the suspects perform the feat we just witnessed?"

I run through the list. Gustave Root—he'd never survive that leap. Mark Romo—pretty sure he lacks the nerve and sobriety. Erica Cain—in her business suit? Please. Vivian Root in her bathrobe—doubtful. Jessica Allen—too short and lacking the necessary muscles. Leo Ivanov—never. Aaron Cain with Rohypnol in him—laughable. Oliver Twist—nowhere nimble enough. His plastic surgery would crack on the spot. Mr. Beale—no idea, but I'll count him as a maybe. That leaves Celeste Wood—she's in good shape with a long swimmer's figure, but she's not Sophie-fit. No one is. And Sophie barely made the jump.

* * *

Scott and I drive to see the medical examiner. I was wrong about McDonald's for dinner. Instead, we breeze through the Chick-Fil-A drive-thru for a quick bite, allowing me to complete the breakfast, lunch, and dinner chicken trifecta. And not for the first time, either.

Alona Mendoza is the murder squad's go-to medical examiner. We don't have the volume of cases to justify our own full-time person, but DeKalb County—prodded by some financial incentives thrown to it by the Governor—lends her to us whenever the need arises.

Jim Walker's naked body rests on Alona's cold table when Scott and I enter the autopsy room. Less than twenty-four hours ago, Walker was living the high life at one of Atlanta's most palatial estates. Now look at him. The swiftness with which murder shatters a lifetime of plans never ceases to get to me—all of Jim Walker's hopes and concerns

79

left discarded on a snooker table. For better or worse, only one bill collector is left for him to worry about—God.

Alona is of Basque descent and has the Spanish looks to prove it. Her long, dark hair is typically in a bun to minimize any distractions, and tonight is no different. She greets us with a friendly smile, and I wonder—as I have on previous occasions—about her odd choice of committing her life to probing the secrets of the dead. Her dedication is intense. Unmarried and in her mid-30s, Alona has the reputation of being the hardest government worker in metro Atlanta. I believe it. But that doesn't leave much room for a social life. She doesn't seem to mind. Not one to waste time, she launches into it.

"Easy diagnosis on this one—a single, deep incision wound into the back that pierced the backside of the heart. Death followed quickly. Did you recover the murder weapon? If not, you're looking for something remarkably sharp."

We tell her about the Nazi honor dagger and enjoy the expression of horror that dots Alona's facial landscape in the aftermath. Her eyes flare, and she pantomimes a spitting motion in disgust. That gets our attention.

She explains, "I hate the fascists with every ounce of my being. Hitler helped Francisco Franco's rise to power in Spain. Americans always forget about Franco, but he ruled over Spain with an iron fist for four decades, even banning the Basque language and culture. My parents fled to escape the oppression."

Alona spits again.

Hemingway's *For Whom The Bell Tolls* takes place during the Spanish Civil War. By my reckoning, the book is his masterpiece. One quote has stuck with me through the years: "There are many who do not know they are fascists but will find it out when the time comes."

So true. I tend to believe that a petty little fascist lives in all of us. Something inside the human psyche pushes a person to want to tell others how to live—the judging gene that allows us to feel superior to our fellow creatures, our own inner Pharisee. I'm no different. I became a prosecutor for a reason.

80

Scott tells Alona, "Since you feel so strongly about it, we won't even tell you about the Hitler painting and the swastika then."

Zero chance that bait isn't going to catch the fish. After her strongly-worded encouragement, we proceed to tell Alona about the Hitler painting and the swastika. A series of exclamations in some strange tongue—Basque presumably—flows with machine-gun rapidness out of the medical examiner's lips. I catch the meaning without deciphering the words.

Before we leave, Alona adds, "One weird note from the toxicology report. He had Rohypnol in him."

* * *

Driving away, Scott asks, "Who do you think did it? My money's on Gustave."

"He's the only one with a real alibi."

"True, but I just don't like the guy."

"You and Alona both."

We sit in silence considering the case. Thinking about Scott's question about the most likely culprit, I keep coming back to the question of the locked door and tell him as much.

"If we're limited to the balcony as the means of escape, we're looking at Mr. Beale or Celeste Wood, right? That jump is no joke."

"I could buy Romo."

"Physically, yes. But otherwise?"

He shrugs and responds, "Let's focus on the possible for the time being. Romo has the physique to pull the stunt off and claims he didn't get wasted until after seeing Jim Walker's dead body. He's in, along with Mr. Beale and Celeste. You already know how I feel about the circus freak—and if he did it, then no doubt he was operating under Gustave's orders. That outcome wouldn't displease me. As for Celeste, she's the only one to actually confess. Maybe she was being clever by hiding in plain sight."

Her parting words come back to me: "*Yes! I confess! I killed him and then used the balcony as a high dive to make my getaway into*

81

the pool! And I would've gotten away with it, too, if it weren't for you meddling kids!"

I don't want to believe it. Celeste may be the only one of the party guests that I actually like. And there's the Scooby-Doo connection. My son Cale and I spent hours watching Scooby-Doo cartoons together, the both of us invariably singing along with the theme song—always out of tune but with full enthusiasm. My wife Amber would shake her head at our antics.

A solitary tear runs down my cheek as I swim in the memory of those stolen from me. For years after the murders, I didn't cry at all—suffocating to death all my emotions, except for the anger and the hate. But that strategy reached its expiration date, and my life collapsed in the aftermath.

A nervous Scott questions, "Are you crying?"

"Thinking about Cale."

He nods and allows me some space. But then a weird thing happens. I realize in the moment that the tear running down my face doesn't come from a place of loss. Usually when I reflect on Amber and Cale, the overriding feeling is sadness. This time, though, is different. Instead of pain, the memory of spending time with my son is a spontaneous injection of joy.

I stare out of the car window and smile.

* * *

Cate is waiting up for me when I straggle in. She says, "You look better than this morning at least."

"Not sure I feel better."

"Want to tell me about it?"

No harm exists in sharing some details of the investigation with her. She's an automatic recusal for any case that comes before the Supreme Court from the murder squad as it is. I give her a rough outline of Gustave Root and his strange assortment of friends. Her focus narrows like a laser beam.

She pants, "Mark Romo? You met Mark Romo? He's hot."

"He's a drunken dolt."

"Still hot. Have you ever seen him with his shirt off?"

Part of me wants to tell her about the kid Romo left for dead. That would burst her bubble. But I'm keeping the information about the hit-and-run still close to my vest. Instead, I just grunt. She changes the subject.

"Thought anymore about what you want for your birthday? You only turn forty once."

"Surprise me."

"That's helpful."

I shrug my shoulders and head to the shower to turn the water on. As I wait for the water to warm, Cate switches gears again.

"You still owe me a honeymoon, you know. Two months from now, my calendar is clear."

The speed of our nuptials made planning a honeymoon impossible. We compensated by celebrating the wedding over a snowy weekend in a suite at the Four Seasons in Midtown Atlanta. Since then, Cate's appointment to the Georgia Supreme Court and the formation of the murder squad has keep both of us busy spinning plates. But she is right. I do owe her a honeymoon and put the question to her.

"Where do you want to go?"

"Australia has been on my mind lately. Have you ever been?"

I blanch. The color in my face must've drained fast because her hopeful eyes die a quick death. With a worried voice, she asks, "What?"

"That's where Amber and I honeymooned."

Cate groans and says, "I'm not competing with that."

"Stop it. If you want to go to Australia, we'll go to Australia."

She shakes her head with great vigor before explaining, "You don't understand. My ex-husband is a cheating scoundrel. Only thing you have to do to be better than him is to keep your penis in your pants. That's a low bar. But Amber is a saint—a martyred saint even. Before you object, you've been wonderful about never making me feel like I have to measure myself against her. I mean that. But it's still a weight I carry around with me, sparring with the memory of a dead woman."

"We can make our own memories there."

"Not for our honeymoon. Later, yes. But our honeymoon needs to be *our* honeymoon. Besides, I don't want to face the situation thirty years from now where we're reminiscing about our honeymoon in Australia, and you talk about something that happened with Amber. Because then I might have to divorce you on the spot."

I breathe a sigh of relief. I would go to Australia if that's what she wants, but a honeymoon trip with a different woman over the exact same ground I traveled with Amber on our honeymoon is begging emotional trauma to punch me where it hurts. Maybe Cate senses that, too. I offer an alternative.

"I've never been to New Zealand."

"Too close to Australia."

Water from the shower pounds on the glass, and steam takes over most of the bathroom. The hot liquid pouring over me would feel heavenly, but the moment requires my full attention. Cate's words about Amber break my heart. Tonight is the first time she has revealed any concern about living in my late wife's shadow, and I can tell that she really was excited about going to Australia. Scurrying for a solution to revive her spirits, I land on a possibility.

"Italy? I've never been there."

Her face lights up, and she responds, "Me, either. And I've always wanted to go. Which part? Rome? Venice? Florence? I hear Lake Como is beautiful."

"Let's do all of it. How much time can you take off?"

Cate approaches me with generous eyes and gives me a light kiss on the lips—much like she did at the end of our first date. A tight hug follows. She whispers, "*Ti amo.*"

"I love you, too."

17

The next day starts bright and early. The murder squad's headquarters occupies the second floor in Georgia's new five-story courthouse—home also to the state Supreme Court and Court of Appeals. Everyone on the team calls our space "the Office." Persons unknown to me decided that the effect of the name packed a greater punch with the "O" capitalized, and the convention stuck. But the name is far less important than the location. The convenience of working in the same building allows Cate and me to commute together the vast majority of the time. This morning we are back in our familiar routine, and I bask in the normalcy. We talk about Italy for most of the drive.

Within fifteen minutes of arriving at the Office, I'm back on the road again—this time with Scott as my traveling companion. We're on our way to question Aaron Cain at the offices of Cain & Cunningham in Buckhead. Last night, Barbara emailed her analysis of the new contract Jim Walker signed with his law firm: "Standard agreement in most ways, five-year term, but real heavy on confidential provisions—basically bulletproof—preventing Walker from ever revealing client or firm secrets. Stronger than anything I've ever seen. Reading between the lines, the law firm sounded worried on that front."

That information fits one of the working theories—Walker's leveraging his knowledge of sensitive secrets to pry cash out of people.

Before we enter the building, Scott says, "You take the lead. These big firm lawyers get snippy when talking to regular cops. Might respond better to you."

"Doubtful. Most of the lot tend to look down on everybody."

We announce ourselves, and an assistant leads us right away to Aaron Cain's corner office. Cain & Cunningham is one of Atlanta's oldest and biggest firms. I reckon that Aaron is a descendant of the original Cain who first put his name on the firm's shingle. A large painting in Aaron's office of a century-old white guy with the name-plate "Sebastian Cain, Attorney at Law" confirms the hunch—the Oliver Wendell Holmes handlebar mustache a nice ode to the by-gone time.

Aaron welcomes us with a smile and open arms. After his wife Erica's chilly attitude toward us the other night—which we gave back to her in return—I expected something in the way of a stiff upper lip. But Aaron is the managing partner of a 1,000-lawyer behemoth. Public relations and fake smiles go with the territory.

After shaking hands, he says, "I have a bone to pick with you, Mr. Meridian."

"Yeah?"

"You are the only lawyer in this town that appears on the front page of the *Daily Report* more than I do."

He gives a hearty laugh. The *Daily Report* is a specialized newspaper that reports on the happenings in the Atlanta legal community. Taylor keeps a scrapbook of the squad's media appearances, including the *Daily Report*, but I don't pay it much mind. That Cain keeps internal score of such things reveals a healthy self-regard or an underlying inferiority complex—maybe both.

I answer, "I really wouldn't know much about it."

"Not a big reader?"

"I read a ton—just not my own press clippings."

If he takes offense at the subtle dig, he fails to show it. Instead, he chuckles again as if we're all old friends. He invites us to sit down, and we accept the invitation. I ask, "How are you feeling?"

"Much better than the other night. Don't know what came over me. But it could've been worse. Terrible about what happened to Jim."

"You really have no idea why you weren't feeling well?"

"No—why?"

"Because you were drugged with Rohypnol."

Cain looks as if he doesn't believe me. He rubs his cheek and frowns before responding.

"A roofie?"

"You know about roofies?"

He doesn't answer the question and just sits there staring down at his desk lost in thought. At last, he asks, "How do you know I was drugged?"

"Hair sample."

"You stole my hair?"

"Picked it off the floor of Gustave's dining room. You didn't seem to mind."

The eyes become sharper and scrutinize us with a growing distrust. More silence. I figure he's searching his brain for any clue as to whether picking up a strand of someone's hair off the ground without consent constitutes an illegal search. But Cain practices corporate law and doesn't swim in those legal waters. The uncertainty makes him appear helpless in the moment. He runs his hand over his hair that remains—maybe to make sure that he still has some left. I wait for him to speak.

"I'm not sure how I feel about you doing that."

"I'd have thought you would be more upset about getting roofied."

"Yes, of course. Who drugged me?"

"No idea. You have any suspects? Remember anyone a little too interested in your drink?"

He shakes his head and retreats again into himself. Everyone at the party is a client of Cain & Cunningham, and I wonder if that angle plays into his reticence. I decide to try a different track.

"Tell me everything you remember about the other night."

"I remember dinner—lamb, I think. But after leaving the dining room, things got real fuzzy, almost dreamlike. Erica tells me that I went upstairs to lie down and stayed there until Jim's body was discovered. But I have no recollection of any of that."

The explanation is awfully convenient. Based on our interviews of all the suspects, Walker and Cain headed upstairs together after the party guests split off from each other upon leaving the study. Aaron would've had Walker all to himself for a few minutes at least—making him one of the most important witnesses. But one of the main side effects of Rohypnol is memory loss. As the drug worked its way through his system, Cain's capacity for remembering much of anything would be compromised—big time.

He adds, "I can't really say that I even understood that Jim was dead until I woke up the next day, and Erica told me. The whole night is a blur."

"Who do you think killed him?"

"I don't know."

"All the guests at the party are clients of your firm, and we know that Jim Walker performed sensitive work for each of them. Surely you have some guess."

Cain chews on whether he has any insight or not for a good minute. At last, he offers, "I would think an intruder killed him."

"That dog won't hunt."

He shrugs his shoulders and keeps any contrary thoughts to himself. I didn't really expect a name out of him anyway. I say, "Interesting contract you just signed on Cain & Cunningham's behalf with Jim Walker. What's the story?"

His features pinken at the mention of a topic so close to home. He grumbles, "How do you know about that?"

"We're paid to know things."

Cain grunts and responds, "Jim wanted more money, and we gave it to him. He was a valuable member of the firm."

"That's one way of looking at it. Another perspective is that Walker found himself drowning in bills because of The Bar's Bar, went to you to bail him out, and made noises about all the damaging client and firm secrets he knew as part of the negotiations."

"You make us sound like the Mafia. We're a law firm, not a criminal enterprise."

"I don't know. Those confidentiality provisions you made Walker sign make it look like you were scared of something. And how many other partners in the firm make seven figures without doing any actual legal work? You doubled Walker's compensation and even guaranteed it for the next five years. Every other partner gets rewarded out of the firm's annual profits, if there are any. But Walker gets paid first, no matter what. Why?"

"I'm not going to talk firm business with you. The end."

"That had to stick in your craw, and two weeks later Jim Walker is dead."

"Not talking about firm business."

The earlier congeniality is gone. The hardness that replaces it reveals the other side of being a managing partner of a giant law firm. Yes, fake smiles have their place but so do withering looks of steel. His is not bad, but having sat across the courtroom from scores of murderers over the years, the effect is lost on me. I point my head to the old painting of Sebastian Cain on the wall and ask, "Was he one of the founders of Cain & Cunningham?"

The sudden change in topics catches him off balance. He swivels his gaze to the picture to make certain it's still there. After gathering himself for a few moments, he answers.

"Yes. My great-grandfather. A Cain has been running Cain & Cunningham for over a hundred years now. It's a family tradition. My son joins the firm in the fall, so we should be good for at least another 50 years."

"That's some legacy. I can imagine how you felt when Jim Walker started demanding money of you like he owned the place."

The grimace is tight, but he lets the comment pass otherwise. No matter. I know who he is already. Cain views power as his birthright, even going so far as to keep score of how often he appears in the newspaper. Walker's repository of prime blackmail material would've roiled a man like that—especially if Walker possessed sensitive information about Cain himself. On that front, I glance over to Scott and leave the last bit of questioning to him. He barks, "What can you tell me about Sylvia Pinker?"

The punch lands. Cain's eyeballs flare but retreat to normal size in good speed. But's he rattled—good and hard. A close look and you can even see the mice in his head spin their furious little feet. He's smart enough to realize that waiting too long to answer is a bad look but also that rushing into the wrong response is even worse. He compromises by buying some time.

"And what does she have to do with anything?"

"Plenty."

The one-word answer packs more ammunition than we actually hold. Scott's serious face tries to bluff the rest. But since Sylvia Pinker refused to talk to Taylor, we're operating in the dark as to the particulars. All we have are Gustave's insinuations, a non-disclosure agreement, and Aaron Cain's concerned manner. But something is there. We sit in Cain's comfortable cushioned chairs and wait with all the time in the world. Aaron tries to out-silence us but gives up the effort in due course.

He says, "Sylvia Pinker is a former associate with Cain & Cunningham, and I'm not going to talk about firm business. The end."

Scott scoffs, "If you think that is the end, then you haven't been around many murder investigations. Which way to your wife's office?"

18

Erica Cain's assistant holds us at bay and wears a suspicious look that we might bull rush her boss' door. The hostility is the likely residue of the rough landing at the end of our first session with Erica—me promising that we would uncover her secrets and all. Scott bears the brunt of the assistant's antagonism. I guess my face is more trustworthy. Or maybe she recognizes me from the *Daily Report*. Either way, I'm fortunate because the scowl she unfurls at Scott is illegal in seven states. She probably works as a bouncer on the side. Undeterred, Scott casually shifts his position to reveal the gun at his hip—a cop power move of the first order. He then smiles at her to rub it in. The assistant turns her back to him and that's that.

A few minutes later, we sit across from Erica—who wears another dark power suit. The vibe in her corner office is more modern than her husband's traditional décor. No portraits of old dead white guys in here. Instead, a bright painting of flowers in a vase hangs on the wall—the intricacy of the work more complex than it sounds. I check the signature and see that the artist is Celeste Wood. Mark me down as impressed. Looking around at the rest of the space, I spy a sleek treadmill off to the side, allowing Erica to jog and bill clients simultaneously. Modern law firm efficiency at its finest.

She snaps, "I don't have much time. Let's get on with it."

I ask, "Any idea who drugged your husband with Rohypnol?"

"Someone drugged Aaron? At the party? I thought it was something that he ate."

Her surprise seems sincere, and I'm puzzled. Cain had to talk to her before we entered the room yet failed to mention the roofie. The only explanation that makes sense is that the other things he told her were more important—Sylvia Pinker being the betting favorite.

91

"He didn't mention that to you?"

She doesn't answer the question, but her annoyance is obvious—whether with me or Aaron is less clear. I prod her again.

"Any ideas?"

"Of course not—that doesn't even make any sense."

"Did Aaron spend a lot of time talking to anyone in the study after dinner? He doesn't remember too much."

"Not really. Everyone was just mingling around, killing time. Why would someone drug Aaron anyway?"

I have no idea but keep my ignorance to myself. Instead, I move on to a different topic.

"So the night of the murder, Aaron goes upstairs to lie down in a spare bedroom, and you head to the kitchen to fetch him a Coke to settle his stomach."

"That's right."

"See anybody in the kitchen?"

"You trying to establish my alibi?"

"Do you need an alibi?"

"No."

"Then just answer the question."

"Fine. I didn't see anybody. I grabbed a Coke out of the refrigerator and went to check on my husband."

If I credit Erica's answer, then Mr. Beale's whereabouts in the immediate aftermath of people departing from the study are a black box. No one saw him, and he won't tell us anything. And while Leo Ivanov verified Mr. Beale's presence in the kitchen a little bit later, Jim Walker could've already been dead by that point. A new thought emerges in the moment—maybe Gustave had Mr. Beale waiting for Walker in the Billiard Room already.

I ask, "Was Mr. Beale in the study with all the guests when everyone broke off to do their own thing?"

Erica picks up a pen and chews on the end of it. Her eyes move skyward—the universal sign for trying to recover a memory, as if the past could be ours again if only we look far enough out in the horizon.

At last, she becomes satisfied with whatever she sees and returns her focus to us to provide an answer.

"I don't think he was. I'm a visual thinker and don't see him when I picture the scene. He was in and out serving dessert earlier, but he wasn't there when the party dispersed."

"What's the deal with Beale anyway? We can't find proof that he even exists. Is he in the country legally?"

"Attorney-client privilege."

That's the second time she's used that dodge with us, and Scott grunts his usual grunt. But that fight isn't worth having. I say, "Speaking of client secrets, could Jim Walker be trusted to keep them?"

"Absolutely. Jim was renowned for his discretion."

"Then why did Cain & Cunningham feel the need to straitjacket him with enough confidentiality provisions in his contract to fill the Pentagon?"

"I'm not authorized to speak on behalf of the firm. Ask my husband. He's the managing partner."

"We did. He refused to talk to us about firm business."

"Well, there you go."

"Walker ever try to blackmail you?"

"Blackmail me? For what?"

"Sylvia Pinker."

Erica puts the pen down and straightens some papers on her desk. Her lips twitch in displeasure. When she does meet our eyes again, the mask she wears is one of deliberate coldness. The guess is that she's shooting for ruthlessness. The attempt falls a little too short but respectable nevertheless. Better than her husband. Except the whole charade is so unnecessary. In the courtroom, performance is half the battle. You have a pliable audience—the jury. Not so in this setting. There's not a facial expression in her arsenal that could move me, and she should be savvy enough to realize that fact. She doesn't want to answer the question—fine. But her ancillary performance is only making me more interested in why the Cain family bristles at the name of Sylvia Pinker. It's bad tactics.

She says, "You're wasting your breath. Sylvia falls under the heading of firm business, and I'm not going to discuss it."

I smile in response to her dropping temperature and respond, "I ask if Walker ever blackmailed you, and you go all lawyerly on me. Not sure that's the right strategy on your end. You're only whetting my interest. And you shouldn't put too much faith in that non-disclosure agreement you required Sylvia to sign. A criminal case takes precedence. You remember what happened to Marsh & McCabe in the aftermath of the Bernard Barton trial? What I did to Roy Winston on the stand? He tried to hide behind a non-disclosure agreement, too. Didn't work."

Erica actually swallows. The Bernard Barton prosecution was my last trial—the one that weakened my faith in the death penalty. Before things went south, I pulled off one of the best cross-examinations of my life against the managing partner of another large Atlanta law firm. Roy Winston's self-immolation—with a large assist from me—made big news around town. The resulting public relations blowback crippled Marsh & McCabe and led to a mass exodus of the firm's lawyers—a large swath of whom ran to the outstretched arms of Cain & Cunningham. One of those was Jeff Yarber, a good friend of mine from law school. I intend to call him later today to see if he knows anything about the mysterious Sylvia Pinker.

Even though they happened less than a year ago, the events from that period feel like a different lifetime. And with Erica not saying much, I allow myself to drift in the memories until she decides to speak again. The clarity of hindsight is crystal—the mistakes I made so obvious. But the best thing we can do with the blunders of our past is to use them to keep us humble. I'm better anchored now—rooted with a firmer footing in my faith, equally yoked to a strong woman, taking each day at a time as it comes.

Erica says, "Anything else? I really am busy."

I turn to Scott and ask, "Anything else?"

"Nah. We know how to find the information we need."

Indeed. I'll talk to my friend Jeff, and Marlon is spending the day doing a deep dive on Jim Walker's home computer. We're also due to pay another visit to Gustave in the late afternoon. One way or another, we'll pry the secret loose from the Cains' tight grip. The good-byes are sparse, although Scott does wave to Erica's assistant on the way out.

19

Celeste Wood lives in Virginia Highlands—an upscale section of Atlanta, steeped in history, close to downtown. Still rich, but much more down-to-earth than the Tuxedo Park neighborhood. The people who live in Virginia Highlands are those who resisted the tsunami that drove so many in Atlanta to Buckhead or the suburbs in the 1970s and 1980s. Other areas in Atlanta have recently regentrified, marking the return of white people to the city limits. But Virginia Highlands had no need. Its residents never left, and the area retains the feel of a true community. I figure it's a good place to live for an artist.

A bright red door greets us, and a smiling Celeste—her overalls covered in paint, a paintbrush in her hand—opens it in good cheer.

"Come on in to the studio. I want to do a few more brushstrokes and then we can talk."

The inside of the house looks like how I imagine an artist's space would—disheveled, airy, bright. The downstairs studio is more of the same. Paint is ubiquitous, and the evidence indicates that she sometimes uses the walls for trial runs before putting color on canvas. The industrial-looking floor, too, receives its fair share of artistic attention. Celeste walks with purpose to an easel to make some more art, and we watch her go about her work. I linger close to the door out of fear that I'll step on the wrong thing. Scott is more adventurous and does a slow stroll along the circumference of the room—until Celeste forbids him from moving into a position where he could see what she's working on. He shrugs his shoulders and rejoins me.

She puts the paintbrush down and says, "I don't normally show anyone my works-in-progress, but I'm going to make an exception for you guys."

Celeste swivels the painting around to give us a good look. The reaction is a mixed bag. Scott bursts out laughing—sidesplitting, in fact. I'm too stunned to do much of anything. The image of what I see doesn't compute.

Me.

Or at least the broad outlines of me. Her talent is striking—the transformation of a worn-out subject into something fresh and vibrant being the proof. Celeste told us before that Hitler had no ability to paint humans, and that critique packs more punch in light of her own obvious skill on that score. The artist goes about explaining her work.

"I hope you don't mind, but I wanted to paint you from nearly the first moment I saw you in Gustave's study. Some quality is there that I wanted to capture. Best way I can say it is this—you have a lived-in face."

The tone is complimentary, but the words are ambiguous enough to give me pause. She continues, "It's interesting—your face."

"My wife thinks so."

Scott snickers some more. Celeste turns to him and counters, "Your face, not so much."

"But I'm much more fun at parties than he is."

I don't argue the point—figuring that he's right. He adds, "Tough market trying to sell that one."

No one argues that point, either.

Celeste leads us to a covered patio and invites us to sit down. Like a good Southern hostess, she pours us some sweet tea. Still way too behind on my sleep, I welcome the quick hit from the sugar-flavored caffeine.

Scott says, "We want to follow up with you about a few things from the other night."

"Go ahead, shoot."

"You mentioned Jim's money troubles. But did he ever talk to you in detail about what was going on with him? We have reason to believe that he was in pretty deep."

"Not hard numbers, if that's what you mean. But I knew it was bad. Selling my paintings was a pretty desperate move. When I confronted him about it, the worry in his eyes was a side of him I had never seen before. Jim always had a coolness about him—refined sophistication even. Never rattled. That kind of thing. In that moment, though, he was a scared animal. He loved money, and financial ruin was about the worst thing that could've happened to him. He should never have opened that stupid bar."

Probably not the worst thing that could've happened to him—thinking of that Nazi dagger in his back. But her description of Jim's deteriorating situation is as vivid as one of her paintings. And I reflect on a truth I learned early on in the trenches practicing criminal law—desperate men do desperate things.

I ask, "Did he give you any indication how he intended to escape his predicament?"

A slight breeze blows, and I feel the lightness on my skin. Celeste shakes her head no in response to the question, and her curly hair—more buoyant today without the late-night swim—travels in tandem with her movement.

"Did he mention anything about a new contract with Cain & Cunningham?"

"A little. He and Aaron Cain were butting heads. Jim complained that the firm wasn't paying him his worth and that he could sink the whole place if he were of a mind to. Also said that Aaron and Erica especially should pay him more out of their own pockets just based on what he knew about them."

The gravity of her words dawns on her in an instant. Celeste draws one knee into her chest and rests her head upon it. She then stares at us with a troubled expression—the first time in my presence that she has shown any serious concern that someone close to her was murdered.

"What else did he say along those lines?"

"You don't think that they—"

The words hang incomplete in mid-air. Her eyes search my lived-in, interesting face for an answer, but I'm not biting.

"I don't think anything. All you need to worry about is telling us the facts. Did Jim say anything else about Aaron and Erica?"

She pauses to give the question a good mental frisking and responds, "Yes—when he asked me to go to Gustave's party. I told you before that he promised to buy back those paintings of mine that he sold. I scoffed and asked him with what money. He bragged that he had just stuck it to Aaron real hard and had a lot more money coming his way. He was back to his old self and in a jovial mood on the way to the party. The fear he had bared earlier was all gone."

Aaron Cain doesn't strike me as an easy man to bully, which points to the probability that Jim Walker had the goods on him. But what?

"Does the name Sylvia Pinker mean anything to you?"

"Never heard of her."

"Any idea what damaging information Jim knew about Aaron and Erica?"

"Not a clue. Jim was always circumspect about his work. No pillow talk along those lines at all, and frankly I don't care much about other people's dirty laundry anyway."

Scott takes over the questioning with an eye to shoring up our knowledge as to how Celeste ended up in the swimming pool around the time someone murdered Jim Walker.

He says, "We want to get a better feel of your movements at the party once you left the study. Where did you change into your swimsuit?"

"The pool house outside."

"See anybody on your way out there?"

"Not really. My sense is that all of us scattered out of the study at the same time, and I obviously saw other people as we were leaving. But after I left that area, I went straight out back to change and didn't see anyone."

"What about after you came out of the pool house?"

"Mr. Beale was heading back toward the kitchen from the garage with giant bags of ice in his hands. I remember that distinctly because the bags appeared pretty heavy, and he was carrying them like they were nothing. With him being so thin and all, I didn't expect that he would have that kind of strength."

That punctures a blow—perhaps fatally—into my theory of Mr. Beale lying in wait on Gustave's instructions for Jim Walker to enter into the Billiard Room. It would've been too neat a trick for Beale to stab Walker, lock the door, escape off the balcony, head to the garage, grab the ice bags, and head back into the kitchen in such a short period of time. Unless Celeste is a slow dresser.

I ask, "How long did it take you to change into your bathing suit?"

"Not long at all. Two minutes tops. After being around those people, I was dying to get into the pool and didn't waste any time. I could feel the grime on me."

* * *

Back in the car, Scott resumes his earlier laughter and says, "I'm going to buy that painting to use for target practice."

"That's a great work of art we're talking about. When it's finished, it should hang in the High Museum for generations to enjoy."

He chuckles some more. I leave him to it, knowing that if the roles were reversed that I would be laughing my head off, too. Why would Celeste choose me as a subject to paint? My face isn't interesting at all, although I'll concede that it's lived in. The cynical side of me reflects that Scott and I are now talking about art instead of assessing Celeste as a murder suspect. Maybe she reasons that if I'm too busy staring at my painted self on a canvas, I won't spend any time looking at her. As false flag operations go, the idea wouldn't be all that bad.

I ask, "Think Beale is out of it now?"

"Probably. It would be stretching probabilities to their breaking point based on what we know. But I'm still going to keep an eye on him. He had the run of the whole place that night and no doubt served plenty of people their drinks, giving him the best opportunity to drug Jim Walker and Aaron Cain. And his absolute refusal to cooperate with us—alone among all the suspects—does him no favors."

"That came from Gustave."

"Don't care. It casts suspicion on both of them. Besides, I don't trust giants who apparently possess super strength. Disrupts the natural order."

20

Jeff Yarber answers on the first ring and pleads, "Please tell me that you're not calling about Jim Walker."

"How did you know?"

"Because when I read in the paper that you were investigating the murder, I said to myself 'that bastard is going to call me.' The only surprise is that it took you this long."

"I've been busy."

He grunts and not in a fun way. Jeff gave me inside intelligence about his law partner Bernard Barton—information that I detonated during my cross-examination of Roy Winston, former managing partner of Marsh & McCabe. Jeff's law firm was one of the principal casualties. I hope he doesn't hold a grudge.

"You don't expect me to spill firm secrets again, do you?"

"Is that a rhetorical question?"

He curses a blue streak but maybe in a fun way. We haven't talked since the end of the Barton trial, and the hunch is that he has been saving the choice words now coming out of his mouth for precisely this occasion. At last, he runs out of steam, and I defend myself against the charges.

"It's your fault—working for law firms up to their elbows in murder investigations. You should hang out with a better class of people."

"Bernard didn't even commit the crime you tried him for!"

Fair point. Except Bernard Barton was still bad news for a whole lot of other reasons.

Jeff adds, "We're supposed to be friends. But the only time you ever call me is when you need something. How do you think that makes me feel?"

"The phone works both ways, you know. But you're right. Apologies. Let's grab a meal together."

"I'm not going to be seen in public with you! People find out we're friends and you do your wrecking ball impersonation again, I'm in fiduciary hot water. I barely escaped suspicion last time around."

Law school is a stressful place, and the sense of kinship forged among law students from surviving the tumult together endures long after graduation. No matter how far we drift away from one another in subsequent years, the closeness remains. Jeff and I were especially close. We escaped the strain of never-ending work by playing cards—poker mostly but also a dash of spades on the side. We even teamed up to win the UGA Spades Championship, which netted me a $100 gift certificate to the local mall. I gave the winnings to my wife Amber as penance for being a miserable law student for a couple of years running. Jeff—who was born and raised in Chicago—bought a pair of Air Jordans in homage to his hero. I hear a deep sigh on the other end of the phone.

"What do you want to know?"

"What did Aaron and Erica Cain do to Sylvia Pinker?"

He groans, "I thought you were going to ask something easy about Jim Walker, but instead you want me to rat out the two most powerful partners at the firm. You always did say, 'Go big or go home.'"

His voice betrays a touch of uncertainty. The disembowelment of Marsh & McCabe must have been difficult for him, and I don't want to put him through a similar ordeal again. But I still give him a friendly push all the same.

"Your country needs you, Jeff."

"Whatever. Have you ever met Sylvia?"

"No."

"Super hot. Total smokeshow. Anyway, a few months ago, shortly after us Marsh & McCabe folks came over, word starts to percolate that Sylvia was raising some unspecified hell about the Cains and was considering filing a lawsuit. After having just lived through a scandal of our own thanks to your overzealousness, the new transplants had no desire for a repeat performance. As a group, we pressured Aaron Cain to make the problem disappear. And he did. Some type

TO KILL A LAWYER

of settlement negotiated by Jim Walker on the firm's behalf. Sylvia had to sign a non-disclosure agreement, of course. Again, I don't know the particulars. But when an attractive female associate negotiates a hush-hush settlement with a big law firm, you know as well as I do what that suggests—something sexual."

Yep. Old male lawyers straying from their wedding vows and forcing themselves on younger women is a fixture in the world of Big Law. The whole David and Bathsheba thing again. Still, if Aaron wanted to pursue that path, someone outside the office would seem the wiser course. Erica Cain is tough as nails, and trying to cheat on her with another woman right down the hall doesn't seem conducive to one's good health. I muse, "You would think Aaron would go farther afield if he wanted to scratch that particular itch?"

"Who said anything about it being Aaron? Could've been Erica. That's who Sylvia worked for. The two traveled together all the time—joined at the hip."

"Really?"

"Rumblings to that effect. But no one really knows—except the parties involved and the late Jim Walker."

He pauses, starts to do the calculations in his head, and begs, "Please tell me Jim wasn't killed because of that."

I make no assurances.

21

Leo Ivanov's house is the picture of order. Just as Celeste Wood's unkempt home reflects the uniqueness of her artistic personality, the same melding of person and space is obvious in the precision with which Ivanov has arranged his private sanctuary. The symmetry makes sense. A man who dedicates his life to mathematics and chess would want to ensure that everything is in its proper place.

He leads us to a sitting room with filled-to-the-rim bookcases dotting opposite walls. In the dead center of the room on a polished brown table sits an ornate wooden chess set—two chairs aligned face-to-face on each end of the board. I eye the set-up with appreciation, thinking back to Daddy and me squaring off in games of intense concentration on our front porch.

Ivanov asks, "You play?"

"Some."

"Fancy a match?"

I jerk my head up to him. The picture of a hungry wolf seeking a fresh lamb to devour comes to mind. But I'm game—even if I'm walking into a slaughter. How often does a person get to play a grand-master in chess? I readily agree to Ivanov's offer.

Scott mutters, "What am I supposed to do?"

Making his way to a chair, Ivanov waves at Scott with a dismissive hand and offers, "Make yourself at home and look around." I repeat Ivanov's words in jest but stare at Scott with great concentration: "Yeah, make yourself at home and look around."

He nods back at me—certain of my meaning, the two of us seemingly born on the same mental wavelength.

In the United States, the Constitution forbids law enforcement searches of a person's home without a warrant or consent. From one way of looking at things, Ivanov just provided consent. Maybe being from Russia he just assumes that the police can stick their noses wherever they want anyway, permission or not. Scott meanders out of the room, leaving me to humiliate myself for the greater good.

The grandmaster picks up a white pawn and a black pawn in each hand, hides his hands behind his back, and brings them out front again with two closed fists outstretched to me. He says, "Choose."

"You should at least throw a guy a bone and let me be white."

"'Throw a guy a bone'—what does this mean?"

"A plea for a small mercy that is in your power to give."

Ivanov laughs, opens the hand holding the white pawn, and tosses it to me. In chess, white gets to move first, providing a small statistical advantage. Emphasis on small. Leo could take a couple of his pieces off the board before we even begin and still wipe the floor with me. Grandmasters are that good. I begin the game by moving my King's pawn to square d4. He answers with pawn to d5. I unleash the Queen's Gambit, offering up the sacrifice of my c pawn to create more operating space on the board. He unfurls a slight smile and declines to take me up on it—an answer known as Queen's Gambit Declined.

We go back and forth for a few minutes. I give each move a fair amount of deliberation—reasoning that the longer the game goes on, the more time Scott has to "look around." Besides, losing too quickly would be a blow to my chess pride. While I'm busy thinking, Ivanov stands up to stroll along one of his bookcases and picks out a book to peruse. When I finally shuffle another piece, he—nose still in the book—asks, "Where did you move?"

I tell him, and he responds, "Queen to e7."

"You're just showing off now."

He half turns and flashes a sheepish grin and offers a slight raising of his shoulders. I transport his Queen to e7 and think hard about how to respond. We repeat this dance over the next several moves.

Studying the board, the foreboding that I'm in grave danger of being subject to a quick checkmate overtakes me. Based on the position of the pieces, that fear seems not to be warranted. But the nagging sense remains. The great chess players have the ability to see eight moves ahead—a dizzying level of foresight only possible for the few geniuses among us with computer-like brains. I stare at the arrangement of pieces before me and finally advance a center pawn, hoping it will be enough. I then tell him my move.

With his back still to me, he observes, "*Da*, excellent. The only way you could've staved off mate in four moves. Only delaying the inevitable, but I commend you nevertheless. Well done. Knight to g4."

His confident voice and command of the situation deflate me, but I take the humbling with good grace. A man should always know when he is licked. Hopefully, Scott is almost finished with whatever he is doing. His search of the house is living on borrowed time at this point.

We play a few more moves, and the hopelessness of my position becomes more evident with each one. Scott returns to the room and gives me a slight nod. I announce to Ivanov: "I should probably concede."

"*Da*, it's the honorable thing to do."

I turn my king over on its side.

* * *

Ivanov finds a third chair, and I let Scott lead the questioning. He starts, "We wanted to talk to you some more about Carliss Sherman."

The genial manner of our host changes quicker than you can say, "Checkmate." He snaps, "How do you know that name?"

Since I've never heard of Carliss Sherman until this moment, my working assumption is that Scott's impromptu search of the premises bore good fruit. He keeps the pressure up.

"No stone goes unturned in a murder investigation. You refused to give us her name, so we went and found it. We haven't talked to her yet, but that's next if you don't cooperate with us."

Ivanov stews in his own juices for a spell—the expression on his face no different than if he had taken a bite of bad goulash. Apparently, his ability to see many moves ahead isn't as strong away from the chessboard. Impregnating a student and forcing her to have an abortion would be a big scandal on a college campus, especially in the #MeToo age. And Jim Walker was smack dab in the middle of helping Ivanov cover it up. Of course, we're going to follow up about the woman. Scott says, "Talk to me about the settlement. How did you settle on the $100,000 figure? Who did you write the check to?"

Asking about the check confuses me, but I remain in character—knowing a good reason exists on the other side of that inquiry.

Ivanov whines, "*Nyet*—why does this matter?"

"I'm probing your possible motive for murder."

The grandmaster makes a noise in the vicinity of a growl. He stands up in a hurried motion, and we watch him closely in case he becomes stupid under the stress. But all he does is start pacing around the room like a caged tiger, mumbling in Russian. My Torts professor in law school would always charge around the classroom like a maniac, adding miles to his pedometer over the course of each class. Ivanov reminds me of him now. Scott keeps up the heat.

"This isn't going away, Leo. Talk to us about that settlement."

More grumbling, but the pace slackens. Ivanov faces us with sagging shoulders, the looming defeat heavy on him. At last, he gives in.

"Mr. Walker handled everything with that woman. Made the deal, negotiated the amount, arranged the abortion. He just told me how much."

"Seems a bit of an overpay?"

"I told you before, it bought me peace of mind. Women these days, they say anything, the man is finished. 'He made me have sex with him against my will.' The nonsense—it is too strong. What choice did I have? She wanted the money. I paid the money. I'm the true victim here."

Poor Leo. He beats upon his chest in indignation, but I'm unimpressed. Even if I grant him that the relationship was consensual as claimed, he was horny and found a willing outlet in the form of a student. Now he wants to cry foul. The nonsense is strong all right. I liked him a lot better when we were playing chess.

"Who'd you make the check out to?"

"No check. Hundred-dollar bills—a thousand of them."

"Cash? You gave Jim Walker a $100,000 in cash?"

"*Da.*"

I share Scott's disbelief. That's an awful lot of walking-around money, and lawyers don't pay off legal claims in cash. Each law firm has a trust account with a bank through which settlement funds must first flow. Even a career criminal law attorney like me knows that. Except Jim Walker paid off Ivanov's lover with a bunch of Ben Franklins. Curious. Scott continues.

"Why cash?"

"Because Mr. Walker told me so. Better no paperwork, he said."

"How do you know Carliss Sherman even received any of that money?"

The question hits Ivanov where it hurts. He pauses in mid-step—the thick eyebrows almost frowning as he peers deep into Scott's soul, not liking what he sees.

Leo sputters, "Because she went away and promised to keep her mouth shut forever. That's how. Done deal."

"But how much did she think the deal was worth?"

"What is this? I followed my lawyer's instructions. I gave him cash to pay that pest of a woman and washed my hands of it. Mr. Walker handled the money after that. You have to take it up with him."

"Except we can't really do that now, can we?"

* * *

"What was that all about?"

Scott and I are on the road again, this time heading back over to Gustave Root's mansion in Tuxedo Park. The business with Leo Ivanov's $100,000 cash payout is a revelation, but I still don't know what to make of it. Scott explains.

"While you were frolicking around playing board games, I was busy doing police work. Made myself at home behind Leo's desk in his office and reviewed some correspondence. One letter was from Carliss Sherman, expressing second thoughts about the $25,000 payment she accepted to keep quiet about doing the deed with the good professor. Carliss felt strongly that she deserved more."

"Wait—$25,000?"

"Exactly. Any guesses where that missing $75,000 in cash might've ended up?"

Jim Walker. And the letter from Sherman not only would've agitated Ivanov about what his former student might do going forward, it also would've alerted him that he had been hoodwinked by someone he trusted. I think out loud.

"So Ivanov knew that Walker stole 75k from him? That sounds like a motive for murder."

"Doesn't it? And him lying to us about it just now doesn't exactly ease my suspicions. He knew Walker stiffed him but played dumb."

Poor Leo.

22

The third visit to the Root mansion in roughly forty hours has me nostalgic for the time when I was blessedly ignorant of Gustave's existence. Two days in and I've already aged a year. Some cases do that to you—usually the ones that have you inspecting dead bodies long after the clock strikes midnight.

Mr. Beale is waiting for us at the front door as we approach. The other night, the giant wore nothing but blank looks. His mood today has taken a surly turn. The disturbing blue eyes carry disapproval and a scowl trickles across the pale cheekbones—mostly in the direction of my companion. We follow the silent man into the house.

Mr. Beale opens the door to the empty study and extends a never-ending arm—he must have the wingspan of a 747—to indicate that we should enter. After we're safely inside, he flashes a departing glare and runs along.

Scott calls out after him, "I don't care what anyone else says. I know you can talk."

The displeased albino disappears, and I observe, "Still sore about him hurting your hand, huh?"

"What do you think?"

While we wait for Gustave, I study the Hitler painting in its honored place directly over the mantle. I have to confess that the Führer had some talent—despite Celeste Wood's strong opinion to the contrary. But her standards are much higher than mine. For someone like me—who can barely draw crooked stick figures—the man could paint a passable picture. I shake my head. The events that create destiny turn on the thinnest of reeds. How would history have changed if the world's greatest monster hadn't been rejected by the Academy of Fine Arts in Vienna? My grandfather fought at the Battle of the Bulge and met my grandmother the same day he set his feet back on American soil. Likely I would never have been born if not for the Nazis.

"Just can't get away from looking at it, can you?"

Gustave finds me now just as he found me the other night—staring at the Hitler. I don't feel obliged to answer his question and don't. He moves to the bar and asks, "What are you gentlemen drinking?"

Given the alarming percentage of guests to this house that end up with Rohypnol in their system, neither of us is drinking anything. But the offer makes the moment a good entry point for asking our host about that particular peculiarity. I get the ball rolling.

"Would it surprise you to learn that both Jim Walker and Aaron Cain were drugged with roofies at your party the other night?"

Gustave—who is drinking—stops his glass tumbler just short of his lips. He lowers the drink back down and asks, "What are you talking about?"

"Two toxicology reports. You can write it down in ink."

"Beats me."

"Mr. Beale was serving the drinks, right?"

"You leave Mr. Beale out of it. He's been off-kilter ever since you guys got your hands on him. Just as I feared. And I can assure you that Mr. Beale didn't drug anybody. He wouldn't even know what a roofie is."

Scott says, "And you do?"

"I make movies, jackass. It is a recurring plot device."

For a host, Gustave isn't being too hospitable, but he raises a good point, though not the one he was trying to make. I really don't know how hard it is to acquire Rohypnol in everyday life, but a Hollywood producer could certainly get his hands on as much as he wanted with little fuss. He eyes us with deep misgivings and takes a sip from his drink—and then another one for good measure. I eye him right back. His hair is as wild as it was the night of the murder. Part of the eccentric brand he works hard to cultivate, I figure. Time to get back to business.

"Who among your guests would be the most likely to deploy roofies against unsuspecting partygoers?"

"Hell if I know. Probably the same person who killed Jim."

"And who would that be? Surely you've put some thought into the question. What's your theory?"

"You're the hot shot murder squad. Do your job. That's why I wanted you guys in the first place."

No one's buying that line. He called Minton to throw his weight around because that's what men like him do. Now he gets to choke on the aftertaste of that miscalculation. I tease, "Talk to the Governor lately?"

He frowns and downs what's left in his glass.

* * *

Root stands at the bar and fixes himself another drink—something brown, straight, no ice. I hand the baton off to Scott, figuring Gustave and I could use a break from one another.

"We need some information from you about the Cains and Sylvia Pinker—to make sure what you know about the situation matches what we know."

"Why? I'm not involved."

"Making you the perfect witness. What did you hear?"

The witness seems dubious about the logic of that reasoning and swallows a few more drops to consider the matter. We wait him out. He holds his tumbler at eye level, stares at the liquid, and says, "You gotta understand—everything I heard was secondhand. I'm not attesting to the truth of anything I'm about to tell you. And I don't even know Sylvia Pinker. Got it?"

"Got it."

"Sylvia is supposedly quite a looker, and she did a lot of work for Erica. One time on an out-of-town business trip, Aaron happens to be there, too. The three of them start drinking at the bar. The next morning, Sylvia wakes up naked in bed with husband and wife, claiming that she didn't remember anything that happened the night before. Aaron and Erica said that's because she was drunk. But Sylvia claimed they roofied her."

Apparently, the incidence of people being drugged with Rohypnol is much higher than I appreciate. The disclosure settles over the room, and all kinds of possibilities do pirouettes in my head. Scott allows the moment to marinate before continuing.

"What happened when everyone returned home from the business trip?"

"Sylvia raised holy hell and wanted to get the *New York Times* in on it. Aaron and Erica paid her to go away quietly."

"And who told you this information?"

"Jim, naturally. He had to put out the fire."

I suppress a laugh. Large law firms have more drama than a daytime soap opera. But who am I to judge? The Bernard Barton trial not only ended as a loss, it was also my moral and ethical nadir. One might think that lawyers should know better, except we're just as capable of spitting into the wind as the next person—and a helluva lot more likely to think we can get away with it.

But how does this new information about Sylvia Pinker factor into my murder investigation? The swiftness with which Marsh & McCabe crumbled as a going concern in the wake of bad press must have given Aaron and Erica a serious case of heartburn when Sylvia threatened to go public. And then shortly after that crisis is resolved, Jim Walker pops up demanding more money to keep quiet about the very fire he helped them put out. Some people would call that blackmail.

I also reflect that Walker sure had a lot of fingers in other people's pies—Gustave, too, for that matter. All the suspects—Celeste Wood the possible exception—had these dual connections with both men. And Walker seemed to share his knowledge of these people pretty freely with Gustave. I decide to ask Root about it.

"Jim was supposed to be a great guy at keeping secrets. But he seems to have told you everything about everybody."

"I am an incurable gossip, and so was Jim. We would talk for hours and hours on end—horse-trading secret for secret. With Aaron and Erica, my interest was more than mere curiosity. They handle most of my legal work—billing me millions in fees annually as part of the bargain. If trouble was brewing—especially trouble where the word 'rape' is involved—I needed to know about it. Jim gave me a head's up."

Gustave pours yet another drink and takes a quick gulp, adding, "He was a treasured friend." An unplanned moment of silence for the late Jim Walker follows.

Scott asks, "Did you know that Walker wanted more money from Cain & Cunningham?"

"Sure. I told him to put the screws to them. Even gave him permission to drop my name as leverage if he had to—that my business might leave with him if he went to another firm. And they paid him, all right."

"How did that go over with Aaron Cain?"

"Who cares? Aaron Cain is a bootlicker. What's he going to do? Ever hear of the Golden Rule? He who has the gold gets to make the rules. I have the gold."

I'm pretty sure that's not the translation in my Bible, but maybe there's a different meaning when spoken in the original Hebrew. The comment, though, paints a picture of Aaron and Erica's heads stuck in a vise with Sylvia Pinker on one side and Gustave's lucrative legal work on the other—with Jim Walker turning the vise tighter and tighter to the tune of a new $1.5 million contract. Things get more interesting when you throw in Aaron's walking up the steps to the second floor at the same time as Walker, Erica's loitering in the hallway outside the Billiard Room, and evidence that the Cains play with roofies in their spare time. Add it all up, and the current feels as though it is pulling me toward a particular direction.

Scott switches tracks to explain that we would like to talk to Vivian some more and even take another stab at Mr. Beale. Root scoffs at both notions and threatens to get lawyers involved this time around if necessary. Like a Pavlovian dog, Scott gets sore at the mention of lawyers and pushes back twice as hard.

"Listen, Gustave. We can't even find proof that Vivian or Mr. Beale even exist. One theory is that they are in the country illegally, and you're holding their lack of legal status over their heads. I could get the immigration and customs folks on the case. They're even less charming than I am. Or maybe the FBI. They might be interested to know if you met Vivian while you were hanging out with your pal Jeffrey Epstein. Care to comment?"

The silence suggests not. Scott presses forward.

"You've told us about how Jim Walker got other people out of trouble but never what tight jam he helped you escape. Being on Pedophile Island can't be good for business."

Gustave laughs before responding, "You leap to the wrong conclusions. My association with Jeffrey is no secret. Everyone already knows I spent time on his island. As did a lot of other people—including presidents and princes."

"Presidents and princes? Is that supposed to be some kind of character reference? Because the record of those guys on issues of this sort ain't great."

Gustave finishes off the remains of his third drink since entering the room. His tongue licks his top row of teeth in a slow burn—like a hungry predator in the wild might do in the presence of prey. He sets the glass down on a table with more attention than the action deserves—the coils of his body ready to spring. But the tension dissipates, and the movie mogul turns toward me with a plastic smile.

"A murder in a Tuxedo Park mansion has gotten the neighborhood tongues wagging. I've decided to do what I do best—throw a party. People want to see the scene of the crime, and I intend to satiate their morbid fascination. Monday night. Mr. Meridian, I understand your wife is a Justice on our fine Supreme Court. Her presence would bring a welcomed measure of sophistication to the festivities. All the party guests from the other night will be there as well as many other luminaries. Evening wear is the attire of choice. Please come. Just make sure you leave your pit bull here at home on his leash. And with that, I bid you adieu. The two of you may see yourselves out."

He turns around, seemingly clicks his heels together, and marches out of the room like a well-trained SS officer. Scott notes, "Pit bull?"

"In fairness, you've been called much worse."

"But never by a Nazi pedophile."

23

The snarl of Friday afternoon traffic delays our return to the Office. I'm already late for taking Cate to our favorite dining spot and curse the congestion. When Scott and I do arrive back, we head straight to Marlon's office to see what intel he gleaned from playing with Jim Walker's cell phone and home computer. Everyone else has left for the day.

Marlon leans back in his chair and announces, "The harvest has borne fruit. You wouldn't believe the things I've learned today about our cast of suspects—starting with Aaron and Erica Cain."

Scott retorts, "That they drugged Sylvia Pinker and raped her?"

"You guys have been busy, too."

He proceeds to give us the rest of the dope from Walker's texts and emails. Aaron and Erica Cain—Walker pressured them over e-mail to double his salary for smothering Sylvia's allegations to death and reminded them that things would turn ugly if that news ever became public. After much indignation, the Cains got the message and Walker got paid. Leo Ivanov—the grandmaster sent angry missives to Jim about being cheated out of $75,000. Walker claimed a misunderstanding but agreed to pay the money back. Vivian Root—she and Jim exchanged a bunch of steamy texts. Mark Romo—according to Walker, the family of the kid killed was making noises about wanting more money, and Romo should prepare himself to pay more cash. Jessica Allen—a journalist was looking into the bullying allegations, but Walker could silence the story by buying the journalist off if Jessica could cough up enough money. Oliver Twist—not much, except that Walker warned him in a recent text not to saw anybody else in half. Twist took offense at the joke. Walker snickered back that Twist should learn how to be a better magician. Celeste Wood—she texted Jim with choice words about what he could do to himself after selling her paintings. Mr. Beale—nothing.

We fill Marlon in on our findings. The three of us agree that the stories about the family in the Mark Romo hit-and-run and the journalist investigating Jessica Allen sound like pretexts for Walker to hustle more money out of the Hollywood stars. Did they realize they were being conned? Marlon doesn't think so based on their responses, but maybe they got wise in the days since.

* * *

Cate and I huddle close over an intimate table in our favorite upscale restaurant—conveniently located in the Serenbe community. Serenbe is hard to describe. Picture a Hollywood movie lot of perfect houses and smiling people dropped into isolated farmland where cows and outdoor theater productions share the same grassland—kinda like *The Truman Show,* but set in the country instead of at the beach. That's Serenbe.

After the Bernard Barton trial, getting away from Atlanta to remake my life topped the list of pressing priorities. Except where to? The Georgia coast was a leading contender, the Maine wilderness not far behind. But after 15 years of working in the city, Atlanta was a hard mistress to cast off. I compromised by moving thirty miles south to the far reaches of Fulton County—the last sliver of the county to resist metropolitan sprawl, a place where rural life still dominates with not a skyscraper or strip mall in sight. Although the same people send me my tax bill now as when I lived in town, the similarities end there.

I somehow missed this oasis during my years as a prosecutor. A late spring hike in Cochran Mill Park last year—where I'm told they film something called *The Walking Dead*—broadened my perspective. Fifty acres and a solid brick house later, I had a new home. Serenbe was included as part of the bargain—right down the road.

Because neither of us is any great shakes in the kitchen, Cate and I eat out most nights, usually in Serenbe. She gladly left the city to join me here after we married. Both of us have country roots, having grown up in neighboring small towns ninety miles south of Atlanta. We didn't know each other back then, although we were both at the same football game once when our high schools played each other—her on the sideline in a cheerleading uniform, me on the field in shoulder pads. From that starting point to the present over two decades later, the twists and turns that brought us together defy the laws of mathematics. But maybe all love stories face similar long odds.

She says, "You look bone-tired."

"That obvious?"

"And then some. You need a day off—like Ferris Bueller."

"Sounds fun but not tomorrow. Re-interviewing suspects. Plus, we're having Scott and Taylor over."

"You still plan on cooking out?"

I make an unhappy face, fretful of adding another agenda item to my long list. Riding to the rescue, Cate offers to throw some chili in a slow cooker to spare me the trouble. My face collapses into an appreciative look of relief, and I squeeze her hand.

Remembering Gustave's invitation, I tell her, "We got invited to a fancy party."

"Exciting—whose party?"

The waiter brings over some bread, and I tear off pieces for us both while relaying Root's macabre desire to give all the posh residents of Atlanta—including all of the suspects in Jim Walker's murder—a chance to pour over the crime scene. She fixates on one point.

"Mark Romo's going to be there?"

A mischievous smile alights her face as she takes a bite of her bread. I shake my head in disapproval and respond, "Calm down, woman. Have some dignity. You're a Supreme Court justice for goodness sake."

"I could get a photo with him at least."

"He's a murder suspect in my investigation."

"Someone else can take the picture."

"Real funny—but someone on the guest list is a murderer. I'm not sure you should go. Jim Walker got killed at the last party in that house."

"But half the town's going to be there, right? I've been working too hard and could use a good party. You can be my bodyguard."

She smiles and finishes off her bread, licking the butter off her fingers—a gesture remarkable in its sensuality. Cate smiles some more and blows me a kiss, signaling the final word on the matter. The waiter brings us our usual appetizers—salad for her, soup for me. Waiting for my lobster bisque to cool, I change topics.

"Another weird thing happened today. Celeste Wood—she's a painter and one of our suspects, although low down on the list. Well, Scott and I went to question her, and she has a studio in her home. She brings us into to the studio to show us her latest work in progress. Any guesses about the subject matter?"

As she's busy eating her salad, an answer is not expected. I wait a moment to build up the dramatic impact.

"Me! Celeste said I had an *'interesting'* face that had a *'lived-in'* quality to it. I think it was a compliment but wouldn't swear to that under oath."

Cate's eyes narrow. I quickly add, "Made sure to tell her that my wife really likes my face, too."

A dismissive snort emanates from the other side of the table. She asks, "Is the picture any good?"

"Not that I can judge that sort of thing, but yeah, I think so."

"I want to see that painting."

We'll have to see about that but certainly not before I catch Jim Walker's killer.

* * *

Cate sips her post-dinner glass of wine with the look of a satisfying meal on her face. She observes, "You still turn forty next week."

"Stop reminding me."

"I don't want to hear it. I beat you to forty a few months ago. It'll be nice to have some company."

"You don't look a day over thirty."

"Charmer."

The two of us sit there, happy and content with the other's company. I reflect on the work before me tomorrow—follow-up interviews with

Oliver Twist, Mark Romo, and Jessica Allen. The Cains are the leading suspects as things stand, but a part of me feels as though I'm spinning my tires in mud until we figure out the mystery of the locked door. Talking to the suspects feels like a misuse of time while doing nothing on the one critical question upon which everything depends. I have no idea, though, what to do about the door. Before I get too far down into that rabbit hole, Cate breaks me out of my reverie.

"We've never talked about having kids and probably should. The whole biological clock thing, you know."

She studies my face with an expression I struggle to read. Meanwhile the pang of a memory strikes me in my side. Amber and I had a similar conversation around the time I turned thirty. Both of us were young professionals at that point, rising up in our respective careers. But after talking it over, we agreed that the time was right to start a family. Except nothing happened—despite our best efforts. A few years later, panic started to set in. We both visited the usual specialists, and Amber started on some fertility drug. My son was born the next year.

Cate says, "I lost you there for a second. What were you thinking about?"

"Cale."

"That's why we should talk. After what you've been through, I don't know where your mind is on having another child—whether the pain would be too much for you."

"I loved being a father."

The answer is ambiguous but not purposely so. She continues studying me with green eyes of luminous intensity. Her raising the topic makes me think she would like to get pregnant. Hers is the biological clock ticking, after all. She once told me that she'd always assumed kids would be part of her life, but her career and a cheating husband got in the way. I consider how much of myself Cate has already restored and remember a mantra that guided my desire to marry her in the first place—the future is what we make it. I offer a suggestion.

"One option is to have lots of sex and let the chips fall where they may. If God blesses us with a child, all the better."

The green eyes now glisten. She smiles and rubs my hand before answering.

"I agree to those terms. We can start tonight."

I hail the waiter and say, "Check please."

* * *

Sweetheart and Bristol sit on the floor next to me in bed hoping to jump up and share the space. I command them instead to their cushions across the room and watch them get settled for the night. Cate pop outs of the bathroom wearing a thin bathrobe that doesn't hide much. She tells me to give her a minute and disappears.

The heavy weight of tiredness hits me with full force in that moment. I close my eyes for what I promise myself will only be a few seconds. Sometime later, I feel a brush of moist lips on my cheek before collapsing into a deep sleep.

24

After the killings of Amber and Cale, work became my refuge—nights, weekends, holidays. I figured to disappear into manic busyness for a few years, wake up one day, and find myself magically cured of my pain. That delusion is almost comical in hindsight—almost. Life has a way of teaching a person the harsh lessons that need to be taught. For me, I learned that running away from your hurt cannot heal your wounds. It only infects them. Better to deal with the pain at the root and let God carry some of the load. By hoarding all my grief for myself, I was both stealing something that belonged to God and denying Him the opportunity to heal me.

Now on the road to recovery, I haven't worked a Saturday for the murder squad yet. Until now. Driving to the Office through the scattershot of an early morning fog, pinpricks of agitation needle me. Regret at leaving a barely-clothed Cate at home doesn't improve my spirits. I toyed with waking her to consummate our plans of the night before but lacked the heart to disturb her peaceful rest and left her to her sleep—although with a sense of paradise lost.

The interstate is empty at least. I make it to the Office in good time.

* * *

Scott's mood is fouler than my own. He has to testify on Monday in one of the cases he cleared while he was the lead homicide detective with the Atlanta Police Department. Today, he gets to spend his time working with a prosecutor in witness prep. A year ago, I would've been that prosecutor. We run into each other on his way out the door.

He grumbles, "I owe you an apology."

"For what?"

"I failed to realize how good a lawyer you were until I started having to work with other prosecutors again. Either they cannot connect the simplest dots or know everything already anyway. Had the most infuriating talk last night with the guy I'm now going over to see."

He gives me the quick backstory, and I feel his pain. By the end of my time in the district attorney's office, both of us were the lead dogs in our departments and handled all of the city's high-profile murder trials together. We were a well-oiled machine until the team sprung a leak—me.

I ask, "Is Sophie here yet?"

Because Scott is out of commission, Sophie will be my partner for the day. He answers, "Haven't seen her. Only one around is Marlon in his office."

"Did he go home?"

"Beats me. He's wearing different clothes but keeps spares here, so I couldn't tell you."

"Where does the old man get the energy?"

* * *

Sophie rides shotgun as we travel to visit the magician—née illusionist—Oliver Twist. Previously a deputy with the Coweta County Sheriff's Office, she used to date Scott once upon a time. Amber and I would socialize with the two of them fairly regularly during that period. I cannot remember what ultimately put a stop to those outings—Scott and Sophie's break up or Amber's giving birth to our child. Either way, a long time has passed since Sophie and I have ridden together in the same car.

She quips, "Going out into the field with the boss. Is today some kind of performance review?"

"Yeah. A lot is riding on it. I need you to solve this murder so I can get some sleep. I'm overdrawn and heading toward bankruptcy."

"Yes, sir."

I could do without the "*sir.*" I'm not yet forty, and Sophie is only a few years my junior—despite our respective outward appearances. I look every bit my age, but she could pass for fifteen years younger.

Her escape from the balcony of the Billiard Room remains fresh in my mind as I continue to work over the problem of the locked door. I ask, "How's your ankle?"

"Fine. A little ice, and it was good as new."

We're meeting Oliver Twist today at his workshop, located in an industrial area west of downtown, only a short drive from the Office. When we arrive, Twist—today wearing an all-white suit instead of all-black—greets us outside with open arms and a smile full of white teeth, a mosaic reminiscent of Mr. Roarke from the TV show *Fantasy Island*. I half-expect Tattoo to pop out screaming, "The plane! The plane!" He would fit right in with the rest of this strange case.

Our host invites us into his magician workshop, and I feel the sensation of stepping into another world—a dark one consumed with dismemberment and torture, almost medieval in character from the appearance of it. I scan around and take inventory of the furnishings—an ominous silver slab with straps to hold the victim in place, a guillotine, a giant water tank with shackles at the top to suspend a person upside down, a wooden table with spikes hovering above it, a large cabinet on wheels helpfully labeled "The Devil's Torture Chamber." The room is packed to the brim with all things magic, and I reflect that this is probably the place where Twist paralyzed his assistant for life when the Bullet Catch Illusion misfired.

The foreboding surroundings give me a slight shiver. Sophie smiles like a kid in a candy shop.

Twists asks, "What do you think? I'm deciding which illusions I should take with me to China."

I respond, "Not the Bullet Catch Illusion."

His body sags as if my words deeply wounded him, but I still can't get a read on his stretched-out face. He whimpers, "I probably deserved that."

He'll get no argument from me.

After finishing with his pouting, he explains, "My newest illusion is called the Inca Tomb. Whoever enters the Inca Tomb forever passes onto the other side of eternity, never to suffer the slings and arrows of outrageous fortune in this world ever again. I could show you how it works, but one of you would need to volunteer."

"No thanks."

Sophie jumps in, "I'll do it."

She walks toward him with brisk steps before I have the opportunity to object. Twist rubs his hands together greedily and leads her to a walk-in, rectangular box. He opens the door to the box and shows me the inside before whirling the entire box around to demonstrate that no means of escape exist from the Inca Tomb.

Before Sophie enters, I shout, "If you hurt her, Twist, I'm going to perform a magic trick of my own where you disappear for good, never to be seen again. I call it, 'The Missing Magician.'"

He laughs—a fake, ventriloquist-dummy laugh, like so many of his mannerisms. After a quick bow, he answers, "Understood, my dear fellow. I researched you and know to respect the sincerity of your threat. You recently killed a man."

Guilty as charged. I wonder if Twist has recently killed a man himself.

He whispers instructions to her, and Sophie steps into the box. The door closes, apparently separating her forever from this side of eternity.

In full performance mode, Twist announces, "All the world's a stage, and all the men and women merely players. They have their exits and their entrances, but the most terrifying exit of all awaits those who dare set foot into the Inca Tomb."

I prefer the original Shakespeare.

Twist spins the box around a full three times—for my benefit, I assume, although the intended effect doesn't move me. He chants some magic spell, opens the door, and sure enough, Sophie has vanished. The magician spins around—pleased as punch with himself—eager for my reaction. I make my voice as sardonic as humanly possible and give it to him.

"Amazing."

At that moment, I feel movement on my right hip and turn around to find Sophie holding my gun in her hand, the handle held out toward me.

"Hi, boss."

Credit where credit is due. The speed in which she escaped from the box, circled behind me in the clutter of the workshop, and removed the gun from its holster is a better magic trick than the Inca Tomb.

* * *

Oliver Twist is effusive in his praise of Sophie's star turn as his spur-of-the-moment assistant.

"Miss Applewhite, you are descended from the gods—Aphrodite herself, I would say. The stage is your rightful home, and I besiege you right now to say good-bye to your current employment and join forces with me as my illusionist's assistant. You'll need a performance name. How about the 'Sensational Sultry Sophie'?"

Wearing a bemused grin at Oliver Twist's protestations of love, Sophie turns toward me and asks, "Counteroffer?"

"We'll put 'Sensational Sultry Sophie' on the nameplate to your door if that's what you're angling for."

With that deal-clincher, she declines to accept Twist's generous offer. Time to hunker down on the business for which we're here. Given Twist's enthusiasm for all things Sophie, I nod at her to begin the questioning.

"Oliver, you have a special gift. Your illusions will bring joy to millions of people in China—if you're not in prison for murder. Therefore, if you ever want to make that trip to Shanghai, nothing but the truth should pass through your lips from this point forward."

The fierceness in her face is all business. Both Twist and I stand surprised at the sudden transformation—him especially since he's on the other end of it. The sense that he would like to hide away in the Devil's Torture Chamber for the foreseeable future takes hold. I don't blame him. I've never seen Sophie interrogate suspects before. Early returns are strong. She continues.

"Jim Walker insulted you in a recent text. Tell me about it."

Twist remains a few seconds behind on the conversation and just stands there. With great effort, he eventually pries open his mouth and offers a response in a clipped tone.

"Mr. Walker didn't appreciate my art. That in itself wasn't a big deal. But he and Gustave were close friends, and Mr. Walker kept putting it in Gustave's ear that I wasn't a talented illusionist. I didn't much appreciate it. Gustave is my most important benefactor."

"Worried that Walker might sabotage your big break in China?"

"The thought crossed my mind."

"Jim was your lawyer, right? Don't lawyers have a duty to look out for their client's interests?"

"Technically, yes. He was my lawyer. But Gustave arranged for Mr. Walker to represent me and paid the bills—if there were any bills. Felt like he was representing Gustave more than me. Mr. Walker didn't try to hide his contempt for my chosen profession. Even said that saving me from prosecution for accidentally shooting Missy was a better trick than any I'd ever perform. He liked fancy things, including hanging around rich and famous people. I know the type well. For him, I wasn't important enough to warrant his attention on my own."

His mood is sullen—like a sad puppy disciplined with a pat from a rolled-up newspaper. The vulnerability makes him more human, and a different interpretation of his eccentricities starts to emerge. The man once named Rupert Ramone—the one who uses big words, quotes Shakespeare, undergoes endless surgeries on his face, and pants for fame to validate his worth—bristles under the weight of feeling inferior to those around him.

While I play Dr. Freud in my mind, Sophie keeps up the full court press.

"Oliver, you know where this is going, right? Jim was a threat to all your hopes and dreams. But then he ends up with a dagger in his back, and you're back on the boat to China."

"I didn't kill him."

"You have no alibi. That's not a good thing."

"Do you want me to lie? I stayed in the study and read sonnets. No one else was in the room. I can't prove a negative. But I'll tell you the truth. When I saw that he was dead, I cheered on the inside. His murder brought me great pleasure. Satisfied?"

Not really. Confessing to one offense to ward off suspicion about a larger one is often a tactic of people who aren't as clever as they think. The tough reality for Twist is that I now have a better feel for his possible reasons for wanting Walker dead. Jim didn't like him and had Gustave's ear, threatening Twist's best chance at stardom. That's a sturdier motive than some fear that Jim would disclose what happened to Missy—an event from years ago that few people would actually care about anyway.

Sophie glances over to see if I have any questions for the witness. I take another stab at the locked door mystery.

"Given any more thought as to how someone would go about getting into and out of the Billiard Room when it was locked from the inside?"

"As I said the other night—"

"I remember exactly what you said the other night: '*Through the power of illusion, of course.*' Except I'm searching for a solution a little less general and more focused on the actual mechanics of how to turn the inside lock from the hallway."

Twist has no answers for me. I confirm that he will be attending Gustave Root's party on Monday night and make him promise to inspect the lock closely at that time. As we stand up to leave, he says, "Miss Applewhite, are you sure you have no interest in metamorphosing into the Sensational Sultry Sophie?"

She replies, "Let's make sure you avoid a murder rap first."

25

When filming in town, Mark Romo stays in a penthouse atop Buckhead's swankiest condo building. He opens the door himself and waves us in, flashing a movie star smile and letting his gaze leer over Sophie for a couple of appreciative seconds. In the living room, floor to ceiling windows offer a million-dollar view of Atlanta in the distance. Romo drops down on a couch, and we take opposite chairs on both sides of him.

After hitting a brick wall initially, Barbara delivered the goods on the details surrounding Romo's hit-and-run. She emailed her report to the entire team early this morning—including gory pictures from the scene. We now have a name, the date, and a pretty good understanding of what happened. In particular, the boy's injuries indicate that Romo was speeding roughly thirty miles over the legal limit at the time of impact, killing the child instantly. With Cale on my mind a lot the past few days, Romo's cavalier attitude the other night about the accident—"*Jim kept my name out of it at least*"—riled the hell out of me on the drive over here. Truth be told, I'm still riled. The man sped away from a bleeding kid sprawled out on the sidewalk. That's a special kind of cowardice.

Sophie handled Oliver Twist so well that I decide to let her take the lead this time around, too—also figuring that the less I say to Romo, the better.

"You were pretty drunk the other night, Mark. How you feeling now?"

He picks up a half-filled glass of whiskey off the coffee table in front of him and finishes it off before answering.

"Good. Feeling good. Seeing that dead body freaked me out, and I had to drink off the memory. But I'm pacing myself today, even though it's Saturday, and I can drink however much I want. Can I fix you something by the way?"

"Have any roofies in your possession?"

The response is not one he expected, and he takes a moment to recover his bearings. With a confused expression on his face, he answers, "Roofies? Me? Come on—I don't need roofies."

The smirk he unleashes is vile. I liked him better as a dumb drunk—and I didn't much like him then. But in the daylight of relative sobriety, he comes across as an arrogant asshole. I want to punch him in the face—the thought of that kid lying in his own blood still a thorn in my flesh.

Sophie counters, "Trust me, plenty of us women out there are capable of resisting your charms, and you still didn't answer the question. Do you have any roofies here in your condo? I can check your medicine cabinet if you insist on doing it the hard way."

"Relax, already. I don't have any damn roofies."

He grabs a bottle of Jack Daniels from off the coffee table and fills his glass to just south of the brim. It's not yet noon.

Under Sophie's direction, Romo again tells the full story of what happened the night of the murder—a necessary exercise to determine if his version of events is different when he's not stone-cold drunk. But today's account pretty much tracks what he told Scott and me the other night. He talked to his agent on the phone, heard Gustave call for help outside the Billiard Room, tried to open the door but couldn't, followed Oliver Twist up the ladder, saw Jim Walker dead, opened the door to let Gustave in, hightailed it out of there, and proceeded to drink himself into a stupor.

With Romo's story about what happened that night again on paper, Sophie transitions to prodding him on his possible motive for killing Jim Walker.

"Mark, we also need to talk to you about Tristan Curry."

"Who?"

His ignorance is sincere. Sophie looks at me almost confused, and I start boiling with righteous fury. Tristan Curry is the name of the boy that Romo ran over and killed. Except this entitled, drunken bastard—guzzling Jack Daniels in his penthouse condo—doesn't even recognize it. I growl, "You lousy son of a bitch."

He turns to me, full of annoyance, and snaps, "Who pissed in your corn flakes?"

I grit my teeth—the cold anger inside of me turning hot. I lean into him with an iron voice and suggest, "If you're going to kill a kid, you could at least do him the simple courtesy of learning his name."

The recognition registers on his face, and he appears slightly embarrassed—but nowhere near as ashamed as he should be. He gives a half-shrug of his shoulders and reaches down for his whiskey. As he brings the glass up to his lips, I spring up like a cobra and slap it out of his hands. The brown liquid splatters in all directions, and the glass bounces off the carpet but doesn't break. He stares up at me in a new frame of mind—no smirks, no shrugs, just fear.

I yell, "Say his name!"

"What?"

"Say his name!"

"Okay, okay. Tristan Curry."

"Good. Now maybe the next time you hear it you'll spare a second and feel a twinge of remorse over what you did."

Sitting back down, I make myself a solemn vow that when the Walker investigation is over, I'm going to unleash Barbara on this clown. Our jurisdiction is whatever I want it to be, and vehicular homicide in Georgia carries penalties up to fifteen years in prison. Romo could use some alone time in a cell—maybe with "Tristan Curry" tattooed onto the wall to remind him of why he is there.

Sophie studies me with a neutral expression. Romo stares at the floor while stealing glances toward the Jack Daniels that remains on the coffee table—as if he wants to take a drink right out of the bottle, but fears what I might do in response. I nod at Sophie that she can resume her questioning.

"Now that we've given you a friendly reminder about who Tristan Curry is, talk to me about where things now stand. Jim was badgering you about having to come up with some more money to keep things quiet, huh?"

Romo remains a little slow on the uptake—frozen in place for a time while we wait for his answer. He does his best to avoid looking at me while at the same time still making sure that I'm not on the move again. Licking his lips after another lustful look at the Jack Daniels, he starts talking.

"Jim said something about that, sure. An email or text. Then mentioned it again at the party and said we needed to meet soon. I asked him how much more were we talking about here. He said probably a quarter million."

"What did you think about that?"

"It wasn't fair. A deal is a deal, you know. I don't want to be bled by this family my whole life."

He turns in my direction, regrets it immediately, and swings back to Sophie. She crunches her thin eyebrows up in confusion and observes, "I thought Jim worked it so you wouldn't ever have to worry about that again."

"I know, right? That's what I told him at the party. He said settlement agreements can buy that kind of peace of mind, but I couldn't very well sign one with the family, could I? The whole point was to keep my name completely out of it. And that means cash with nothing in writing. Made the deal harder to enforce, he said."

"How much cash did you pay the first go around?"

"Two million."

"All cash?"

"Yeah! Took a couple of suitcases."

Jim Walker certainly had a nice racket going—skimming off secret settlements that only he knew about is borderline foolproof. I wonder how much of that money—if any—Tristan Curry's family ever received. The family didn't even know Mark Romo was involved. What leverage did they even have over him? Walker could've lied about the whole thing and pocketed the entire amount. And how much does it cost to run a bar anyway?

Sophie asks, "What if I told you that Jim Walker kept some of that money for himself?"

Even allowing for the fact that Mark Romo is an actor, the belief on my end is that the suggestion takes him by surprise. He even looks back toward me to confirm the veracity of what Sophie just said. I nod my head to resolve his doubts. He fumbles for a response.

"Why would Jim do that to me?"

Sophie answers, "Why would he steal your money? Either he needed the cash for himself or just didn't like you or possibly a little bit of both. The bigger question is what would you do to him if you found out."

"What do you mean?"

"Somebody killed him. You've already killed one person. Why not two?"

Romo grabs the Jack Daniels, takes a slug, and proclaims, "I didn't kill anybody!"

He ventures another peek at me, and I arch a questioning eyebrow. One swallow and a bite on the lips later, he sputters, "I mean—except for Tristan Curry. But that was an accident."

* * *

We stop to grab lunch at The White House Restaurant, but I lost my appetite somewhere in Mark Romo's condo. Maybe Sophie stole it. While I nibble at an omelette, she scarfs down the Presidential consisting of hot cakes, two eggs, and an eight-ounce ribeye—the meal an energy boost before she runs a half-marathon tomorrow morning.

Between bites, she says, "Got kinda intense in there."

I just nod. The boundary line between righteous anger and sinful anger is not a clear one to me. Romo more than deserved a good scolding, but I'm less sure that knocking the drink out of his hand came from a Jesus-honoring heart. The instant I set foot in that condo—and likely a little bit before—the evil of Romo's desertion of Tristan Curry had me out of alignment on the inside. But this work requires me to be a hard man at times. And therein lies the rub. How do you love others when you want to punch them in the face?

26

Jessica Allen's residence of choice in Atlanta is a downtown condo adjacent to Centennial Olympic Park. The Georgia Aquarium is right across the street. I remind Sophie on the elevator ride up that anything she says can and will be used against her in the court of social media.

Allen takes her time coming to the door. Whatever the reason for the delay, it didn't involve making herself more presentable. Her hair is as wild as an unbroken mustang, the pajamas she wears even worse. I marvel again at her tiny frame and conclude that she, among all the people there that night, is the unlikeliest of suspects. Unless she's some kind of clandestine ninja, she didn't exit the Billiard Room by way of the balcony. And even though the Nazis designed their honor daggers with the sharpest of tips, I'm unsure whether she would even have the strength to jam the thing with enough force into Jim Walker's back.

When we cross the threshold and sit down in the living room, Allen tries to focus by wiping the sleep out of her eyes but ends up smearing day-old mascara, giving the effect of a tiny, hungover football player. She asks, "Can we talk on the balcony? I could use the fresh air."

I respond, "You're not smoking a joint in front of us if that's your plan."

She makes a disagreeable noise, confirming my suspicions. Giving up on the fresh air idea, she sprawls in a cushioned chair in the living area. We find seats for ourselves and get down to business.

I say, "You told me the other night that you were doing weed on Gustave's front porch at the time of Jim Walker's murder. That still your story?"

"Why wouldn't it be?"

"The weather. I got to thinking afterwards that the temperature was pretty cold. Your outfit—which showed plenty of skin—didn't really fit the conditions. No way you sat outside for twenty minutes dressed like that. Unless you're part-Eskimo—which you're not."

Jessica yawns. I fight the urge to yawn, too—although a Saturday afternoon nap sounds heavenly right now. She sits there weighing her choices, almost certain to make the wrong one. I try to give her an extra little incentive to even the odds.

"Lying to law enforcement is a crime. You don't want to go to jail, and I don't really want to put you there because I have bigger fish to fry. So here's the deal—if you tell the truth right now, I'll give you a mulligan for the other night."

"What's a mulligan?"

"A free do-over to blot out your previous sin. Take the deal. Jail is much worse than what you see on television—especially on a Saturday night."

"I'm a pretty big fish."

"Did you kill Jim Walker?"

"No."

"Then you're not the big fish I'm looking for."

She yawns again, and I desperately want to join her. Sophie watches us with a wry smile. If she yawns, too, I'll probably falls asleep on the spot. Allen stretches her arms over her head as far as they can reach and then some more over the back of the couch. When the stretching routine is over, she stares at me and sighs.

"Fine. I did smoke a joint but not outside. Like you said, too cold. I took one step out the front door and knew that wasn't happening. How well do you know the house? There's a little window nook recessed into a wall near the kitchen across from the back staircase. I camped out there under some blankets and popped open the window to kill the smell. It's a pretty good hiding place as long as nobody is looking straight at you."

I remember walking by the spot when the team searched the mansion. It's tucked away like she says—and provides an excellent view to the entrance of the kitchen. But first things first.

"Why did you lie to me before?"

"Gustave bragged how he was good friends with the Governor. I supposed that you were doing his bidding and would tell him everything I said. That was a problem. While Gustave's cool most of the time, he is really into all that junk he collects and doesn't want it smelling like weed. He's warned me before. And honestly, I'd rather lie to the police than get on Gustave's bad side."

"And yet you still smoked marijuana in his house?"

"A girl's gotta do what a girl's gotta do. The whole party was headass, and I needed to take off the edge."

Pretty sure I've never heard the word "*headass*" before, but I think I get the gist. Her story about the window nook rings true to me, but that's only the preliminaries. Now comes the important part—what did Allen see from this vantage point? I put the question to her but have to wait for the answer after she finds an unused joint in the cushions of her couch. Putting it to her nose, she breathes it in and looks to me in the hope that I may relax my earlier edict against her smoking in my presence. But no. If word got out that I let a Hollywood actress do drugs right in front of me, that wouldn't do much for the murder squad's reputation.

Jessica compromises by putting the weed in her mouth unlit. Only then does she tell me what she saw.

"The lawyer chick—Erica, maybe that's her name—walked out of the kitchen just after I got comfortable. A few minutes pass and here comes good old Mr. Beale carrying a bunch of ice into the kitchen. The Russian with the beard—the one who plays chess—stomped down the stairs after that and went into the kitchen. Then Gustave descended the stairs a few minutes later, which scared the hell out of me, of course. He turned into the kitchen and came back out pretty quickly. He didn't see me, thankfully. After that close call, I hid under the blanket until I finished the joint and didn't see anything else."

"You saw Leo Ivanov coming down the stairs?"

"That's the Russian dude, right? Most definitely."

Everything she said about Erica, Beale, and Gustave is consistent with what we already know, but the Ivanov bit adds a new wrinkle. He told Scott and me that he used the bathroom before heading to the kitchen. I assumed that meant he used one of the bathrooms on the first floor—of which there are many. Instead, he was upstairs, right down the hall from the Billiard Room. Interesting.

I hand Allen off to Sophie to probe whether Walker tried to steal from her, too. But I don't pay much attention. Jessica already passed the test. She couldn't have known that Erica, Mr. Beale, Ivanov, and Gustave all were in the kitchen over a twenty-minute period unless she herself was snugly tugged away in the nook as she claims—which means she wasn't upstairs killing Jim Walker. Unless she really is a ninja.

For her part, Allen avows that she isn't going to pay another cent to anyone because some girl in middle school killed herself years ago—and if a journalist wants to out her as a bully, so be it. She told Jim as much at the party. After a few more questions from Sophie along these lines, we leave the diminutive actress alone so she can smoke her weed in peace.

27

I walk through the door of the house fifteen minutes before Scott and Taylor are due to arrive. The comforting smell of chili greets me—the dash of a jalapeno scent triggering my appetite after a light lunch. Sweetheart and Bristol dash over and lie on their backs for a quick belly rub. Cate—wearing a "Kiss the Cook" apron—stirs the chili on the stove. She turns her head toward me, and I kiss the cook.

She asks, "Long day?"

"Something along those lines. I slapped a glass of Jack Daniels right out of Mark Romo's hands. He's lucky I didn't hit him—or maybe I'm lucky."

Cate stops stirring and turns around to get a better read on my temperature. She smiles a little and says, "Because I think he's good-looking?"

That garners a laugh, and I feel better already just by being home. I answer, "No—although he did leer at Sophie like a slab of meat. Except she can kick his ass on her own without my help. Something else set me off."

"You want to talk about it?"

"Not now—too long a story. Later maybe. I need to change before they get here."

"Did he at least deserve it?"

I think again of Tristan Curry dying on the sidewalk and say, "He deserves far worse."

* * *

When I decided to move out of Atlanta, the peacefulness of the country drew me to this area. But one unique feature more than any other led me to make this particular piece of property my home—a detached automobile garage. Large swaths of my youth were spent working on cars at the side of my Uncle Ernie. Most of my family are Baptists, but he was always a Chevrolet man—the black sheep of the Meridian clan. By purchasing the place, the thought was to spend the rest of my life restoring old cars.

Fate had other plans, but I did manage to finish bringing one old car back to life—a Silver Blue 1963 Chevy Corvette Stingray. Pure American muscle and a bona fide work of art. On the open market, it could fetch $100,000, but I'll never sell. Sentimental reasons—mainly that my intimate knowledge of the vehicle saved me from a car bomb a few months ago—ensure that I will always keep the Corvette close by.

My current reclamation project—if I ever again find the time—is a 1977 Pontiac Firebird Trans Am LE, complete with the classic T-Top so you can feel the wind in your hair. The car has long been a source of fascination for me, ever since I was a young boy. But with a new job and a new wife on my plate, work on the restoration is languishing.

I take Scott out to the garage to show him the bones of the new project. Even though the car is without an engine and wears more dents than a golf ball, he immediately recognizes the iconic piece of movie history.

"The Smoky and the Bandit car?"

Not the real one, of course. But I am restoring the piece of metal now in front of him to look just like what Burt Reynolds drove in the film. I nod yes in answer to his question with a proud gleam in my eye. Scott is less impressed.

"Every time I think you couldn't be more of a redneck, you go and prove me wrong. An educated and remarkably articulate redneck—but a redneck all the same."

In my defense, Scott believes that everyone born in Georgia outside the city limits of Atlanta is a redneck. But my rural roots are deep enough that he's not too far off the mark in his diagnosis of my condition.

He says, "Now there's something I want to show you. Anywhere we can shoot around here?"

I lead him and the dogs to a clearing in the woods about a hundred yards behind the garage. Picking a target, he explains he wants to demonstrate his new gun for me. I ask, "Is it loud?"

"Loud enough. Why?"

"The dogs and their training. I want to see how they react."

Sweetheart and Bristol loiter near me but immediately sit dead still when I call out, "Halt!"

Scott takes his position and fires ten rounds, making a smiley face in the bark of a tree a couple of first downs away. The noise is pretty stout, but the dogs don't jerk an inch. To release them from the position, I yell, "Freedom!" They bound toward me with tongues wagging. Scott reloads the gun and hands it to me.

"Your turn."

I take aim and fire, but the trigger doesn't move. After making sure the safety's off, I try again with the same result. A third attempt with me using as much finger pressure as possible meets a similar end.

"What am I doing wrong?"

"A biometric pistol, synced with my fingerprints. Only works when I'm holding it. Some perp takes my gun, he's out of luck. You should think about getting one."

"No thank you. Revolvers are simple. I like simple."

On the walk back, he says, "Sophie called me and explained what happened with Mark Romo."

"Was she appalled?"

"Nah. She's not that kind of girl. Awe would be closer to the mark. Said it was badass as hell—like something you'd see John Wayne pull off in a movie. But she did worry that it wasn't like you to do that kind of thing—being a lawyer and all."

"Am I still a lawyer?"

"Your official title is 'Special Counsel.'"

And so it is. When the murder squad formed, everyone got to pick their own titles. The result is a motley assortment of designations before our names that bear little relationship to each other or any discernable hierarchy. Chief Detective Scott Moore. Inspector Marlon

Freeman. State Attorney Barbara Hsu. Lead Agent Sophie Applewhite. Lieutenant J.D. Hendrix. Executive Administrator Taylor Diamond. The incongruence fits the vibe of the team.

And I'm Special Counsel Chance Meridian—even though I don't feel much like a lawyer these days.

Before we join Cate and Taylor, I return to the Jim Walker murder.

"Had a crazy thought about the case on the drive home today. What if we're being played? What if all of them did it? Like *Murder on the Orient Express* by Agatha Christie. They all had motives. He was blackmailing Aaron and Erica Cain, stealing or trying to steal from Ivanov, Romo, and Allen, having sex with Gustave's wife, threatening Oliver Twist's big chance for stardom, and hawking Celeste Wood's paintings on the side. Only Vivian lacked an obvious motive, and Gustave made her stay upstairs. Now we may know why. Gustave invites everyone to the party. They all conspire together beforehand, concoct the lie about the locked door, and stage a crime that's impossible to solve."

"You think Celeste would've been in on it? Gustave didn't invite her. Walker pressured her into coming as his date."

"She's the iffy one. But since she was outside swimming anyway, they could've pulled it off without her knowing anything about it."

He leans back on the red brick of the house and gives my theory a good think. Two things about my idea really appeal to me. First, it solves the locked door problem. Second, except for Celeste and Vivian, I really don't like these people and nailing the lot of them for murder would be emotionally satisfying.

Scott says, "That's a lot of people to keep together in a conspiracy. Surely one of them would crack, right?"

"Maybe we just haven't found the weakest link yet."

* * *

Work is off limits as a topic during dinner, and the reprieve is a welcomed respite. To much merriment, Taylor shares stories about me all the way from elementary through high school. I tell her she's fired.

After the meal, we gather around the fire pit in the backyard. The women drink wine, Scott nurses a beer, and I work on a Coke to help me stay awake. I offer to make s'mores, but no one bites. I make one for myself anyway—consistent with my lifelong habit of consuming too much sugar when the world gets a little too sideways for my taste. S'mores especially are a common vice. Something about the combination of roasted marshmallows and Hershey's chocolate realigns my soul with the best version of me. I take the first bite and smile.

Scott regales us with tales of when he worked the beat as a uniformed cop—a couple of which I've never even heard before. His loose license with the facts is forgivable in light of his great skill as a storyteller. Both German Shepherd pups make their way to my lap, and I gaze at the distant stars above in the clear night air. The moment is perfect. The touch of the dogs, the smell of the burnt wood in the fire, the sight of the boundless universe, the aftertaste of chocolate on my tongue, the comforting voice of a good friend in my ears—all five of my senses at work with each other to deliver one juncture in time where everything fits. I like to think that's what Heaven is like—fullness of heart and being for all of eternity.

When Scott and Taylor leave, Cate kicks her shoes off and nestles up next to me on the couch. I drape my arm around her, thankful again that we found each other. She asks, "So what happened with Mark Romo today?"

I relay the story and feel her stiffen at the various low points of Romo's bad behavior, all up to the moment where the actor shrugged his shoulders with bored indifference after his failure to recognize the name of Tristan Curry.

"And you just knocked the drink out of his hand?"

"Yep. And then I yelled at him to say Tristan Curry's name."

Cate jerks her head off my chest to get a better look at me and exclaims in an incredulous voice, "You didn't! What did he do?"

"He said the name."

A disbelieving laugh follows, and she returns her head to my chest while murmuring, "I wish I could've seen that." We sit quietly together for a while, each of us in our thoughts. I finally let out the yawn with which I've been wrestling ever since being in Jessica Allen's condo. Cate asks, "You're not going to let him get away with killing Tristan, are you?"

"Feel free to divorce me if I do."

She pats my leg and says, "Good boy." I hold her tighter, and another spell of silence lingers. Her turn to yawn is next. We should really head to bed, but moving requires more effort than I care to spare in the moment. Besides, my wife feels too good leaned up against me. After a spell long enough for me to wonder whether she's fallen asleep, she says, "What's bothering you about today?" I give a lot of thought to the question and answer.

"Even before I got to Romo's condo, my heart felt black. Angry. Furious with him about leaving that boy to die. And then everything he did after opening the door just made me more lathered up—the smirks, the shrugs, the leering at Sophie. Like he was rubbing my soul with sandpaper. There I was, sitting right next to this guy, knowing that I hated him. That darkness I felt scares me."

"Seems to me that you did the Lord's work in confronting him."

"Trust me, Jesus wasn't in my heart in real time."

"But you were angry because you saw the injustice of it all. And where do you think you get your sense of justice if not from God?"

I chew on her response and kiss the top of her head. *Justice*. What does that word even mean in a fallen world where the laws are written by flawed humans who may or may not have consulted God in the writing? I remember Danny Davis strapped to that gurney and ponder whether he received justice. In Georgia, maybe. But in the twenty-two states that have abolished the death penalty, maybe not. And where do I best fit in the delivery of this elusive *justice*? In the courtroom making legal arguments? Or on the streets with a gun at my side knocking whiskey out of the hands of murder suspects? And does it even matter? After all, law and force are two sides of the same coin.

The next time I open my eyes, my watch informs me that the hour is an ungodly one. I check it again to make sure. Cate's head no longer rests on my chest, opting instead to use my thigh as a pillow. After getting to my feet, I scoop her up and manage to get the both of us to the bedroom without dropping her.

I kiss her still sleeping cheek and whisper, "I love you."

28

We miss church the following morning. I hope the preacher—my brother Ben—isn't too mad. Ben serves as a senior pastor in my hometown ninety minutes south of Atlanta. His reputation in preaching circles continues to grow, and bigger churches often throw more money and a larger platform at him as a lure to join them. But Ben remains content to minister to his modest country church, firm in the belief that he is where God wants him. He is also the happiest person I know.

Since getting married, Cate and I usually make the drive in the Corvette every Sunday morning to hear Ben preach and have lunch with the family, including Cate's mom. Given my sleep deficit of the past week, today would've been an excellent time to stay home—except I still have to tell my mother about the Governor's impending engagement to Susan Benson. And that requires an in-person trip. The compromise was skipping the sermon.

We're the last to arrive when we pull up to Ben's house. One step out of the car, and I can smell the cooking of Ben's wife, Sally. Mom and Tammy Wilson—Cate's mother—rock gently in white chairs on the front porch. My nephew and niece run up to me with hands out to receive their customary dollar from Uncle Chance. This ritual was more fun when my visits were intermittent. But as an every weekend routine, the price isn't right. I need to re-negotiate. Ben comes out to greet us and gives Cate a welcoming hug. After giving me the same, he notes, "Missed you this morning."

"A wise pastor once told me that sometimes the most spiritual thing you can do is to sleep in on Sunday mornings."

"Is that right?"

"Straight out of Habakkuk, I think."

He laughs. I motion him with my hand to take a walk, and we head off to a murky pond a little way behind his house. After confirming that we're alone, I explain, "I have some unpleasant news to share with Mom, and I'm not doing it alone. You're going to be there with me."

"That sounds ominous."

"Something like that. Minton and Susan Benson are getting married."

Pastors hear all kinds of strange confessions from the members of their flock. Ben is no different, and surprise is almost a foreign emotion for him as a result. But this particular bit of news does the trick of jarring his senses. The Governor might as well be part of our family, and his marrying Susan Benson is akin to a Capulet marrying a Montague. A carousel of questions travels around my brother's punch-drunk face. Finally, he settles on one.

"How long has that been going on?"

"Not sure. Some time since Ruth died."

"Why doesn't he tell Momma himself?"

"He and I had that exact conversation. He begged me to take the bullet."

"I bet he did."

Ben's consternation almost makes the hard task in front of me worthwhile. But not quite. The Governor's impending engagement to Susan Benson will poke Mom in the exact spot where she hurts the most—not to mention trigger a whole host of ancillary memories that could unleash other wounds. Minton and Ruth McReynolds were a constant presence in the life of my parents, and when Ruth died, Mom lost one of her best friends in the whole world—a mere six months after my father passed away. Nothing about today's conversation is going to be pleasant.

Assessing the tactical landscape, Ben suggests, "Let's wait until after lunch for you to tell her."

"For me to tell her? Thanks, brother."

"Thoughts and prayers."

* * *

"What were you and Ben talking about?"

Mom is a born detective and has always had a nose for situations that don't smell right. My taking Ben behind the house for a private chat fits the bill. Now I get to hear about it from her. I answer, "I was telling him how much I love him."

She scoffs and presses me some more. I stick to my guns and say only, "It was between the brothers, Mom."

Lunch is pleasant, but the sensation that the scene is not quite in tune pervades the air. Nothing tangible that anyone could ever point to, just the feeling of something slightly crooked. After some delicious peach cobbler, I ask Ben and Mom to join me in his study. My mother's eyes land on me like a heat-seeking missile—her hunch that something is amiss confirmed. The three of us excuse ourselves, and I shuffle out the door as if my feet were chained in shackles. When I glance back for one last look, Cate mouths "Good luck."

Ben closes the door to his study, and Mom immediately demands of me, "Do you have cancer or something?"

"No!"

The question stuns me. I stare at her as if she's crazy but relent when I see the relief in her eyes at my answer. She has endured a lot of loss within the past five years—Daddy, Amber, Cale, and Ruth. Burying one of her sons might break her. That she spent all of lunch worrying about my health is both touching and heartbreaking at the same time. As I contemplate this poignant dichotomy, Mom interrupts.

"What is it then? Some kind of bad news, I know. Spit it out."

I freeze. Spitting it out is difficult with the object in question stuck firmly in my throat. After much effort, I manage to cough it up.

"Minton and Susan Benson are going to be married."

Her reaction is more confused than anything at first, as if I'm speaking some exotic foreign tongue. Finally, she asks, "To each other?"

The nod I give is short but enough. That slight gesture starts the avalanche. A cacophony of stream-of-consciousness profanity erupts from my mother's lips, including some words I've never heard her utter in the nearly forty years that I've known her. I glance around for a place to hide but come up empty. Ben's eyes bug out to twice their normal size. He prepares his sermons in this room and views the space as almost sacred. But Mom's tirade will no doubt echo in the walls for the foreseeable future. As the uncomfortable monologue continues, I am wistful for the good old days when I was back in Gustave's study scrutinizing Adolf Hitler's artwork.

Mom finally pauses to catch her breath. Ben and I remain silent—afraid of dousing the fire with any more gasoline. Without warning, the rant begins anew.

"What is the deal with men and that woman? Does she have some magic dust that she sprinkles down there on her pu—"

Ben exclaims, "Momma!"

The interruption spares me a lifetime of psychiatric counseling. It also takes a little bit of wind out of Mom's sails. She stands there defiant, but a little of the invective begins to leak out. I know she won't cry. Maybe later in the privacy of her bedroom but not in front of her two sons.

She says, "Did you two know that Minton was seeing that woman?"

"First I learned of it was right before lunch when Chance told me," interjects Ben with remarkable speed.

Thanks, brother. Both of them turn their heads to me, and I feel like an accused criminal in the dock at the Old Bailey—the hostile eyes of the crowd casting judgment on the cursed and the damned. I take a deep breath to buy time. One of my core values revolves around an ancient truth: A man should not lie to his mother. But that doesn't mean the truth can't be massaged.

"I had some suspicions but hoped the whole thing would just go away."

"You knew!"

My arms turn upwards at my side, and I say, "Who knows anything anymore?"

A saying among trial lawyers goes like this: if the facts are on your side, argue the facts; if the law is on your side, argue the law; if neither the facts nor the law is on your side, bang the table. Hiding behind existential philosophy is my version of banging the table. Mom snorts. She was married to the man who taught me that saying. But she does divert her focus back to the Governor instead of me.

"Ruth must be turning over in her grave. She couldn't stand that woman. Absolutely hated her. What in the blazing hell is Minton thinking?"

The question is likely rhetorical, and I choose not to answer on that ground. She frowns, no doubt racking her brain to figure out more aspects of the situation to be angry about. The search doesn't take long.

"He doesn't expect me to go the wedding, does he? Please tell me he's not that far gone."

I shake my head. Minton didn't mention anything of the sort. If he does have a thought along those lines, then he's going to have to do his own damn bidding on that score. I'm out. But no. Susan Benson herself would put a stop on her end to inviting Mom. We're safe from that catastrophe at least.

More dead air follows. Mom seems resigned that her Sunday afternoon is now spoiled, but she is as tough as they come and has endured worse than this. With the fight seeping out of her, the three of us rejoin the rest of the family.

* * *

"How did it go?"

The Corvette is still in Ben's driveway when Cate presses me for the scoop about the big reveal to Mom.

I respond, "Ben learned a lot of new words that he can incorporate into his sermons and some mention was made as to whether Susan Benson sprinkles magic dust on her private areas to attract men—except she started to use a different term for private areas. Ben threw himself in front of the train before she could get the whole word out. Thank God for small miracles."

She laughs uproariously and asks, "Where can I get some of this magic dust?"

The engine of the Corvette roars, and I spin the tires on the way out to the open road. I shake my head at her in mock disappointment but finally smile. Cate's sense of humor is wicked, and I get a greater glimpse into it every day I'm married to her. She does ask whether Mom's going to be all right, and I offer my best diagnosis.

"I don't know. Sometimes the best thing for a person is to blow off their excess steam. Better that she gets it out of her system on me than walking around all week with it bottled up, nursing a grudge. But a helluva lot of past hurts were unleashed today."

We have the leftover chili for dinner—comfort food that comforts. Afterward, I decide the best therapy would be to spend some time exercising my muscles working on the Trans Am. As I head out the back door, Cate says, "Let's make sure we head to bed at a decent hour tonight. Together." Her manner is overly suggestive, and I happily catch her drift.

In the garage, I mess around with the pistons in the engine a bit. The work is rote, allowing me to dwell on my *Murder on the Orient Express* theory—the idea that most everyone in Gustave's house that night had a hand in killing Jim Walker. The hypothesis is a direct affront to my belief that the simplest solutions are most often the correct ones, but nothing about this case is simple. After mulling the whole thing over in my head, I move from working on the engine to fooling around with the transmission, no closer to the solution to the murder and giving up that particular chase for the rest of the night.

I return instead to yesterday's confrontation with Mark Romo and pray a silent prayer for God to purge the hate out of my system. While I eventually forgave the unknown man who murdered my family—someone I once named Mr. Smith to give my hatred a better focus—what I've learned since is that spiritual cleansing is a never-ending process of renewal. Kinda like how I have to shower every day to wash the dirt off of my body. But ever since watching Danny Davis die, the grime inside of me has accumulated without any action on my part to flush it out. Feeling a nudge to do something, I decide to reflect on the fruit of the Spirit as laid out in Galatians. I drop into the passenger seat of the Trans Am and go about renewing my mind.

Love. Joy. Peace. Patience. Kindness. Goodness. Faithfulness. Gentleness. Self-control.

So beautiful and obvious on the pages of the Bible. So hard to capture when people like Mark Romo get in the way. I sigh. Jesus pegged the problem a long time ago: "The spirit is willing, but the flesh is weak." Me most of all. I remain, as ever, a work in progress—half-finished like Celeste Wood's painting of my lived-in face.

Hours later, I jolt awake and check my watch. For the second straight night, I fell asleep for far too long in the wrong place. My body feels like a pretzel in the aftermath. I manage to reach the house only to find Sweetheart and Bristol on high alert when I enter through the backdoor.

"Relax."

They don't move, and I search for the right command in the coma-like fugue that is my brain at the moment.

"Freedom."

They rush toward me with big smiles and receive hearty pats on the head for following their training. I kick off my shoes and sling them somewhere. With German Shepherds on my heels, I stagger back to the bedroom in the darkened house. The outline of Cate's body shows in the scant light created by the various electronics in the room. The heaving of her chest in tempo with her breathing makes my heart feel full. I lie next to her, knowing I should shower but lacking the will. The last thing I remember is kissing her bare back.

29

Cate jostles me awake to say I need to get a move on. I crawl to the shower and hope for the best. Twenty-two minutes later, I'm behind the wheel, and we're on the move to Atlanta.

She asks, "What kept you in the garage last night? I thought we were on the same wavelength about engaging in some sexual congress."

"We were. Except I fell asleep in the passenger seat of the Trans Am."

"And me waiting in bed with bated breath while you're out there snoring in the redneck mobile."

"The best-laid plans of mice and men often go awry."

"That's the problem—I was trying to get laid."

"Want me to turn around and head back to the house for a quick dose of morning delight? We're both awake for a change."

"Tempting, but I have a meeting, and we're already leaving work early to get ready for the party tonight."

Cate pulls out a legal pad and starts to make a to-do list for the hours ahead—one of her rituals when I chauffeur us into work. I turn on some R.E.M. and lose myself in the noise since I'm too tired to drive and think at the same time. Right about when "E-Bow The Letter" starts to play, my wife turns pensive and asks me to mute the music.

She says, "I don't want to grow apart from you. That's what happened with my first husband. We started working too hard, drifted away from each other, stopped having sex. And then one day I caught his secretary on top of him in our bed. I lived through that once and couldn't bear to go through it again."

Her eyes plead for reassurance. Now off the interstate and stopped at a traffic light, I tell her, "Kiss me." She obliges, and I hold her lips until the light turns green. As we approach the judicial building, I say, "Not for a single solitary second since we got married have I regretted it. You're perfect the way you are—smart, funny, beautiful. And being with you has shown me that I still have lots of good life to live—something I never thought possible after what happened to Amber and Cale. You lifted the cloud that I assumed would follow me forever, and you foolishly said 'yes' to marrying me in a fit of impetuousness. Now you're stuck with me for the duration."

When I pull into our parking space, Cate kisses me again and then holds up her legal pad to show me the last item on her to-do list: "Have sex with Chance!"

I say, "The exclamation point is a nice touch."

* * *

Barbara is waiting for me at the Fulton County Courthouse when I arrive for our meeting with Judge Mary Woodcomb. Before Cate came along, Mary owned the distinction of being my favorite judge. She sat on the bench for my first trial ever and treated me with a gentle hand. She also presided over my last trial—the Bernard Barton one—the both of us wizened veterans by that point. Woodcomb now handles all judicial business for the murder squad.

But more than the courtroom memories we share, the thing about her that resonates with me the most is her presence at key moments in my life—both tragic and joyous. Mary was one of the few judges to attend Amber and Cale's funeral—a thoughtful gesture that still carries special meaning. She also married Cate and me a couple of months ago in the same chambers that Barbara and I are about to enter.

The purpose of our meeting today is to procure Woodcomb's signature on a warrant to search Leo Ivanov's residence. Carliss Sherman's letter—seeking more money to keep quiet and revealing that Jim Walker only paid her $25,000 instead of $100,000—is a critical piece of evidence that we need in our possession. Sophie and J.D. are camped outside Ivanov's place right now waiting for the go signal.

Barbara by herself is overqualified to babysit a search warrant in need of a signature. The two of us being here is overkill. But I haven't seen Mary since the marriage ceremony and wanted to take the opportunity to get my face in front of her again. The timing also worked out since I have another meeting in the courthouse afterwards.

As we wait for the summons, Barbara says, "I heard about what happened with Mark Romo the other day—about how he didn't even know Tristan Curry's name."

"Word spreads fast in the Office."

"Something like that. We're going after him, right? I want to be the one that takes him down so I can see his dumb, smug face when the jury brings back a guilty verdict."

I sometimes think that all prosecutors have a little bit of the Puritan in them—Barbara more than most. I understand the feeling, having always been more of an Old Testament kind of guy myself, an eye for an eye and all that. But Barbara takes it to another level. As a straight arrow who has always played by the rules, she takes a dim view of those who think that the law doesn't apply to them. At least she comes by it honestly. As an Asian female, any deviation from society's expectations on her part would meet with disproportionate disapproval—unlike the Mark Romos of the world who are given more latitude than they deserve. From Barbara's perspective, turnabout is fair play.

The judge welcomes us and asks me, "How's married life?"

"Wonderful."

"Good. I'm always relieved to hear about happy marriages. I handle too many divorces in this job. Always a sad business. Marrying you off to Cate Slattery is probably the most satisfying thing I've done in my black robe all year. That—and adoptions. Adoptions are the best. Divorces and murders—another story entirely."

She directs us to a sitting area on the other side of the room from her desk. Mary insists on informality when meeting with lawyers in private—a far cry from some judges who actually wear the black robe in chambers. With the proposed search warrant, the judge asks for a summary of what we're after. Barbara tells her about the Carliss Sherman letter.

Woodcomb asks, "How do you know the letter is there?"

I answer, "Detective Scott Moore saw it when we questioned Leo Ivanov."

Her eyebrows raise a hair, and she says, "How did he see it?"

"Ivanov is a grandmaster at chess. He challenged me to a game. When Detective Moore wondered what he was to do while we moved pieces around a chessboard, Ivanov told him to '*make yourself at home and look around*.' Detective Moore did just that."

"Meaning you already searched the place without a warrant?"

"With the explicit consent of Mr. Ivanov, yes. We need the warrant to assume possession of the letter before it disappears by unnatural forces."

Mary grunts. She generally gives me a long leash but is not a rubber stamp by any stretch. But whether Scott stretched the bounds of Ivanov's consent is not a contested issue at this point. Woodcomb signs the search warrant and sends us on our way.

* * *

Judge Ella Kemp gives me a warm hug in her chambers. Ella is my former trial partner—and a little bit more. But the romantic relationship between us never actually took flight. Some bad behavior on my part broke her heart and ended up breaking my own heart as part of the deal. Half a year later, Cate helped me pick up the pieces. As for Ella, she is now engaged to Trevor Newman—a United States Attorney in the Justice Department.

Even though both of us are now in better places than when we last worked together, Ella's suspicion that I rejected her as a love interest because she is black still bothers me—mostly because I fear she may be right. Subconscious forces of which we are barely aware often guide our choices, and I've learned the hard way that lots of ugly things lurk beneath the veneer of my respectability. While I eventually confessed my love to her on my last day as a prosecutor, by then it was too late.

But the unchangeable past is just that—unchangeable. I'm here to seek help in trying to do some good in the present. In particular, I want to pick Ella's brain about Vivian Root.

Before trying homicide cases with me, Ella cut her teeth as a prosecutor in the sex crimes unit. Her empathy with female victims, forged from standing side by side with them in the pursuit of justice, made her a force of nature in saving women from the ravages of abuse. Wanting to lean in to her expertise, I explain the situation with Vivian to her.

"Picture a Nazi sympathizer with actual artwork from Adolph Hitler's own hand on his wall. We'll call him Gustave. Rich guy. Famous. Powerful. Even thinks he owns the Governor, although he's recently been disabused of that notion. The worst of it—he was pals with Jeffrey Epstein and hung out with him there on Pedophile Island. That's one side. On the other side, we have this young woman— Vivian. Married Gustave when she was only nineteen years old. He was in his late fifties at the time. Now she's having buyer's remorse and wants out. Why did she marry him in the first place? Because, in her words, she *'was trapped in an awful situation surrounded by horrible people who didn't have my best interest at heart.'*"

"You think she was a sex slave on Pedophile Island?"

"Can't discount the possibility, especially since we can't even find proof that Vivian actually exists. I know we're only a lowly state agency and all, but something should be there."

Ella chews on a pencil as she gathers her thoughts—a longtime habit she's had at least since the time I've known her. She asks, "What do you want from me?"

"Guidance. Advice. Anything. I want to help her but don't know how. And I worry that Gustave might hurt her. Complicating matters on that front, Vivian was having an affair with the man whose murder we're investigating."

Ella whistles—another trademark of hers.

"You think Gustave killed the guy?"

"Probably not. We'd love nothing more than to put the collar on him, but it doesn't really fit the facts."

"Let me talk to Trevor. With his contacts in the U.S. Attorney's Office, he might be able to scare up some more information about Vivian. If she really was hanging around all those pedophiles, the feds probably would have an interest in protecting her. See if you can find out whether or not she was on that island and how determined she really is to escape her situation."

I give her as many particulars about Gustave and Vivian as I can. When I mention that Vivian is black, Ella's eyes narrow and a grim determination fills the entirety of her face. I've seen that look before, and it has always meant bad news for someone.

She seethes, "Old Nazi-loving white guy marries teenage black woman he met on Pedophile Island? How messed up is that? Too close to the old slaveholders treating female slaves as their sexual property for my taste. We need to get Vivian out of that environment."

Sounds about right. Vivian intimated as much to me: "*Gustave worships his collectibles, and I'm the finest piece in his collection.*" Mr. Beale and his many talents likely fall into the same category—an exotic specimen of memorabilia to parade before Gustave's astonished guests. That gives me another thought.

"As long as Trevor is willing to dig up information on people, any background he can unearth about an eight-foot albino named Mr. Beale would also be appreciated. From somewhere in Europe. Used to be a part of the circus, now works for Gustave."

"You're not joking, are you?"

"I never joke about eight-foot albinos."

Ella shakes her head at the madness of it all. I explain about the upcoming party at Gustave's mansion that night in the hope that Trevor might uncover something before then.

As I head out the door, she says, "I'm surprised you're now consorting with murder suspects at posh parties. Doesn't strike me as your scene."

"True, but it seemed impolite to turn down the chance to see how my suspects behave out in the wild."

30

The Fulton County Courthouse is a block away from the State Capitol, and I head straight over for my bi-weekly lunch with the Governor. The magnificent dome—decorated with gold stolen from the Cherokees—shines bright in the mid-day sun. In keeping with the prophecy of Georgia's resident groundhog, winter ran long this year, although the worst now appears over.

The groundhog's name, of course, is General Beauregard Lee—because everything in Georgia at one time had to pay appropriate homage to the state's Confederate past, even the naming of fat rodents. But those days are long gone. I figure that if Oliver Twist can't make Stone Mountain disappear for good, someone else will—at least the defiant carvings of Jefferson Davis, Robert E. Lee, and Stonewall Jackson that adorn the mountain's face. At one point in my life, trying to erase the façade off that exposed granite would've struck me as profoundly absurd. But scenes like the one just now with Ella have taught me that the stain of slavery endures still and causes real hurt in the living. More than that, my Bible instructs, "Give to everyone what you owe them." And for those who committed treason in defense of human bondage, what's owed is not honor, but a reckoning.

When I reach the outside of Minton's office, Martha Towns is not at her desk—which may be a first. I knock on the Governor's door and hear a gruff noise I take as permission to enter. He gives a half-smile when he sees me, but his heart isn't really in it. He looks much too tired for a Monday morning. I ask about the absence of his gatekeeper of nearly fifty years.

"Martha's not out there. She didn't quit, did she?"

"That's not funny."

"Didn't realize I was kidding."

He growls and directs me to a table with a spread from Doc Chey's Noodle House on it. I help myself to the BiBimBap and Mongolian Chicken. My customary bottle of Coke already sits in its usual place. Given Minton's foul temper, I decide to exercise my right to remain silent until spoken to. The food is better than conversation anyway. I always eat well during these little luncheons.

The Governor chews on some Shanghai Dumplings. Between bites, he says, "You told your mother? How did it go?"

"Don't expect her to attend the wedding."

"What did she say?"

"Some of the words would get me arrested, so I'll pass."

"Give me something."

I stare up at the ceiling and wonder how I got drawn into this soap opera. After a deep sigh, I say, "Some mention was made about Ruth turning over in her grave."

He nods as if that was expected and says, "Martha said the same blasted thing. You knew Ruth. What do you think? Is she turning over in her grave?"

Trying to summon up something approaching sympathy on my face, I put on my theologian hat.

"I hope that upon our deaths we are forever free from again caring about the concerns of this world—seems incompatible with my idea of Heaven. In other words, don't worry about Ruth because I don't really think she's worrying about you anymore."

His expression tells me that he's not so sure. Fair enough. When I was hitting my various low points during the Bernard Barton prosecution, the burden of disappointing Amber pressed on my heart like a sudden loss of oxygen. But that anchor was a weight of my own making. The dead don't care. I help myself to one of the dumplings. Minton changes the subject.

"How's your investigation going? Do you realize that nut Root keeps calling my office here demanding to speak to me? Leaving messages about firing you and demanding his campaign contributions back."

"He's having a big party tonight at his place to show off the exact

159

spot where someone murdered Jim Walker. Cate and I are going. You should come, too. You and Gustave can then catch up."

"Were you always this sarcastic? I remember you as more respectful."

In response, I pull out my phone to show him the pictures I took of Root's autographed copy of *Mein Kampf* and the framed swastika on his wall. The Governor grabs his glasses and perches them on his nose to see better.

"What's this?"

"Scenes from your friend Gustave's closet."

He turns up his nose at me and shoos the phone away. After checking his watch, he says, "I'm too busy for this nonsense. Get out of here."

I finish off my BiBimBap and head on my way.

* * *

Martha Towns is ensconced in her usual place when I exit. Her once vibrant dark hair is now gray, and she's more hunched up than she used to be, but I don't care. Martha has long been one of my favorite people, and I don't reckon anything will ever change that. I go over to give her a hug, but she turns her shoulder away and refuses to look at me. I whine, "What did I do?"

"As if you don't know. The Governor and that woman! And you smiling at me with that sweet smile all the time hoarding that information to yourself. The Governor told me that no one knew about the relationship except *you* and his bodyguards."

I turn my head and stare at the now-closed door to Minton's office. That dirty, rotten snake—running me over with the bus and then backing up for good measure in case he missed a spot. No reason at all existed for him to tell Martha I knew about his little dalliance except to divert a measure of her hostility my way—after I took the bullet for him in telling Mom, too. I'm of a mind to bring Gustave to my next Governor's lunch in retaliation. That might be fun. But in the meantime, I turn my attention to mending fences with Martha.

Flashing my sweetest smile, I say, "You know you can't stay mad at me."

"Don't push your luck, Chance. You're on thin ice."

160

She looks like she might mean it. I reassess my approach and decide to re-frame her perception of events.

"Listen—you're looking at it as a secret that I was keeping from you. From my point of view, I was jumping on a grenade to protect other people from getting hurt. Learning that news was a bitter pill for me, not some sweet lollipop I refused to share. And as I will remind you, a whole host of people kept my father's affair with Susan Benson secret from me for over two decades—you among them."

Daddy wanted it that way—for me to maintain my respect of him in the midst of his disgrace. I was the only person close to him not to know, and stumbling on the knowledge a couple of months ago wrecked me for a spell. Martha was part of that conspiracy of silence and has unclean hands now to hold a grudge against me for similarly keeping my lips sealed on a secret not my own.

Still, she maintains, "You didn't need to know that."

I flash a skeptical expression her way, and she shakes her head in a sign of submission. Pulling open one of the bottom drawers to her desk, she withdraws a jar filled with her famous cookies. She opens the top and holds it out to me.

"Here."

Chocolate chip is her specialty and also my favorite. I devour the cookie and say, "The Governor tells me that Gustave Root is being a thorn in your side."

"That man is awful. Why does he want you fired so bad?"

"Because I don't know my place."

She doesn't seem surprised.

31

Scott slumps into the visitor's chair of my office after spending the morning testifying in his murder case—probably his 10,000th such trial at this point. Anytime he appears in court, he wears his shiniest badge on the outside of his coat to convey the authority of his position. Plain-speaking and to the point, he makes a good witness. He also looks the part—the years of experience that wrinkle his face adding gravity to his words. I ask him how it went.

He waves a hand and grumbles, "Fine. We'll get the conviction, despite that new prosecutor's lack of instincts. That's the advantage of being the government. Home-field advantage and the presumption of guilt."

Pretty much. Presumed innocent sounds nice in the stratified air of constitutional law, but trials take place in the real world, and juries want to convict—especially in murder cases. He asks, "How's your Agatha Christie notion going?"

"I gave up on it sometime last evening."

"Probably for the best. Anything new on the case?"

"Sophie and J.D. retrieved Carliss Sherman's letter from Ivanov's place. Apparently, he raised hell and yelled a bunch of Russian at them. Also mentioned something about the Gestapo."

"Don't think the Gestapo relied on warrants."

With his hands behind his head, he leans back in his chair before putting his feet up on my desk. That's his musing pose, and I don't have to wait long to hear it.

"Here's how I see it. You know I'm big into motive, means, and opportunity. Not in this case. Everyone in that house had a motive, and everyone had access to the means."

"Vivian didn't have a motive."

"She was cheating on her husband with the victim. Rest assured, a motive is in there somewhere. Human Nature 101. You would see that except you're way too trusting of women as a rule. That's bitten you in the ass before."

"Low blow."

"Tough love. Anyway, what I was saying—motive and means are an even playing field for everyone. Practically useless in this case. Instead, everything hinges on opportunity. Who had the best opportunity? Aaron and Erica were in a bedroom right next door to the Billiard Room. Ivanov was somewhere on that floor before he came down the steps and was spotted by Jessica Allen in her hidden nook. Vivian was standing right outside the Billiard Room with Walker's dead body on the other side. That's my top four. Romo is next. His pacing around the whole house is a little too convenient for me, but I confirmed with his agent that they were on the phone together during most of the relevant time. He's still on my list, though—as are Celeste Wood and Beale. They were both outside in close proximity to the balcony. Maybe one of them jumped and decided to act normal from there—her swimming, him fetching the ice."

I consider protesting on Celeste's behalf but don't want to be accused of trusting women too much again. Instead, I say, "Beale wasn't really near the balcony. Didn't we already determine that the garage is too far away given the timing issues?"

"We did, but I want to keep him on the list anyway. Call it my policeman's gut."

"Gustave, Jessica Allen, and Oliver Twist are out?"

"No opportunity—it is what it is."

"Where do the roofies come in?"

"Some connection to the issue of opportunity. Figure that out, and we probably crack the case."

* * *

Marlon joins us and places a small plastic bag on my desk that contains three tiny metal dots—listening bugs for tonight's party.

I complain to him, "They're microscopic."

"All the better to be hidden."

"But I'm going to lose them."

He's all out of sympathy. I take one of them out of the bag and immediately drop it to the floor. A minute later, I manage to find it.

Scott asks, "Did you get a warrant?"

I shake my head. He raises his eyebrows and says, "Really? We'll make a cop out of you yet."

"No need for a warrant where there's no reasonable expectation of privacy. It's a party with tons of people there."

That's the argument at least. No way Judge Woodcomb would approve a request for me to drop listening devices in Gustave's house wherever the mood struck me. But sometimes creativity carries the day. When he found out about my invite to Gustave's party, Marlon—a technological wizard who loves playing with his electronic toys—had the idea of leaving eavesdropping spyware around the house where our suspects might congregate. In his words: "You never know." After a consultation with Barbara on the various legalities, we decided to make our own luck and leave the bugs in areas of the house well-populated enough to avoid any claims of privacy.

The kitchen is the obvious first choice—if for no other reason than determining if Mr. Beale can actually speak or not. With the other devices, the plan is for me to make executive decisions about the ideal placement in the heat of the moment. At the end of the party before I make my way home, I will simply reacquire our property, and no one will be the wiser.

Marlon explains, "I'll be here with J.D. and Sophie monitoring the bugs—one for each of us. You can even talk into them if you need help in a pinch."

I turn toward Scott and say, "Jealous? I get to play cloak-and-dagger at a billionaire's mansion tonight. What are you going to be doing?"

"Waiting for you to call me to ride to your rescue."

"That'll be the day."

* * *

Being the boss means trafficking in paperwork. My desk is full of the stuff, and I lack the will to pay it much mind. When my cell rings and the caller ID shows Ella Kemp's name, I rush to answer, thankful for more important business than the busywork in front of me. Ella's excited voice barely gives me time to spit out a greeting.

"Are you sitting down? Trevor came through for you in a big way. Vivian Root—real name Madeline Moses—is originally from the Bahamas but spent a good chunk of her adolescence on Little St. James Island as a de facto ward of the late Jeffrey Epstein. Little St. James Island has other names of which you might have heard—Pedophile Island and Epstein Island being the most common. Do I need to draw a picture for you?"

"Please don't."

"At some point during her stay, she aged out and became too old to interest the clientele. Except for Gustave Root. He made arrangements with Epstein and took Madeline Moses off the island with him. They were apparently married in Barbados, and he brought her into the country. She now goes by Vivian Root, but no record of any official name change exists anywhere. Legally, she's still Madeline. That's why you couldn't find her. Her immigration status is still unclear."

The pieces fit like I suspected, but patting myself on the back is out of the question. Sometimes the best thing for everyone is to be way wrong. Ella continues, "Trevor is interested in talking to her. She must know things. Witness protection is a possibility if she's worried about her safety."

Vivian's first thought upon seeing Jim Walker dead on the snooker table flashes through my mind again: "*I thought Gustave had killed him.*" But when I offered her a free escort away from her husband, she responded, "*One day I might take you up on that offer—if I think I can trust you.*"

Through Trevor and the feds, I now have something more tangible to give her than a free ride in a police car. Here's hoping she agrees to the terms. I say, "Let me try to talk to her tonight. Anything on Mr. Beale?"

"Not his real name, either."

"You don't say."

"Shocking, right? Anyway, Mr. Beale is none other than Friedrich Bellingshausen—once a circus attraction in Europe billed as the 'World's Tallest Man.' Came over with Gustave on a visa years ago and has disappeared off the government radar ever since—no official documentation of any kind. The visa has long expired. A credible rumor exists that Bellingshausen killed a man with his bare hands. That's supposedly why he left Europe with Gustave."

"Did he ever kill anybody with a knife?"

"Don't know. But you should be careful all the same."

32

"Zip me up."

Cate walks over my way wearing a short blue dress with a lot of sparkly things. She turns her back to me, and I slide the zipper up easily over her smooth back. Moving my hands to her bare shoulders, I start to give her a deep massage—topped with a gentle kiss to her neck.

"That feels good," she says.

"Let's just stay here and complete your to-do list. I promise not to fall asleep."

"Are you crazy? I love a good party—being all dressed up and going out on the town. Should be fun."

Having met many of tonight's partygoers, I don't share her same level of enthusiasm. I check myself in the mirror to straighten my tie and feel a wave of tiredness sweep over me like an unexpected wind. Putting on my shoulder holster is the last touch before securing the revolver in its hiding place for the evening. I usually prefer wearing the gun on my hip but opt to be a tad more discreet owing to the formality of the event. No matter. The bulge under my coat is visible all the same if you know what to look for. Satisfied that I look presentable enough in my nicest suit, I head to the kitchen for some caffeine.

My wife emerges a few minutes later—a necklace of many blue stones adorning her neck as the final piece of her outfit. I pay her appropriate homage.

"Glad I'm carrying a gun. I'm going to need it to keep the men away from you tonight. You look incredible."

I move toward her for a kiss, but she rebuffs my efforts on the grounds of protecting the integrity of her lipstick. Foiled again, I lead her to my state-issued SUV and help her up in the seat for the drive to Tuxedo Park and Gustave's mansion.

167

Around the time we pass the airport, I give her a stern warning.

"The following is a public service announcement—be extremely careful of what you put into your mouth. Guests at Gustave's house have a disturbing tendency to end up drugged with roofies. Don't accept any drinks handed to you. If there's a bartender taking orders, watch him pour and keep watching until the glass is in your hand. Don't put your drink down at any point or otherwise leave it out of your sight. Keep your guard up, and trust no one. We are foreigners entering a hostile land."

"You sound like my dad. 'Never take a drink from a strange man.'"

"That's good advice in general, but especially tonight. Remember—someone at this party is a murderer."

The seriousness of my tone makes the impression I intended—that this is not a game. She nods, and we head into downtown in silence to face the meat of the traffic. After a few minutes of my dodging cars through various lane changes, Cate says, "You've given me your warnings, now I'm going to give you mine."

"Yeah?"

"Whatever happens at the party, no matter how late we get home, I'm having my way with you at the end of it. No ifs, ands, or buts. We decided the other night to try to get pregnant but haven't had sex since. That's not how it works. Understand?"

"Thanks for the warning."

She punches my arm. I grab her hand and bring it to my lips to kiss her knuckles, ready again to forget the festivities completely and head straight home.

"Hey—my offer from earlier still stands. We can skip the party and advance to Go right now. Just give me the word."

"True. But I want to have my cake and eat it, too. First—my night on the town, then my night on you."

She blows me a kiss.

* * *

A valet outside of Gustave Root's mansion tries to commander the SUV, but that's out of the question. Too much expensive equipment inside and too many shotguns hidden in the back. I flash my badge and explain that I'll park the vehicle myself. I take the spot closest to the house.

After I help her alight from the car, Cate takes a look at the classic white façade in front of her and proclaims, "So this is how the other half lives."

"Champagne wishes and caviar dreams."

"Ooh—you think they'll be caviar here? I love caviar!"

"Fish eggs?"

She nods excitedly. I stare at her like she's an alien and realize how much of my new wife I have yet to discover. *Fish eggs.* I shudder.

Gustave—his turbulent gray hair particularly tempestuous this evening—greets me at the door like we're a couple of old friends. After that charade, he pivots to Cate and deploys all of his European manners on her as if she were royalty. Heeding my warnings, she is polite but skeptical. The host then maneuvers us further inside for introductions to two of his other guests, some envoy from Switzerland and his much younger date. He explains to the other man, "Ah—you are *très* fortunate tonight, my good friend. Here is Chance Meridian, the head of the Atlanta Murder Squad and his wife, Cate Slattery, a leading jurist on the Georgia Supreme Court. A power couple of the first order. Mr. Meridian also killed a man recently. How exciting! You'll even notice the bulge in his jacket where he carries his gun."

Grinning from ear to ear in awe of his own cleverness, Gustave pats my chest on that exact spot. I reflect that's a good way for a man to lose a hand. Cate's expression does a fair job of maintaining a Swiss-like neutrality in the uneasy aftermath, and I flash a fake, diplomatic smile to defuse the provocation. For her part, the envoy's date—who may very well have been born this century—eyes me with a strange new respect. But killing a man ain't all it's cracked up to be. After Cate and the envoy exchange a few pleasantries, Root ushers us to another set of people for more introductions, repeating most of the same routine as the first go around. He doesn't pat my chest this time at least.

The dichotomy of Gustave's excessive friendliness with his angry phone calls to Martha to have me kicked off the case is puzzling at first. After the third set of introductions to more of his guests, I grasp that I'm part of the show—Cate, too. Root is ingratiating himself with his wealthy friends on the backs of our perceived status—trophies to be paraded around, just like Vivian and Mr. Beale.

That realization doesn't sit well, and I cut short an ongoing conversation to steer Cate away from any more of our host's machinations. Gustave watches our departure with condescending bemusement—the face of a man convinced he can get away with anything.

She says, "I need a drink."

"Let's go to the kitchen."

We retrace the steps of Erica Cain as she made her way to get her husband a Coke shortly before someone jammed a knife into Jim Walker's back. When I pass the nook where Jessica Allen sneaked a joint the other night, I peek in but find no sign of the actress. When we reach the kitchen, Mr. Beale towers over a host of other kitchen helpers as he directs them in preparation of the meal—using hand signals from the look of it. Leo Ivanov sits in a chair off by himself, his eyes staring down at his phone. The movement of his fingers suggests that he is in the middle of an online chess match.

Beale analyzes me with those ocean-blue eyes of his, narrowing them to express displeasure with my intrusion. Cate tries not to stare at him and succeeds for the most part but still manages to steal some quick glances toward his direction every few seconds. On the drive up, I tried to put Mr. Beale into words for her, but some things belie description and must be seen to be fully understood.

Ignoring the big man's irritation with my presence, I head toward a row of wine bottles on one of the counters. He watches all of my movements about the room—his hands remaining suspended in mid-air. I pour Cate one of the reds—a Pinot Noir—and hand it to her. From the refrigerator, I help myself to a Coke. Mr. Beale continues his silent vigil.

I ask him, "What's wrong?"

He doesn't answer and resumes his work.

The sound of my voice causes Ivanov to jerk up from his game. He doesn't wear the appearance of a man happy to see me—his black eyebrows puckered in frowning contempt. No shock there. Search warrants can have that effect on people. Needing to talk with him, I try to make amends.

"Cate, I want to introduce you to one of the world's great chess players, Professor Leo Ivanov. Also moonlights as a math genius at Georgia Tech on the side. Leo, this is my wife, Cate Slattery."

Showing good manners despite his ill feelings for me, Ivanov rises to his feet and makes a slight bow in Cate's direction. She returns the favor. A waiter approaches us with some type of black substance on a small plate and presents the plate for Ivanov's inspection along with a small fork. I watch mesmerized, uncertain as to what's happening. Leo can't be intending to eat that. But Ivanov picks up the small fork and, sure enough, performs a taste test of the tiny black circles clumped together like jelly. A glazed-over look of profound satisfaction populates his face in the aftermath.

Cate asks, "Is that caviar?"

"*Da*. Beluga caviar from Russia—the best in the world. Care to partake?"

"Hell yes!"

Ivanov motions the waiter for more forks. Cate takes one and scoops a generous helping of the black goo right into her mouth. Moans of culinary delight follow. She says, "Damn that's good! Don't think I've ever had Beluga before. How much does that cost? A couple of thousand dollars per pound?"

"*Da*."

"Chance, you have to try it. A once-in-a-lifetime opportunity."

"That stuff looks like spider droppings."

She shakes her head in mock disapproval. Turning to Leo, she laments, "I can't take him anywhere."

The Russian bellows a deep laugh. I reckon he prefers her company to mine. Makes sense. Both of them turn to me with expressions of expectation on their faces. Cate holds out a tiny fork in my direction, and I take it with the reluctance of a man on his way to the gas chamber. At a couple of thousand bucks per pound, I wonder what prison officials would've done if Danny Davis had requested Beluga caviar as his last meal. Ever so gingerly, I put a small amount on the fork and put it into my mouth. The effect is immediate.

"It's like slurping salt!"

I grab my Coca-Cola with great haste and drown the foul-tasting slime down deep into the pits of my stomach. I've never been more confused in my life—do they really find those disgusting fish eggs appetizing? I don't have anything approaching a refined palette, but still. The two of them share a chuckle at my expense and finish off the rest of the caviar. If nothing else, Leo is now in a much better humor than when he first heard my voice a few minutes ago. Maybe I should make Cate a part of the murder squad to soften up all my suspects. After finishing off the last of my Coke, I tell it to Ivanov straight.

"We need to talk."

He nods his head in grim resignation.

33

The kitchen opens up to a keeping room. Leo and I move that way to talk in private. Cate remains a discreet distance from us on the border between the two areas, working on her wine. Not wanting to leave her waiting too long, I jump to the point.

"Leo, Jim Walker stole $75,000 from you that was meant for Carliss Sherman. You knew he stole from you and yet lied to us about it. That's a problem."

"*Da.*"

"Why?"

His hand disappears into the underbrush of his thick beard. The Russian heaves a deep sigh before explaining himself.

"The foreigner—he always gets the blame. You find out that Mr. Walker defrauded me, and Professor Ivanov becomes suspect Number One. I lied to keep myself out of jail. I made error."

"Well, now's the time for redemption. What happened when you confronted Walker about it?"

"He started talking in the lawyer-speak—claiming some kind of misunderstanding. That he was holding the rest of the payments back lest Carliss became too greedy too fast. I demanded my money back, and he agreed but tells me that I could deal with my Carliss problem by myself going forward."

"Did he pay you back?"

"*Nyet.* The night of the party, he promised to bring a check around to me the next day. This never happened since he gets murdered. Do you think I could still get my money now that he is dead?"

"No idea. Ask your lawyer."

The answer about Walker's paying him back the day after the party is a convenient one. No one's likely to kill someone about to hand over $75,000 to them. It's bad business. But Leo's word isn't gospel on this point. Could be that Walker changed his mind and told the good professor to jump in a lake. Could be that Leo decided that if Walker was going to stab him in the back through some elaborate double-cross, he could return the favor.

And that means the next minute or so is an important one for Ivanov to get right. Jessica Allen places him on the second floor at the time of the murder, and I have every reason to believe her. Leo is about to receive the opportunity to buy himself a bucket's worth of credibility by volunteering that information free of charge.

I say, "You told me the night of the murder that after leaving the study with everyone else that you went to the bathroom and then the kitchen. Remember?"

"*Da.*"

"We're trying to pin down where exactly everyone was and should've asked you which bathroom you used—just so we can understand the traffic patterns of people's movements through the house."

Without hesitation, he answers, "Upstairs. Right up the staircase next to the kitchen. Want me to show you?"

"Please."

He moves with purpose, and we head back toward the kitchen. I gather Cate on the way and ask, "More wine?" She nods yes and hands me her glass. I stray again into Mr. Beale's airspace and receive the same stare of disapproval before he returns his attention to the food. I pour another red for my wife—this time from a different bottle because you can never be too careful. As part of the refilling process, I leave behind the first bug to give the folks back at the Office something to sink their ears into.

On the way out, I watch Mr. Beale's knife skills as he chops vegetables into small shapes with remarkable dexterity. He catches my stare and meets my eyes but continues carving the items with the speed of a jackrabbit. A crack of a smile on his face expands into something more jagged and grotesque. I notice for the first time that one of his upper front teeth is slightly chipped. The rapid chopping continues, even though his eyes remain fixed on me. I wink at him and say in a low voice, "Friedrich Bellingshausen." Beale's eyes go wide at the sound of his own name and he loses his concentration, nicking his finger with the knife in the aftermath. A piercing groan—half-anger, half-pain, half-hatred—emanates from the man holding a sharp object in his hand, along with a glare of pure malice directed my way. Deciding discretion is the better part of valor, I leave before ingesting a knife for my trouble.

Cate whispers, "That was creepy."

"You wanted a night out on the town."

With Leo in the lead, the three of us exit the kitchen, and I again pass Jessica Allen's nook hideaway without seeing her. We ascend the back staircase, and Leo takes a sharp left at the top, away from the direction of the Billiard Room. He directs us to an unoccupied powder room and says, "Here."

"What path did you take to get here that night?"

"Same staircase—up and down."

"Seems a little out of the way."

Ivanov shrugs and makes some comment about wanting to get away from the other people at the party. I choose to give him the benefit of the doubt for the time being. Highly doubtful that he knew a witness from the nook saw him coming down the stairs and yet he acknowledged being on the second floor of his own free will. He passed this part of the test at least.

"See anyone else up here during that time?"

He shakes his head. The response makes sense. The Billiard Room is not visible from the area where we now stand and requires navigating a couple of hallways to get from here to there. No reason apart from using the powder room exists for anyone to be hanging around in this part of the house. Before letting him go, I ask, "Carliss Sherman giving you any more trouble?"

His Slavic features cloud over in disgust. Leo's a pleasant enough fellow until the subject of his former student comes up. He spits out an answer.

"*Nyet*. But she will. Nasty woman. Mr. Walker should've paid her all the money to keep her away."

Out of questions, I watch him waddle down the stairs with his hunched shoulders leading the way. Cate asks, "Who's the '*nasty woman*'?"

"A former student he impregnated and persuaded to have an abortion in exchange for a payoff. Ivanov tends to think that he was the victim instead of the other way around."

Cate sadly stares down the now-empty staircase after her caviar buddy. I pat her on the back for comfort and ask, "Ready to see where Jim Walker got himself murdered?"

34

A sullen Oliver Twist leans on the bannister overlooking the grand entrance to the mansion. The foyer below is chock full of people, and a steady stream of folks enter the nearby Billiard Room, too. Looking down, I notice the Mayor of Atlanta standing just outside the study talking to Gustave and hope that the Governor doesn't get jealous. I consider taking a picture and sending it to him but resist the urge.

Twist turns and sees me as we walk up—the sullen look graduating into a more energetic sulk. His face lacks its typical tautness, and dark bags sabotage the shine of his makeup. He groans, "Not you."

He's back to wearing all black tonight. The design choice worked for Johnny Cash, but on Oliver the wardrobe feels forced—a naked confession of the man's awkwardness.

"Cate, this is Oliver Twist. He's a magician. Oliver—Cate, my wife."

Without any of his usual flair whatsoever, Twist offers a limp hand but little else. He doesn't even bother to offer his customary retort of "*illusionist*" to counter the "*magician*" slur. He slumps against the balcony again, making me wonder if he's contemplating making a jump for it. I assess the distance to the marble floor below. The fall would be decent but hardly a cinch for someone seeking a quick exit. As a suicide bet, it's a fifty-fifty proposition. I decide to be nosy.

"What's eating you?"

We both know that I'm not his favorite person, but it seems Twist needs a friend and any port in a storm will do. After a brief moment of hesitancy, he says, "Gustave told me tonight that the China deal is off as things now stand."

"Did he give a reason?"

"He suspects that I might've killed Jim."

That's an attention-grabber. Even Cate's eyes rise as she drinks her wine while nonchalantly listening.

"Why on earth would he think such a thing?"

"That confounded door! He thinks that since I'm an illusionist, I must have performed some trick to lock the door from the inside. The same thing you told me the night it happened. Did you put the idea into his head?"

A little bit of life flushes in his face at that thought, and he stands a tad straighter. The accusing eyes darting out of his head make me think he's now more interested in throwing me off the balcony than jumping himself. I try to talk him off the ledge.

"No dice. Gustave's the last person with whom I would share my thoughts. And you have to realize that your talents make you a prime target for suspicion. Who better to pull off the impossible than someone whose entire job is making the impossible seem all too real?"

"But I didn't do it!"

"Did you take another look at the door like I asked you to?"

"Yes! The only way to lock it is from the inside! If there's some trick otherwise, I sure as hell don't know what it is!"

I could do without the whining. The rising of his voice a couple of octaves and decibels draws interested looks from various spectators congregated in the vicinity. Noticing their interest, Twist huddles closer to me and lowers his volume to a whisper.

"Do you think he could've killed himself and locked the door to make sure no one stopped him?"

"We considered that. But no fingerprints were on the knife, and Walker wasn't wearing gloves. We dusted the snooker ball you said he was holding when you entered through the balcony. That had his prints. Yet nothing on the knife. That rules out suicide."

The news hits him hard, and he retreats back into a morose state of mind with his head again hanging sadly over the balcony. Without much hope, he leans in again and says, "What if he was stabbed before he went into the room? And locked the door trying to get away?"

"Gave that some thought, too. Biggest hurdle is the lack of blood."

"Secret passage in the walls?"

"We looked—nothing."

More dejection follows, and he says, "Maybe some kind of mechanical device from within the room launched the dagger—like a spring gun or something, only with a knife."

That's a new theory but one not worthy of a response. The Billiard Room was searched up and down, backwards and forwards in the aftermath of the murder. The rest of the house, too. Nothing along those lines ever turned up. Even Twist doesn't put much credence in the possibility. He also looks as though he's spent all the ideas he could come up with. I decide to try out my *Murder on the Orient Express* hypothesis on him.

"Have you given any thought to whether some of the guests conspired that night to kill Walker?"

He perks up and asks, "Like who?"

"Don't know. Maybe all of you. Everyone seemed to have a motive to want Jim Walker dead, which strikes me as both convenient and strange."

If Twist takes offense at my raising the notion that he engaged in a conspiracy to commit murder, he doesn't show it. He also doesn't dispute the charge that he had a motive for the killing himself. Instead, Oliver has a question.

"How would that work?"

"You tell me."

"Like some of the people got together to pull a trick on the rest of us? I don't see it. I have a good eye for tricks."

"Or could be that all of you were in on it."

This time he does react to the implication and sputters, "Including me? Surely you cannot believe that at this late date. 'Upon my soul, a lie, a wicked lie.'"

I think for a second and respond, "*Macbeth*?"

"*Othello*."

Close enough for government work. He sags some more and takes his face with him—the plastic surgery not holding up its end of the bargain tonight. He whimpers, "Wish I'd never gone to that stupid party. But Gustave asked, and he holds my career in his hand with this China business. Now I'm a murder suspect and not even going to be an international star for all the trouble. 'To be or not to be'—always not to be for Oliver Twist. That's the story of my life."

Cate looks almost sad for him, but she doesn't know about Missy the Paralyzed Assistant. As for me, I've heard enough and am ready to move on. I gather my wife to extricate myself from him. Taking the hint, he mopes down the grand staircase as we watch him descend from our perch on the balcony. Cate asks, "Oliver Twist? Like David Copperfield?"

"Don't mention that name to him. He's real touchy on that score."

"Oliver Twist isn't his real name, is it?"

"Take a wild guess."

She shrugs and finishes off the rest of her wine. I ask what her woman's intuition tells her about Twist.

"He's a sad sack. Got depressed just listening to him. Does he really perform in front of crowds?"

"Allegedly. Usually he has more panache. He did make Stone Mountain disappear one time."

"That was him?"

"The one and only. As he told me, he *separated people's perceptions of what they were seeing from the reality.*"

"That's deep. Meanwhile, I need a refill on my wine and you promised to show me where a man was murdered."

"Right this way."

35

The Billiard Room is full of curiosity seekers—or ghouls. Take your pick. Anticipating the level of interest in the now infamous snooker table, Gustave took the thoughtful step of placing one of the drink stations right in front of the massive fireplace. I walk over, help myself to the Malbec, and pour a generous glass for Cate. The bartender protests, "You're not supposed to do that." I flash my badge, grab another Coke for myself, and that's that.

Cate whispers, "Mark Romo just blanched when he saw you walk into the room. I think he's scared of you."

"Try not to stare."

She tries but makes a mess of it—her attention seemingly drawn to him like a tractor beam. Hoping to be more subtle, I glance over and see a fidgety Romo making time with a blond taller than he is. Mirroring Cate, Romo keeps looking over to us, despite his best intentions. I raise my can of Coke to him in a mock toast. He averts his gaze. I muse to my wife, "He couldn't get out of this room fast enough after seeing the dead body. Surprised he returned to the scene of the crime."

"You know, he's not that good-looking in person. Must be all those Hollywood special effects. Too short, too."

"I know you don't mean that, but I love you for saying it anyway."

"Well, he is too short."

A crowd gathers around the snooker table, and we walk over to join the fun. A tape outline meant to replicate the position of Jim Walker's corpse decorates the green felt. An amazed Cate says, "He left the tape around the body in place? That's tacky."

"Worse than that. The police don't do tape outlines any more. Gustave added it for sport."

In a similar display of poor taste, some of the partygoers take a picture of the tableau with their camera phones. The whole scene is one giant farce being played out by fundamentally unserious people. But rich folks have always had the luxury of indulging their silliness—one of the curses of having too much. Cate shakes her head, and I say, "Let's go say hi to Mark."

"Be sweet."

When I turn around, though, Romo is exiting stage left. He stops at the open door to the Billiard Room and inspects it for a good couple of seconds—wearing a preoccupied look on the side of his face visible to me. The moment passes, and he disappears.

Cate says, "He got away."

"So he did."

I scan the crowd in the room and don't find anyone that particularly interests me. Cate checks out the décor and notices the wide assortment of weapons and other strange fare that serve as wall decorations—including the razor-sharp mammoth battle axe I saw on my initial visit. For the first time, my attention stays on a suit of knight's armor occupying one corner, and I wonder about its feasibility as a hiding place. The thought borders on the absurd, but I'm getting desperate.

The throng of people increases, and more folks take out their phones for pictures with the tape outline, even a few selfies. The whole atmosphere starts to make me feel a tad claustrophobic. I steer Cate outside to the small balcony for a dose of fresh air.

The night is warmer than the first time I stood here. I scan the surroundings hoping to spot a fresh clue. But all I see is a long drop to the ground.

I ask, "You think someone can make this jump?"

She stretches her head over the balcony and does the calculations in her head before answering.

"What do you mean by '*make*'? Survive? Sure. Land without breaking an ankle or some other bones? Not likely."

That's how I figure it but do note, "Sophie lowered herself on the bars and jumped the rest of the way. Jarred her ankle a little on the landing."

"She's a unicorn. Any of your suspects unicorns like her?"

"Not really. Celeste Wood—the artist that painted the picture of me—is in decent shape. She's a swimmer. And Mr. Beale is some manner of mythical creature. His height makes the distance down a lot less than it is for us mere mortals. Maybe Mark Romo—although I don't think he would risk his pretty face."

Cate looks down again before dismissing the idea: "I still don't see it."

Me neither. Grasping for any straw that I can get my hands on, I again study—fifteen-feet away—the balcony off the bedroom in which Aaron Cain was supposedly lying down. I remind myself that Aaron and Erica Cain are both too old and lawyerly to make such a leap—immediately banishing the thought.

We head back inside. A waiter approaches with some hor d'oeuvres, and Cate pounces. I ask, "What is it?"

"Escargot. Take some."

"Snails? No thank you."

After the caviar, I'm beyond gun shy about taking any more exotic food journeys with her. But a determined Cate thrusts a small gray blob right under my nose—the blob swimming in enough butter to drown a puppy. She insists, "Try it. At least once. You might end up liking it."

"You sound like my mother."

"I can be mean like her if necessary, too. Try it."

The buttery smell is pleasing to the nostrils at least. To get over my last bit of resistance, I reason that slurping butter is better than slurping salt. I open my mouth and let Cate deposit the dark matter straight into my mouth. After I take my medicine, the doctor checks me for signs of an adverse reaction. Surprisingly, the news is all good.

"Not bad at all."

Cate smiles in triumph, and I help myself to a few more snails. Between the two of us, we clean the waiter's plate for him. Fresh out of reasons to stay in the Billiard Room, we start to make our exit. On the way out, I study the door just as Romo did—trying to see it through his eyes, wondering if he solved my locked room riddle. But the inside bolt is as sturdy and dependable as they come. I give a parting forlorn glance to the knight's armor and leave the room as stumped as when I entered it.

36

As we exit the Billiard Room and make our way back toward the balcony, a loud noise assaults my ear drums. I peer down over the railing to see the partygoers crowd around Gustave. Mr. Beale is nearby, a large mallet in his hands. He raises the mallet and strikes an adjacent golden gong—the offensive result being the same piercing sound of seconds before.

The mansion settles into a curious quiet in the aftermath, and Gustave flashes a broad smile full of white teeth as he prepares to deliver some remarks. I search for the rest of my suspects. Vivian is almost hiding behind the gathered crowd, about as far away from her husband as she can politely manage. I wondered whether Root would let her out of her bedroom tonight. Oliver Twist—still carrying his frown around with him—leans on the wall just outside the study. Leo Ivanov stands a few feet from the gong and is a good candidate to lose some of his hearing if Beale uses that mallet again. Mark Romo huddles in deep with Aaron and Erica Cain near the front door entrance. Celeste Wood, to my surprise, is a few people down from us along the balcony, about ten feet away. She gives me a little wave. No sign of Jessica Allen anywhere, but finding her only requires locating the marijuana smell and following the bread crumbs to wherever they lead.

Cate whispers, "Who is the woman that just waved to you?"

"Celeste Wood—the painter."

"Really? You didn't tell me Celeste was good-looking."

"Is she? I try not to objectify women with such misogynistic observations."

My wife makes a disbelieving snort just as Gustave begins his speech to his guests.

"Friends, what a delight to share my home with you tonight. Any excuse is a good excuse to have a party—even if it means a dead man with a dagger sticking out of his back in the Billiard Room."

Hearty laughter ensues, and I start to take a dimmer view of my fellow humans. The host continues.

"Make sure to check out the murder scene upstairs. Use the moment to contemplate the fragility of life and the darkness that lurks in the heart of man. But I warn you to be careful about what you say. Special Counsel Chance Meridian—the leader of the Atlanta Murder Squad—is on the premises and still on the hunt for the killer."

His arm swings up toward me, and all eyes in the place follow his lead. Except mine. They remain locked on Gustave, who is well-pleased with himself. He wears the satisfied expression of a great director who knows he just choreographed a critical, winning scene. When the guests return their attention to him, he concludes his little talk.

"A buffet is set up in the banquet hall for your culinary pleasure. And remember, my dear friends—eat, drink, and be merry, for tomorrow we may die."

Applause accompanies the end of the talk, but my hands stay where they are. So do my eyes—affixed to Gustave after that dog-and-pony show at my expense. He looks up my way one last time and performs a sarcastic salute to rub my nose in it some more. I despair that if the feds couldn't nail him for his inordinate number of trips to Pedophile Island, then I'm not going to have much luck getting a charge—any charge—to stick, either. But boy I want to. Maybe tax evasion. That's how Eliot Ness got Al Capone.

Celeste Wood comes over and diverts my concentration away from Gustave. She says, "This must be your beautiful wife that you were telling me about the other day."

"The one and only."

Introductions are made, and Cate wastes little time telling her that she would love to see that painting of me when it's finished. I let the two of them talk and notice that Vivian remains off by herself away from the clustered masses. Deciding the opportunity to talk with her without an audience is too good to pass up, I ask my wife, "Can I leave you with Celeste for a minute? There's someone down there I need to talk to."

Mimicking Gustave, she responds, "On the hunt for the killer?"

"Not funny."

* * *

I hurry down the steps and find a vacant-looking Vivian standing in front of a painting of stark distortions that looks like a Picasso and is. She gives me a side glance but doesn't show much interest, leading me to take the initiative.

"You get to attend this party I take it?"

"Something like that."

"Is your real name Madeline Moses?"

Not having a lot of time, I opt for the quick strike. The strategy delivers early returns. The turn of Vivian's neck is sharp and sudden, the eyes distrustful. But the reaction confirms the supposition that Madeline Moses and Vivian Root are one and the same. I follow up.

"That's a pretty name. Why change it?"

"Not my decision. Ask my husband."

"Why would Gustave want to change it?"

"Because he can—just like he toyed with you a minute ago."

Her eyes challenge me to dispute the allegation. I don't because the charge is true enough. But I do counter, "Well, he may come to regret that yet."

She laughs at me and takes an indifferent sip of her wine before launching another sortie against me.

"I owe you an apology. The other night I assumed you were corrupt—bought and paid for like the rest of them, ready to do Gustave's bidding at the drop of a hat. But I was wrong. You're just stupid. Sincere but stupid. And that makes you even more hazardous to my health."

The sneer she wears is as sincere as my apparent stupidity. Her manner is different than when we met before—more resigned to her fate, less plotting an exit strategy. She was scared the night of Walker's

187

murder but still retained an undercurrent of resolve to escape her situation. But all I see now is a jaded woman who has relinquished the buoy of hope.

"Last time we talked, you seemed ready to bolt and start over. Tonight, you're putting off a different air. What happened? Did Gustave confront you about Jim? Make any threats?"

"Maybe I've gotten religion, and no longer believe in the morality of divorce. Maybe I realized that the grass isn't always greener on the other side. Maybe a lot of things. But at the heart of the matter are the facts of life—you don't bolt from a man like Gustave."

"Still think he killed Jim?"

"No—but even if he did, you'll never pin it on him."

Vivian moves down and stands in front of another painting—this one with a disembodied face alone in the desert. The face is corpse-like—gnawed and withered by time. Serpents and jagged skeletons fill its mouth and eye sockets. I study the canvas and wonder about the type of artist that views the world through such a haunting prism—as well as the type of person that would freely choose to hang a depiction of that sort on his wall. Noticing my bewilderment, Vivian comments, "Lovely, isn't it? It's like living in a freak show in this house."

"You don't have to stay. I know people in the federal government that are eager to help you. They—"

"The federal government? The same people that were looking after my old friend Jeffrey Epstein when he died under mysterious circumstances. Good God—you're even stupider than I thought. Are you insane? I'm not talking to the FBI or anyone else with a badge about what happened on that island. Never. Here's some advice. You lead the murder squad, not the damsel-in-distress squad. Stay in your lane, and stop trying to swim in waters too deep for you. You're going to drown."

"They can offer you a new start, a chance to—"

"Believe me, I've been in worse circumstances than staying in this mansion, and Gustave won't live forever. I'm going to ride it out and would ask that you not take me on as a charity case. You're only going to make my life more difficult. You already have."

That last comment confirms the hunch that Gustave didn't react well to being asked about Vivian and Walker. Something happened. No signs of bodily abuse exist that I can see, but the physical stuff doesn't strike me as Root's style. His type of warfare would be more psychological—the fear of what he might do. Honoring her wishes, I decide to stop pursuing the interests of the feds and focus instead on the case closer to home.

"All right, I'll stay in my lane. Any idea who killed Jim?"

"Everyone at that party had a motive to kill him. Your guess is as good as mine."

"Including you? Did you have a motive?"

"I wasn't at the party, was I?"

The answer doesn't quell my interest, and she inspects me with an appraising eye. "*Human Nature 101*," Scott said. Wanting to prove I'm not that trusting of women, I decide to push Vivian on any possible reasons for wanting her lover dead.

"That's not really an answer."

"No, it's not." She pauses and adds, "I tried to break it off with Jim, except he didn't want to listen. Even before the night of the party, Gustave was dropping hints about Jim and me. I told Jim we needed to cool it. He didn't mean anything to me anyway—just a way to pass the time because life in this house can get real boring real fast. But he kept wanting to hook up—giving me a burner phone, coming over to visit Gustave more than usual, pouncing on me whenever we were alone for a second. It was becoming uncomfortable. I didn't kill him, though. The only reason for me to murder Jim would be to hide the affair from my husband, but Gustave already knew."

I credit the answer because I cannot fathom a reason why she would remain lurking outside the Billiard Room if she had just killed Jim Walker on the other side of that door.

"The night of the murder after you told us about the affair, we mentioned to Gustave that one of the guests suggested that Jim had a thing for you. His response was curious. He said something along the lines that you could do whatever you want and that he would even gladly film Jim having sex with you in exchange for more Hitler paintings."

She emits a dismissive grunt and responds, "I think we both know that I'm not at liberty to do whatever I want. As to the other, Gustave would have no problem pimping me out to a friend. And he would certainly enjoy watching it, too. You know why? Because it would fuel his sense of power—to orchestrate other people's degradation. That said, it's bad manners for the same friend to pursue me behind Gustave's back."

"Why didn't Jim just go to Gustave and ask then?"

"Half the fun of illicit sex is the sneaking around."

An uncomfortable-looking Mark Romo heads our way down the long hall. No other people are in the vicinity, so we must be his intended target. Before he gets in hearing range, I ask, "What about Mr. Beale? Did he have a motive to kill Walker?"

"Certainly. They hated each other. Now, Mr. Beale doesn't like anyone—except perhaps Gustave. But he detested Jim with special vigor. Probably because of some bad jokes at Mr. Beale's expense over the years. Gustave enjoys the dissension and fans the flames for his own perverse pleasure—another way for him to exercise his power over people."

Romo arrives and, without glancing at me, mumbles to Vivian, "Been talking to Gustave. He wanted me to find you so the two of you could eat together."

She says to me, "Duty calls."

I watch their huddled conversation as they walk away—Romo becoming more relaxed with each step the further he gets from me. Neither of them looks back.

37

The ascent back up the stairs to Cate and Celeste takes more energy than the trip merits. After the talk with Vivian, I feel the need for a cleansing shower. Everything about the house makes me sick—its owner, the darkness that lines its walls, and all the people in it. Vivian excluded—she only makes me depressed. I give some more thought to the tax evasion angle and wonder if Gustave's failure to ever pay Social Security taxes on Mr. Beale would be enough to land him in Club Fed. But the idea crashes before takeoff. Billionaires don't go to jail for such trifles.

My wife and the painter are joking together like old friends when I reach them. Cate says to me, "A gallery in midtown sells Celeste's art. We're going to visit and buy something for the house."

Celeste adds, "I'll talk to the curator and get you a healthy discount, too."

The both of them—quite pleased with themselves—wait in anticipation for my response. I offer a smile born more of courtesy than feeling and offer them an answer.

"Excellent. The place could use a woman's touch."

I try not to dwell on the cost. Jim Walker's selling of Celeste's paintings to raise emergency cash only makes sense if they fetched a pretty penny. But that thought does remind me of something to ask Celeste.

"I'm surprised to see you here tonight. How did Gustave ever wrangle you into attending?"

"He bought the paintings back that Jim sold. Had them delivered to me today. That was one of my conditions."

"And he did that just to have you come to this party?"

"Don't look a gift horse in the mouth."

The women give each other a little hug good-bye, and Celeste leaves us to go downstairs. With most of the party now interested in the food, Cate and I now have the balcony to ourselves.

She says, "I like her."

"Don't get too chummy. Celeste is still a murder suspect."

"Stop it. You don't believe she did it."

"Maybe, maybe not. But she's still about the only one physically capable of escaping off the balcony."

The old Sherlock Holmes caution remains, "Once you eliminate the impossible, whatever remains, no matter how improbable, must be the truth."

Someone got out of that room after killing Jim Walker, and Celeste's pulling off a Sophie-like maneuver to let herself down off the balcony—improbable, but not impossible—remains one of the only bets on the board.

The front door opens, and a stoned but otherwise happy Jessica Allen enters the mansion. Cate recognizes her at once and exclaims, "The Dark Witch!"

"What?"

"Jessica Allen. She plays the Dark Witch. My favorite superhero."

"Caviar and the Dark Witch? You're turning out to be full of surprises tonight."

"I have not yet begun to surprise you, lover. You better be on your guard for the rest of your life."

* * *

The Dark Witch doesn't appear happy to see me. When we walk up to her, she gives me an indifferent shrug that is the exclusive property of the young. The scent of marijuana emanates off her like a fragrant perfume. With the warmer weather and more people in the house, I figure she decided to partake outdoors tonight and avoid all risk of incurring Gustave's wrath.

She says, "You, huh? I was headed to get something to eat."

"Have the munchies?"

"Hilarious. You should do stand-up. What do you want?"

"My wife wants to meet you. She's a big fan of the Dark Witch."

Jessica thinks the comment to be another joke, but Cate's earnestness quickly shows that the words are on the level. After they exchange a few comments about Hollywood and superheroes, I bring the conversation back to murder and seek her opinion on the ultimate question.

"Who do you think killed Jim Walker? I've just about ruled you out as a suspect, so your opinion has some credibility with me."

Her chemically-addled brain takes a while to comprehend what I'm asking.

"Why did you eliminate me as a suspect?"

"Because you're too small to have pulled off the killing and too inhumane to be bothered by a middle school girl's suicide from over a decade ago, meaning you had no reason to want Walker dead."

She nods and says, "That's right." Allen's quick embrace of her own inhumanity would be another strike against her—except I'm not entirely sure she's firing on all mental cylinders after her drug score. Cate watches the interaction between us with great interest—like a zoologist in the field studying the wild animals in their natural habitat. She doesn't know about the Dark Witch's teenage turn as a terrible bully, but that'll keep. She knows enough to give me room to operate. I remind Jessica of my question and wait for an answer. I don't have to wait too long.

"Oliver Twist."

I didn't actually expect to get anything interesting from her, but that's why you ask the questions.

"Why do you say that?"

"The door was locked, right? That means no one could've killed Walker and gotten out, right? So like he couldn't have been dead when Twist climbed the ladder, right? That means Twist had to do it, right?"

The logic is hard to fault, and we floated the idea to Twist ourselves when we talked to him the night of the murder. But we dropped the thread as soon as we picked it up. Since Walker didn't answer the knocks on the door, the rush to assume that he was already dead is a hard current to swim against. But what if he was alive? I think again: "*Once you eliminate the impossible, whatever remains, no matter how improbable, must be the truth.*"

Despite her general rottenness, I must confess that Allen's brain is not as muddled as suspected. I shake my head. Out of the mouth of babes.

38

Time to eat. I say to Cate, "Remember what I told you about food and drink."

"Yes, dear."

The buffet is help yourself, which decreases the odds that it is spiked for my benefit. The menu is fancy Southern—shrimp and grits being the star attraction. After the snails, I'm half way to being full, but that doesn't stop me from piling the plate with a generous sampling of each dish. With food in hand, we search for a place to sit. Cate leaves the choice to me, in case I have strategic reasons for the company I would like to keep.

Scanning the crowd, I land on three choices. Two spots are open next to Cate's new best friend, Celeste Wood. The rest of that table is occupied by people unknown to me. Gustave and Vivian anchor another option with availability—including the opportunity to sit right next to Aaron and Erica Cain. Lastly, Mark Romo sits between Leo Ivanov and Oliver Twist—who both appear miserable. Since Cate hasn't had her chance to meet Romo yet, I head that way.

He grimaces when we put our plates down. I make a quick introduction. The reaction of both Cate and Romo to each other is of strained politeness—hers because of what she knows about Tristan Curry, his because she's my wife. I leave to go fetch Cate and me some fresh drinks.

When I return after taking the usual drink safety precautions, Romo is gone. I scan around and find him now sitting between Celeste and Jessica Allen—which I have to admit beats being in the middle of Ivanov and Twist. Wanting to ensure that I touch base with all of the suspects tonight, I chose this table to speak to Romo specifically, as only he and the Cains remain on my to-do list. With my immediate plan thwarted, Cate and I keep to ourselves and focus on the eating.

By the time we finish, the rest of our dining companions have moved on. Gustave approaches with Vivian in tow, and they take two chairs across from us. The host beams and asks Cate, "Madam, I trust that the food meets your culinary approval. Mr. Beale is an excellent cook in his own right, but I took the added step of flying up one of the region's top chefs from Savannah to help with tonight's menu."

I miss Cate's answer. Out of the corner of my eye, I spot Mr. Beale talking to Romo—the giant nodding his white head in acknowledgement at the other man's words before walking away. Gustave turns his attention to me.

"And you, Mr. Special Counsel?"

"Sure, everything's top notch. But may I make an observation? You don't give off the feeling of a man too upset about the murder of his good friend. The party's a bit too jovial for the occasion, isn't it?"

"A fair comment. Two points in response. First—consider that perhaps Jim wasn't the good friend that I thought he was."

He turns his head toward Vivian and unleashes a grin of frightful smugness. She bows her head in a gesture of docile submissiveness. Returning his focus back to me, he begins again.

"Second—Hollywood is about image, and everyone has a brand. My brand is eccentricity. How do you think I can get away with having a painting by Adolph Hitler on the wall? Because people already know that I walk to the beat of my own drummer. They say, 'That's just Gustave being Gustave.' I make movies, Mr. Meridian. Usually peculiar movies that stretch the bounds of believability beyond the confines of reality. Nothing is real, though, except being part of the conversation. This party tonight may raise a few eyebrows, but people will be talking about Gustave Root all the same—and not in a boring way. In my business, that kind of publicity is as good as gold."

"I notice you keep your swastika well-hidden in your closet. That would generate plenty of talk if you brought it out into the open."

"Ha! Even bad taste has its limits."

* * *

Walking out of the banquet hall, Cate leans in to me and whispers, "That guy's insane."

"No doubt. And you gorging yourself on his caviar—a Supreme Court Justice no less. Shameful."

She punches me in the arm. Down the far reaches of the hall, I see Aaron and Erica Cain, deep in spousal conversation. Figuring now is the time to pounce, I say to Cate, "I need to speak to some people alone. Can you entertain yourself for a few minutes?"

"You're going to talk to the Cains? I read about them in the *Daily Report* all the time but have never met them. Can I watch?"

"Afraid not. The chat needs to be unfriendly, and your presence might encourage everyone to behave."

I kiss her on the cheek and set off in the right direction, locating another of Marlon's listening bugs in my pocket on the way. Erica Cain spots me first and halts speaking in mid-word—her eyes almost bulging out of her head.

Aaron turns around in response to her stare and spits out upon seeing me, "What the hell do you want?"

"Sylvia Pinker and Rohypnol. I mentioned both of these things to the two of you the other day. Didn't know at the time, though, that you had your own supply of roofies and drugged Sylvia—"

"Did she tell—"

"Shut up, Aaron."

Erica's command halts her husband in his tracks. She is clearly the smarter of the two. I direct my focus to her and start to speak again, while at the same time placing the bug behind a lamp on a nearby table.

"Sylvia claimed that the two of you raped her, and Jim Walker knew about it. He blackmailed you to the tune of a new $1.5 million contract—"

Aaron can't help himself and blurts out, "I swear that if you somehow breached the sanctity of the attorney-client privilege, I'll have your law license."

"Shut up, Aaron!"

I study Erica. She studies me—the both of us ignoring her husband for the time being. I pick up the lecture.

"You're smart enough to realize that the situation doesn't look too good for the Cain family. Jim Walker's murder made life a lot easier for you, and y'all were right where the murder happened at exactly the right time. The Rohypnol angle is just another brick in the wall against you. On my side of the street, Erica and Aaron Cain are the leading suspects. So here's the deal—you need to talk some sense into me before you find yourself on the wrong end of a murder indictment. That happens, and the ensuing publicity will sink you—even if you're innocent. Because I'm a fair guy, I don't expect an answer right now without the two of you having an opportunity to confer. I'm going to walk away and give you that chance. If you want to unburden your souls, come find me. That's assuming you didn't really kill Jim. If that premise is erroneous, keep your mouths shut, and go find yourselves the best criminal defense lawyer in town. My recommendation is Jack Millwood."

True to my word, I leave them as soon as I conclude my speech. With the trap set, the whole enterprise hinges on whether the heat makes them crack in the moment or whether they can hold their powder dry until they get home. Aaron's likely to be bursting his buttons to express the opinions Erica didn't allow him to express to me. But she is the circumspect one. Not that she has any inkling of the bug. No fear there. Her hesitancy would be rooted in the recognition that it's always bad policy to share secrets outside of home base. I set aside the pesky legal question of whether the Cains have a reasonable expectation of privacy standing alone together in Gustave's hallway. If the bug does catch something incriminating, we'll cross that bridge when we come to it.

When I rejoin her, Cate notes, "That was quick. How did it go?"

"You probably shouldn't expect any campaign contributions from them."

39

Still on the hunt for the opening that will allow me to corner Mark Romo, I lead Cate on a tour of the various rooms of the mansion, starting with the study. Proving Gustave right that the artwork of homicidal maniacs is a natural attention-grabber, the first thing I show my wife is the painting by Adolf Hitler. She stares at it for a good half-minute before asking, "He applied to art school and got denied, right?"

"Yep."

"Some people just cannot handle the truth about their own shortcomings."

After making the rounds in a few more rooms on the first floor, the urge to go home starts to win the battle over my desire to talk to Mark Romo. But right before I suggest an imminent departure to Cate, I spy Romo—drink in hand—leaning against a wall near the grand staircase at the front of the house. He looks drunk—the flush face a dead giveaway of his condition.

Our eyes lock, and the earlier wariness with which he regarded me is gone. I take that as a positive sign. Now or never.

I gather Cate, and we cross the foyer toward him. The closer we get, the more obvious that the wall behind Romo is more of a crutch than merely a convenient place to lean his back. The support appears to be the only thing keeping the actor off Gustave's floor—meaning that Romo is a lot more drunk than when I introduced him to Cate over the dinner table.

He watches my approach with blurred eyes. When I stop a few feet before him, he mutters, "Wanted to tell you something."

"Yeah?"

His red face turns purple in a hurry—followed by raspy, gagging sounds. The speed of the metamorphosis is alarming, and I watch the spectacle before me, unsure of what to do. Romo drops his drink, and the glass shatters on the hard marble below. The purple is now of such a dark shade that Romo's head appears ready to explode. The body lurches forward, and he losses the support of the wall. I catch the falling mass before it reaches the ground and manage to ease him down the rest of the way. When I turn Romo over, the gasping sounds stop. I yell for a doctor.

A short, bald-headed man scurries up, and I turn the patient over to him. To the rest of the people in the vicinity, I order, "Everyone stay calm and please make your way to the banquet hall immediately. No one is to leave the property. Your prompt compliance with these instructions is much appreciated."

Aaron and Erica Cain emerge from the nearby study. I repeat the order for their benefit. Oliver Twist and Celeste Wood peer down at me from the balcony. Jessica Allen walks through the front door after another marijuana run. Leo Ivanov arrives from the direction of the kitchen. With Mr. Beale and Vivian by his side, Gustave is the last of the suspects to reach the foyer. I study each of them—a hard grimness decorating my face. The thought that they are all in it together as conspirators again floats to the surface. Maybe Mark Romo was the weakest link in the chain.

The mild-mannered doctor looks at me and shakes his egg-shaped head. Gustave strides up and demands, "What's this?"

"Tell your guests to go the banquet hall. No one is to leave."

"What's wrong with Mark?"

I walk up to him, lean in tight, and repeat my instructions in a voice full of kerosene—adding a few vulgar imperatives for full impact. He backs away with a neutral expression but fulfills my request.

Mr. Beale starts to head back to the kitchen. I yell at him, "Beale!" He turns and stares at me—the startling blue of his eyes particularly discomforting in the moment. I point to the banquet hall and snarl, "That way." The giant waits on Gustave for further instructions. When Root nods, Mr. Beale lopes to the banquet hall with everybody else. I take out my phone and call Scott. He answers on the first ring.

"You can scratch Romo off the suspect list."

"How so?"

"He's dead, right in front of me. Poisoned by the looks of it."

Scott lets the news soak in for several seconds before asking, "You didn't kill him, did you?"

"No such luck. And I'm by myself with around eighty possible witnesses floating about. Send in the cavalry. We're going to need a lot of help on this one. Also see if you can get Alona Mendoza out here. I want her to inspect the body in its natural habitat. And Cate needs a ride home if Taylor is willing."

"On it. Didn't I predict that you would be calling me to ride to your rescue before the evening was up?"

"You're a regular Nostradamus."

A shaken Cate meanders over to me when I end the call and stares down at the now fresh corpse. I put my hand around her shoulder to draw her close and observe, "Someone should've told him about watching his drink. He learned the hard way."

40

The murder squad gathers in the foyer—mere steps from Mark Romo's dead body. Alona Mendez is on her way, and a uniformed officer stands as a sentry to make sure no one touches the deceased until she gets here. Taylor and Cate have already left for the rural countryside of Fulton County. Barbara is in the process of obtaining a new search warrant for the mansion as well as a warrant to enter Romo's condo. Spending another all-nighter in this house of horrors counts as cruel and unusual punishment, but heavy is the head that wears the crown.

I give the team the lay of the land.

"Here's what I know about what happened tonight. Upon exiting the Billiard Room earlier in the evening, Mark Romo inspected the door with great interest, looking concerned as he did so. After that moment, Romo talked to each of the suspects over the next couple of hours. Shortly after Mr. Beale sounded the dinner gong, Romo was conferencing with Aaron and Erica Cain near the front door. Roughly fifteen minutes later, he approached Vivian Root and me down this hallway, explained that he had been talking to Gustave, and that Gustave wanted her to join him. During dinner, Romo was initially seated between Oliver Twist and Leo Ivanov—later between Celeste Wood and Jessica Allen. As the meal was winding down, Romo spoke some words to Mr. Beale, who nodded back at him. A little less than an hour later, I approached Romo right here, and he said to me quote, '*Wanted to tell you something*.' He immediately turned purple and dropped dead. The best assumption is that the same person killed Walker and Romo."

They absorb the rundown in silence and allow the implications to marinate. Just repeating it makes me tired all over, and I wish for an alternate reality in which I was now heading home with my wife so that she could have her way with me. Scott speaks first.

"How do you want to handle it?"

"You and me can tackle Gustave first, then Mr. Beale. After that, we'll conference with Alona once she gets here. Marlon and Sophie—question Jessica Allen, Vivian Root, Aaron and Erica Cain, Leo Ivanov, and Oliver Twist. You decide the order. Two things you want to know from the lot of them. Did they see anyone slip anything into Romo's drink? And what did each of them talk to Romo about at the party? J.D.—the Atlanta Police Department has kindly lent us a few detectives. Take them and question the rest of the guests and caterers to see if anyone saw anything. Start with the bartenders and try to track Romo's drink intake over the course of the evening. Did our bugs pick up anything interesting?"

Marlon grins like a Cheshire cat. He explains, "The one you left in the kitchen captured a great deal of cross-talk and other sounds. I'm going to have to scrub the collateral noise out to get a clean read on everything said there. But the other one revealed some growing dissension in the House of Cain."

He takes out his phone, and we all huddle tight together as he presses play. The first sounds capture the end of my conversation with Aaron and Erica—followed by an extended interlude of silence as I walk away. When I'm gone, Erica is the first to speak.

"I want to ask you something, Aaron. Did you kill Jim? You were up there alone with him while I went to get you that Coke—the Coke you specifically asked me to fetch for you. Did you kill him?"

A lot of different ways the conversation between the Cains could've gone after I left them, but Erica's accusing her husband of murder wasn't one of the choices on my bingo card. I lean in closer to catch Aaron's response.

"How could you ask such a thing of me?"

"Well, you're the one who suggested slipping Sylvia a roofie in the first place. You've been full of bad ideas lately."

A grand jury might be interested in that tidbit. And with a rape indictment hanging over his head, Aaron Cain's picture would grace the front pages of the *Daily Report* for weeks on end—above the fold, too.

Aaron sneers back to his wife, "You didn't need too much convincing as I recall it, and someone drugged me the night of the party. Remember?"

"You could've swallowed the roofie right after killing Jim to give yourself a perfect alibi."

"Damnit, Erica! I didn't kill anybody! And what about you? Did you murder Jim? You had as much opportunity as I did, hanging out there in the hall right where it happened. How come you didn't see anybody go into that room? Awfully convenient. You're ruthless enough to do it, too. And you sure as hell didn't like him blackmailing us."

The conversation ends with a vigorous exchange of expletives. One of them walks off—Erica's high heels from the sound of it. Still sporting a satisfied smile, Marlon stops the recording. At least we now know that Aaron and Erica didn't conspire together to kill Jim Walker. That's progress.

Sophie quips, "Remind me never to get married."

I ask Scott, "What do you think?"

"We have to question them separately but at the same time and seed the distrust. Which one is more likely to break?"

"Easy—him."

"All right. Marlon and Sophie—we'll take Aaron off your plate. Should we start with the Cains?"

Without hesitation, I answer, "No, Gustave first."

41

Scott and I set up shop in the study. A weary-looking Gustave settles himself into a chair across from us—the same seating configuration as the other night when we first did this dance. Before I have the opportunity to speak, Root asks me the first question.

"Have you seen the movie *Goldfinger*?"

"Of course."

"Goldfinger has a line in that movie—'Once is happenstance. Twice is coincidence. Three times is enemy action.' I tell you right now, Meridian, that I disagree with Mr. Goldfinger. Twice is enemy action. Twice now someone has used my home as their personal killing field. The first time was mildly interesting—a fresh experience for me so to speak. But tonight is beyond the pale. Someone is making a laughing stock of Gustave Root. I won't have it."

That he would see himself as the victim, instead of the two dead men, seems on brand for Gustave. But his anger dovetails nicely with why I wanted to speak to him first before the others. I put the issue to him.

"Glad to hear you say that because now you have the opportunity to help us out. Who do you think is responsible for these killings? Your answer carries some weight with me for a number of reasons. First, you have the strongest alibi of anyone for Jim Walker's murder. Given your confirmed movements that night, you simply didn't have the time to kill Jim, meaning I don't have to worry about you lying to me out of self-preservation. Second, you know all these people the best—understand their personalities, their hidden motivations. No doubt you've given the matter plenty of thought. Give me a name."

He looks much older now than he did earlier in the night. The wild hair has lost some of its buoyancy—the wrinkles in his face more pronounced. He runs both hands through his hair before bringing them back down to rub every square inch of his face. After a deep, discontented breath, Gustave gives us a name.

"Aaron—has to be Aaron."

"How so?"

"Jim went up the stairs, and Aaron was right on his heels. Gave him the perfect chance with no one around. Jim also knew that Aaron and Erica raped Sylvia Pinker. That's a powerful motive. It all makes sense, doesn't it? Aaron feigned sickness, followed Jim up to the Billiard Room, and stabbed him in the back. Somehow managed to lock the door from the inside. He then headed to the bedroom to continue his charade and swallowed a roofie out of his stash to make his sickness all the more believable—probably fed one to Jim, too, to incapacitate him. At least, that's my best guess."

The pieces do fit—at least for the Walker killing. And Gustave is now the second person of the evening to accuse Aaron Cain of murder—first his wife, now his biggest client. I ask the natural follow-up.

"Why would Cain kill Romo?"

"No earthly clue why he would want Mark dead—unless Mark threatened something related to Cain & Cunningham. The thing that you have to understand about Aaron Cain is the hold that law firm has over his life. His great-grandfather founded it, you know? Aaron was destined to be managing partner before he was even born. That kind of weight on a man's shoulders can lead him to do all manner of disagreeable things. The curse of birth can be the hardest chain in life to break. Probably why he killed Jim—couldn't stand the idea that Jim was dictating his salary to him."

Gustave leans back in his seat, satisfied with his explanation. Everything he says makes sense and tracks my own already-formed theories about Aaron. But something in Root's manner still bothers me. I finally realize the disconnect and put it to him.

"You came into this room riled up beyond measure and talking about enemy action by some unknown killer. Yet when asked to put a name on the murderer, you deliver a calm recitation of the evidence and point the finger straight at Aaron Cain. That dichotomy rings a false note with me."

"Suspicion is one thing. Proof is another. My anger is generalized. When you do your job and make an arrest, I will focus it accordingly."

"What about Oliver Twist? He told me earlier tonight that you thought he killed Walker."

Gustave waves his hand away at the thought and responds, "Mr. Twist was beginning to annoy me through his neediness, and taking him to China began to feel too much like a chore. I told him that to get him off my back."

Scott takes over to cover the events earlier in the evening, but that's tilting at windmills. Sure enough, Gustave didn't see anyone spike Mark Romo's drink, and the only thing the two of them discussed about in a brief conversation was an upcoming film. I expect more of the same from all the other suspects—plain vanilla talk with the dead man and no useful eyewitness testimony.

The discussion turns to a more contentious matter. Scott explains, "We know Beale talked to Romo shortly before Romo died. He has to account for what was said. We're going to bring him in here, and you're going to tell him to write down the conversation."

"Don't be absurd. Mr. Beale couldn't harm a fly."

I counter, "Really? Word on the street is that Friedrich Bellingshausen killed a man in Europe with his bare hands. Soon thereafter, he followed you to America."

Gustave's look turns sour, as if he just sucked on a lemon. I keep a hard stare aimed in his direction until he answers.

"Someone's been busy. Pity that you waste your time digging up ancient history instead of catching the killer."

He stands up and announces that he will retrieve Mr. Beale. Scott responds, "Sit tight. We'll get him. Best to hear what he has to say without any undue influence."

A few minutes later, a uniformed officer brings Mr. Beale into the study. Almost immediately, Gustave barks something at Beale in rapid German. The giant nods and moves over to a desk. Root returns his attention to us, wearing an Oscar-worthy smirk straight out of central casting. I feel Scott's temperature rising next to me, and it's even money as to whether he slaps the smirk right off Gustave's face. For my part, I sneer right back at Root and proclaim in my version of the appropriate accent, "*Ich spreche deutsch.*"

Translation: "I speak German." Except I don't. Not really. High school and college required me to study a foreign language, and German was my choice at both stops. Any comprehension skills I acquired along the way, though, were lost shortly after I finished my last German exam. And listening to Gustave speak to Mr. Beale right now, he might as well have been speaking Mandarin.

But Gustave doesn't know that. He frowns at my fraudulent boast while Mr. Beale scribbles away on a piece of paper on the desk. Once finished, Beale brings the paper over and hands it to me. The artistic quality of the writing on the page is impressive—calligraphy apparently another of Mr. Beale's many talents. I say to him, "You should have your own font."

No response. I read the statement.

"Mark Romo approached me after dinner. He complimented me on the food. He especially enjoyed the peach cobbler. I nodded my thanks and returned to the kitchen."

After handing the paper over to Scott, I ask Gustave, "Am I supposed to believe this nonsense?"

"Mr. Beale never lies."

I stare up at the silent man but don't see much in the way of honesty.

42

Marlon brings Aaron and Erica Cain out together. I watch them from the doorway of the study. The married couple hesitates when Marlon tells Erica to head upstairs to the Billiard Room while sending Aaron over to me. We planned the scene, of course—hoping to drive a bigger wedge of mistrust between husband and wife. They stare at each other for a couple of seconds. Erica is the first to turn away, and she marches with purpose up the staircase. A moment later, Aaron starts to shuffle over—suddenly feeling pretty lonely by the look of him. Before reaching the door, though, he regains his sea legs—likely remembering that he's the managing partner of a prestigious law firm, just like three generations of Cain men before him.

After sitting down and crossing his legs like a true gentleman, Aaron repeats his threat to me from earlier in the evening, "My wife may be soft, but my warning from earlier tonight stands. I'll have your law license if you don't watch your step."

I laugh at him and retort, "Erica soft? She's twice the man you are." Remembering Aaron's own words to his wife caught by Marlon's bug, I add, "Ruthless, too."

He lets the matter drop without further debate. Scott starts off the questioning with a softball.

"Did you witness anyone slip anything into Mark Romo's drink at any point during the party?"

"No."

"Did you slip anything into Romo's drink?"

"No!"

"Did Erica?"

"No!"

Three questions in—easy, routine questions at that—Aaron already appears ruffled. That the bad guys know about Sylvia Pinker must be too much heat for him to handle. Whatever the cause, his growing lack of composure forces me to conclude that his success in life stems more from privilege than natural talent. Scott goes on.

"What did you and Romo talk about earlier in the evening?"

He digests the question with a puzzled look on his face, almost as if he is deciding whether to take offense or not. The break does him some good, and he returns to a more businesslike manner when he answers.

"Oh, not much. Client relations. Erica did most of the talking. We were letting him know that even though Jim was gone, the law firm of Cain & Cunningham was still there for him."

"And what did he say?"

"Nothing really. Something about lawyers being too expensive, I think."

"What about when you talked to him later in the evening? Just the two of you—when Erica wasn't there."

Cain bunches up his face in a suspicious sort of way—his distrust on high alert. Scott's question is a bona fide fishing expedition. We have no proof that such a second conversation ever took place. Just testing a hypothesis. But Aaron is not having it.

"What are you talking about? I didn't talk to him again."

"A witness says otherwise."

"What witness? That person is lying. What are you trying to pull?"

He swivels his head away from Scott toward me—his accusatory expression saying that I'm exactly the type of person to try and pull something. The rising blood in his face is a particularly unflattering shade of red. So much for his newfound businesslike demeanor. I decide to give him some advice.

"Pro-tip—ration your outrage in smaller doses. If you spend too much of it too soon, it loses all its effectiveness."

My tone doles out as much condescension as I can muster. The meaning is not lost on him. The tenseness in his body tells the story. Aaron wants to explode but realizes such histrionics would only prove my point. He chokes on his anger instead—wobbling pretty darn close to going on tilt, which is exactly what we want.

As planned, Marlon knocks on the door with a solemn expression worrying his face. A wave of his hand motions me over, and he stares bullets at Cain with judgmental eyes. When I reach him, Marlon whispers, "The wife says she and her husband were talking to Romo about continuing to utilize the legal services of their law firm. Said she also talked to Romo later without Aaron around about how filming was going on his new movie."

I join Marlon in directing my focus squarely on Cain—hoping that he gets squirmy from the unwanted attention. Although rattling Aaron is the purpose of the current performance, the revelation that Erica had a subsequent conversation with Romo without her husband around—providing her with a possible poisoning opportunity—is good information to have in my back pocket. I make small talk with Marlon for Aaron's benefit—to make him wonder some more about what we might be discussing.

"She didn't admit to poisoning him, did she?"

"Denied it actually."

"She would."

After some more parting comments. Marlon heads back upstairs to continue his interrogation of Erica. I walk back to Scott and Aaron like a man with a lot on his mind—wearing pensiveness like an extra layer of skin. Sitting down, I take a deep breath and restart the questioning.

"We have a problem, Aaron. A big one."

"What?"

"Why does Erica think you killed Jim Walker?"

The recent color drains from his face—replaced by a pale whiteness. Not as white as Mr. Beale but in the same zip code. He sputters out a number of unintelligible noises—all of which I take to be indications of disbelief. Finally, he manages to gasp, "Did she say that?"

"She did. Damn curious don't you think?"

He honestly looks like he might pass out from the shock. In times of stress, the mind shuts down—a glitch in the normal functioning of our mental processes. Cain is enduring something of the sensation right now. The strain of Erica's seeming betrayal paralyzes him, and he struggles for words that don't come. I dumb down my next question so that even in his diminished capacity he should be able to answer.

"Did you kill Jim Walker?"

"No! I was drugged! I could barely stand up!"

"Erica suggested that maybe you drugged yourself after killing Walker to give yourself an alibi."

That one threatens to send Aaron over the edge. He stomps his feet in petulant frustration—like a child who doesn't get his way. I don't take him to be much of an actor, and his inability to handle the pressure of the moment rings the bell of authenticity. And that makes him a poor candidate for Jim Walker's killer. That murder required a lot of nerve—spiking Walker's drink, removing the dagger from the study, seizing the opportunity when the target would be alone in the Billiard Room, stabbing the victim, and somehow locking the door from the inside on the way out.

The jellyfish in front of me seems incapable of being that bold and decisive. In the moment, I decide that Erica is the better bet of the two and shift the direction of the questioning her way.

"Aaron, I'm going to be honest and tell you that I don't believe you administered a roofie to yourself. The idea is stupid even. But Erica is a smart woman, and her telling us such nonsense leaves me really confused. Why would she do that?"

"I ... I don't know."

"Can I share a theory with you? If she really doesn't believe the things she is saying, then why say them?" I pause to allow the question to breathe a little bit. I then continue and answer my own question, "To throw suspicion elsewhere."

Deer are ubiquitous in Georgia. They are also stupid—frequently stopping still in the road wearing a confused stare as the headlights of an approaching vehicle speed toward them. Aaron's expression after hearing my theory is of the same mettle. He sits there, mouth open, looking at me like a dumb, soon-to-be-dead deer. Words fail him, and I move to fill the void.

"One of the big brick walls of this case is figuring why anyone would drug you. It makes no sense, right? But suppose that Erica decided that Jim Walker needed killing. She would want both a diversion and something to get you out of the way. The roofie accomplished that—put her right next to the Billiard Room and laid you out flat on your back. And who better to slip a drug into your drink than your own wife?"

Makes sense on paper, but the timing bothers me. Gustave announced to the group that he and Jim were going to talk alone upstairs in the Billiard Room. But did that give Erica enough notice to roofie her husband and have him feel the effects of it that quickly to justify his need to lie down?

These nuances are lost on Cain—who remains stupid with surprise. He manages to get out, "I can't believe it."

The words tell one story, the delivery another. And no matter what he says, Aaron sounds like a man slowly coming around to my point of view. I keep the attack up.

"Use your brain. Erica had plenty of opportunity to pull it off. She camped out in the hall right next to the Billiard Room—a stone's toss from the murder scene. Given her location, she should be our best witness as to who was in that room. Except she says nobody entered or exited. Is it possible she would've missed that? Doubtful. But what if she was the only person to go through that door? As for motive—we both know the math on that. Jim Walker was putting the screws to the both of you, and Erica didn't like it."

He doesn't dispute any of that. Nor could he since I basically cribbed all of it from his own words to Erica caught on Marlon's bug. Perhaps taking my advice to use his brain to heart, Cain adopts a contemplative posture and chews on the state of things. I give him a little time to do the necessary heavy lifting but not too much. When it becomes obvious that he's not in the mood to say anything, I ask another question.

"Did you know that Erica talked to Mark later tonight? Closer to the time he was poisoned. Without you around."

"What?"

"Witnesses saw her, and she admitted it to the detectives upstairs."

Aaron doesn't like that at all. The realization that whoever killed Walker also killed Romo dawns on him. His face contorts into something approaching panic as he contemplates Erica's possible responsibility for the growing body count. He studies me for answers, but I shrug and jab him again.

"You have some exposure here. People are going to have a hard time believing you didn't know what she was doing. A count or two of conspiracy to commit murder could be in the cards. And Erica strikes me as the type to want to take along as many other people as she can on her way to the bottom."

The instinct of self-preservation runs strong—innate to our natures and a key to our survival as a species. Aaron Cain's reaction to my floating of a conspiracy charge is another data point along these lines. The possibility that he could be on the hook for Erica's crimes sobers him up quick. A shrewdness recently missing from his manner is evident in the seriousness of his eyes and the tone of his voice.

"Nonsense."

"Sure—because no one innocent has ever been convicted of murder for hanging out with the wrong people."

"What do you want?"

Excellent. He's ready to deal. Nothing like facing a life sentence in prison to get one in the mood to cooperate. And even assuming that Aaron actually meant "till death do us part" when he made that vow to Erica—every promise has exceptions.

"I want my murderer."

He straightens his tie and runs his hand over his thinning hair before speaking again.

"While I still refuse to believe that my wife is capable of such brutality, I'll concede—for the purposes of argument only—that certain circumstantial facts may point in her general vicinity. But you know as much as I do. I have little memory of anything that happened the night Jim was killed. And Erica hasn't confessed to me in the days since if that's what you're thinking. Nor did I witness her have any suspicious interaction with Mark Romo this evening. I didn't even know she talked to him a second time tonight. So while as a responsible citizen I'm willing to do my part to see any killer brought to justice, I remain in the dark as to any way I can possibly help you."

He's sounding like a lawyer again at least. Except a good criminal defense attorney—or even a bad one—would instruct him not to say a damn word to me. But lawyers are a helluva lot better at giving advice than taking it. Law school professors spend three years convincing students that they don't know anything. By the time those same students graduate, they suddenly know everything.

"You can record her and try to get a confession."

"Madness!"

"Up to you. If you want to go down with the sinking ship, so be it."

"But you couldn't use what she says to me anyway. Husband-wife privilege."

Expecting a corporate lawyer to understand the rules of evidence is a lost cause. I explain to him the facts of life.

"Wrong. The privilege doesn't protect what she says to you. It protects you from having to testify against her against your will. Except it's in your best interest to talk freely."

I take the last of Marlon's bugs out of my pocket and place it on a coffee table between us. Aaron stares at the tiny speck, more in fear than out of curiosity. I explain its purpose and tell him what I want him to do with it. If he were smarter, I would worry that he might deduce that—instead of his wife spilling her guts upstairs to Marlon—a similar bug captured Erica's suspicions of him when the two of them talked to each other alone. But he isn't smarter, and I don't worry.

After putting up a half-hearted fight without much conviction, he picks up the bug and leaves the room.

43

Alona Mendoza—wearing jeans and a sweatshirt—studies Mark
Romo's dead body with scalpel-sharp eyes. The dead actor's face remains purple—although the hue is now a lighter tint than at the moment of death. Scott and I stand back to give Alona plenty of room
to work. She bends down, inspects each of Romo's hands, and asks
me a question.

"How sure are you that he was poisoned at the party?"

"Call it a strong hunch."

She leans over the dead man's head, close to the mouth, and
smells—her sniff audible enough for me to hear. After a quick nod
to herself, she delivers a verdict.

"Cyanide."

My guess was arsenic, but that's just because I read a lot of mystery books. In real life, poisons aren't a strength of mine. At least I've
heard of cyanide. I turn to Scott, and he just shrugs. Alona gives us
more of a primer.

"One of the fastest-working poisons. Quickly soluble in water. Can
kill in minutes. Cyanide pills are what secret agents place under their
tongues when they can't afford to be taken alive. Bend down close
to his face and have a smell. Don't touch him, though. For your own
sake. A little cyanide goes a long way."

Scott and I do as instructed. I go first and maintain a healthy distance after her warning, detecting a faint whiff of something I couldn't
possibly begin to identify. Scott follows me and stays with it for a good
fifteen seconds—straying far too near Romo's lips for my comfort.
After standing up, he observes, "I smell almond."

An impressed Alona nods and responds, "Bitter almond—a telltale
sign of cyanide."

I ask, "What does it look like when we search the house?"

"Depends on the form. As a liquid, cyanide is a pale blue or white. As a solid, it would look like any other medication—probably a bit smaller. I smelled the broken glass, too. He was drinking whiskey if that helps you any. How many people had an opportunity to slip it into his drink?"

"He was in a room with around eighty other folks shortly before he died—although we can safely strike off my wife and me as suspects. And based on your description, I don't like our chances of finding cyanide in the house."

"That's your problem, not mine. Happy hunting."

* * *

Eighty or so people may have had the opportunity to kill Mark Romo, but my entire focus is only on nine of them. Gustave Root. Vivian Root. Leo Ivanov. Oliver Twist. Jessica Allen. Aaron Cain. Erica Cain. Mr. Beale. And just to be thorough—Celeste Wood. Somebody with a badge has now questioned everyone in the mansion. The leading suspects currently remain together in the banquet hall under quarantine—with three uniformed officers keeping plenty of eyeballs on them. We sent the rest of those in attendance home—assuming they can even get clear of the property. Word from the patrol cars out on the street puts that possibility in doubt. Just outside the gates, media of all stripes are frothing like dogs trying to breach the grounds. I'm not surprised. The murder of a famous actor makes good copy.

The team gathers in the study—minus Alona who left along with Mark Romo's corpse. Barbara managed to get through the crowded gates with our search warrants and rests in a chair after surviving the ordeal. But the search of the mansion can wait. First—a de-briefing of what the witnesses have to say. J.D. begins by summing up the interviews of all the non-suspects: "No one saw anything."

That's the least surprising news of the night. J.D. throws up his hands in a helpless gesture. He doesn't add any further gloss to the information—which is just as well. Bad news should always be succinct. Especially when all of us are already tired with a long night ahead of us.

217

Marlon stands up to provide his summary.

"The situation on my end is only a little better. All of our suspects admit talking to Mark Romo during the course of the party, but that's about it. Small talk only—all the way up and down. With one exception—when Romo sat between Leo Ivanov and Oliver Twist at dinner. Both of them tell the same story. Romo cornered Twist and wanted to know about the locked door to the Billiard Room—how the murderer escaped. Twist didn't have any answers for him. Romo then asked, 'It's impossible, right?' Twist shrugged, and that was the end of it."

That the dunce-headed actor figured something out about the door that has eluded everyone else defies all probabilities. But someone felt compelled to murder him—right at the same time that Romo started making noises about how the murderer escaped the locked room.

Coincidence? Doubtful. While correlation doesn't always equal causation, sometimes it does.

43

We release the suspects back onto the streets—Gustave grumbling again about being put out of his own home for a second time. I'm decidedly unmoved, and he leaves with everyone else. While the rest of the murder squad searches the mansion for cyanide, Marlon and I eavesdrop on Aaron and Erica Cain. The first thing we hear is the distinct sound of a car door slamming. The both of us smile. I instructed Aaron to place the bug immediately in his car and start questioning Erica about her involvement in the murders of Walker and Romo. I wondered if he would, but he apparently followed instructions like someone interested in saving his own skin. Erica is the first to speak.

"What a nightmare! I never want to set foot in this house again. I don't care how much business Gustave brings the firm."

Cain grunts in the form of a reply. Hiding the bug in the car is one thing. Having the stones to challenge his formidable wife is another. The ride home is quiet for longer than I would like, but Aaron finally works up the nerve to put the issue to her.

"You need to level with me, Erica."

"What are you talking about?"

"About you and Jim. His murder."

The comment is met by a wall of silence at first, but I can hear Erica's stare crystal clear. When she does respond, a few choice words of profanity leave no doubt as to her reaction. But I warned Aaron that he should expect a fierce amount of pushback.

He says, "We need to play it straight with each other. Jim gave you plenty of reason to kill him. I wanted the bastard dead, too. But you gotta stop trying to save yourself by trying to pin the blame on me. I'm your ally, not your enemy. Let's work together and navigate out of this mess as a team. I don't care that you killed Jim. He deserved it. Now is the time for damage control."

"Killed Jim? Are you insane? What did those rent-a-cops tell you?"

I glance at Marlon. He laughs. Rent-a-cops? That hurts. Cain answers, "Nothing you hadn't already told me yourself."

"You didn't talk to them about me, did you? Please tell me that you're not that big of an idiot."

"Stop it! You threw me under the bus first! You flat-out told them that I murdered Jim!"

"That's a lie! Why are you so gullible to believe that?"

I told Aaron that she would deny accusing him to Marlon. Let's hope the lesson took.

"You're the liar! The black guy that was questioning you came into the room and talked to Meridian. And all of a sudden, Meridian started parroting the very same lines you told me yourself earlier tonight—practically quoted you verbatim. You sold me out!"

Good boy—although I hope his thirst for vindication doesn't cloud the big picture that the goal is for his wife to incriminate herself.

Erica snaps, "You're lucky your last name is Cain because you're too stupid to make it on your own otherwise! I never share family business with outsiders. Never! Remember that it was you—not me—who told Jim about Sylvia. And look where that has gotten us."

"We needed help—"

"No! We needed to keep the situation to ourselves—instead you blurted it out to Jim who decided to blackmail us with the information. Well done! If I were going to kill anyone, it would be you. And you have the nerve to accuse me of murder! Those cops are trying to get us to turn on each other. I thought even you would realize that. But I gave you too much credit. Such a sap!"

Aaron mumbles a weak reply and retreats into an unappealing defensiveness. They bicker some more back and forth over his merits as a lawyer. Listening to the exchange, Erica has the better argument—and Cain knows it. His earlier resolve retreats, and he scurries quickly back into being a spineless jellyfish. After diminishing his professional worth, Erica puts a question to him.

"What exactly did you tell them about me?"

The only response is more hemming and hawing. I shake my head at Marlon. We've lost Aaron for good now and with it any chance that Erica might confess to him. Even worse, both husband and wife figure to lawyer up and go into a deep hibernation. She'll make sure of that—as a hedge to prevent more stupidity on his end if nothing else.

Erica sneers, "You still haven't told me what you said to Meridian. Did you tell them that I killed Jim? Are you doing the police's bidding for them right now?"

Something in Cain's face must have given the game away. Because although he doesn't answer his wife with any audible response we can hear, she whispers in a cold and halting tone, "What ... did you ... do?"

I can feel the chill clear across town and have little doubt that Erica has made scores of lawyers wilt across the negotiating table over the years. A pathetic sigh croaks out of Aaron, and he mutters, "Stop talking."

"What ... did you ... do?"

"Now is not a good time to talk."

"What the hell does that mean?"

Loud bumps follow, as if someone is tapping on the bug itself. Then an irritating static takes over—which suggests that the bug is on the move. Through this din, I hear Erica gasping, "What is that?"

"Don't talk."

"You assh—"

The sound of power windows in motion is quickly chased away by the whipping of the wind—resulting in a prolonged hissing, unpleasant to the ears. When the noise dissipates, the signal from the listening device returns to its earlier clarity—treating Marlon and me to the swoosh of cars whisking past our obviously-discarded bug somewhere along the roadway.

The Cains are long gone.

45

The search of the mansion yields a whole bunch of nothing. No suspicious liquids. No suspicious white pills. No anything. Evidence techs dusted the fragments of the glass Romo dropped out of his hand but found only one set of prints—Romo's. The morale of the team is at a low ebb. Two unsolved murders, the last of which occurred literally under my nose. And not a hint of a break in sight.

I send my people home. Patrol officers will keep an eye on the place in the interim in case we want to double back to check things over again, but I'm doubtful. Scott and I loiter in the study after everyone is gone, a lingering habit of ours formed from canvassing murder scenes together in the past. I ask, "Thoughts?"

"We've been resisting a balcony escape, but what else is there? And that means we need to go harder at Celeste Wood. Not many of our other suspects could pull that off—and Romo was one of them."

"Beale."

"Except Celeste herself provides the freak an alibi. She saw him carrying the ice from the garage to the kitchen. Too far away from the balcony. He didn't have the time to kill Walker. But Celeste did. We're running out of other options."

"And why on God's green earth would she kill Mark Romo?"

He doesn't pretend to have an answer for that one. And I still don't buy Celeste as my murderer. Although I've tried enough capital cases to know that motives can arise from the most superficial of perceived offenses, killing your erstwhile boyfriend for selling some of your paintings strikes me as being on the extreme end of things. As if reading my thoughts, Scott adds, "Maybe Celeste found out about Walker and Vivian. We're assuming that Celeste wasn't that into Walker, but only because that's what she told us. Time to look at things with fresh eyes."

Cate will be beyond disappointed if the tide turns against Celeste, but I tell Scott to go forth and find the proof.

When we exit the mansion, the early morning sun tells me that the day is well past dawn. Going home is pointless at this hour—the couch and change of clothes in my office seeming like the better bet. Maybe I can grab a few hours of sleep there. At least I'm not hungry. The snails combined with the shrimp and grits is enough to get me to lunch.

If not for the murder, the party wasn't half bad.

* * *

Someone's hovering above me, but I lack the will to investigate. I'm a side-sleeper, and currently my face is buried in a cushion on my office couch. The past couple of hours have been rough from a rest standpoint—thoughts of the case merging with fragmented dreams to mush my brain into a whirling dervish. The figure standing next to the couch, though, is real enough. Given the dead bodies that keep piling up around me, a slow realization that I could be in danger suggests itself to my percolating consciousness. Except self-defense would require too much effort. I keep my eyes shut tight, hoping to sleep myself out of whatever's now happening around me. I don't get far into the effort when my nose solves the mystery for me.

The presence lurking about smells like my wife—in particular, that Coco Chanel No. 5 perfume she likes to wear. I debate whether to acknowledge her, realizing that playing dead would likely buy me a reprieve. But after another night of my failing to come home, I figure she deserves better.

I groan, "What time is it?"

"It's alive!"

"Objection—counsel is assuming facts not in evidence."

"You wake up spouting evidentiary objections. Amazing."

I don't feel amazing. The turn of my neck toward her is laborious—and painful. The rest of me tries to follow. A dull throb punctuates every move I make, no matter the body part. Two days from turning forty, this coming-attractions preview of the rest of my life feels like a horror film. I decide on the spot to treat myself to a new hot tub as a birthday present. When I finally adjust myself to an upright sitting position, I wrap my arms around a standing Cate and lay my head on her stomach. She strokes my hair and asks, "Catch the killer?"

"Nope, and we're running dry on ideas, too. Except Scott thinks Celeste did it."

"Why on earth does he think that?"

"Absence of feasible alternatives."

She snorts and hands me a Chick-Fil-A coffee. I take a couple of sips and chase the caffeine with a bite of a spicy chicken biscuit—ditching the earlier plan of waiting until lunch to eat. Cate drops next to me on the couch and says, "Celeste didn't kill anybody—and certainly didn't jam a dagger into her boyfriend's back."

The judge delivers the verdict with an air of finality that doesn't leave room for an appeal. Not that I have much interest in appealing anyway since I agree with the ruling. But I wonder what else her woman's intuition is telling her about the other suspects.

"What about your caviar pal Ivanov?"

"He's a teddy bear. However—"

Cate hesitates, and my attention perks up a hair. She grimaces as if hesitant to say anything derogatory about someone who shared Beluga caviar with her. After some prodding from me, she gives up the goods.

"Leo is adorable. I just have the sense that he could become disagreeable if someone wronged him and got on his bad side. That doesn't mean I think he killed anyone or anything."

Not exactly a ringing endorsement. I put Ivanov down as a maybe and move on the next one.

"Mr. Beale?"

"Well, I thought he was going to kill *you* in the kitchen for a second there."

Fair enough. And since the United States government already believes that Beale disposed of a man in Europe, that's good enough for me that he is capable of murder—if only Celeste hadn't given him an alibi for the Jim Walker killing. But what about Beale's boss?

"Gustave?"

She puts on her thinking face and recedes into deep thought. I take another bite of the biscuit and wait.

"I don't think he has any morals, so conscience wouldn't stand in his way. Not sure that murder would be his preferred style, though. Torture would be more up his alley—like setting a puppy on fire or something. More sadist than psychopath."

The imagery doesn't put me in the mood to eat anymore, and I set the biscuit to the side. Cate majored in psychology as an undergrad, and I'm learning to credit her insights on such things—although I don't see why a sadist is less likely to kill someone than a psychopath and count Gustave as a maybe. Running over the roster of suspects in my head, I skip past the Cain family and Vivian since Cate wasn't with me when I talked to them last night. That leaves two others.

"Oliver Twist?"

"Too whiny."

"Jessica Allen?"

"Too tiny."

Remembering my earlier thought about Allen and how she could've pulled off the murder despite her wee frame, I suggest, "Maybe she's a ninja." My wife pats me on the head in sympathy and stands up to leave. She says, "Drink some more coffee."

Sounds about right.

46

After washing up and changing clothes, I reacclimate myself to the living. The coffee helped. The rest of the murder squad is off doing police work things related to the recently-deceased Mark Romo, and I ponder how to add value to further that same endeavor. One option is off the table. Taylor informs me that the media keeps asking about a press conference, but I'm not in the mood. My only statement on the case is short and succinct: "The investigation is ongoing."

I decide to start from scratch and re-watch the interviews from the suspects in the immediate aftermath of Jim Walker's murder. We questioned all of them in Gustave's study except for Aaron Cain, who had too much Rohypnol in his system to be of much use to anyone. No need to bother with him. The same holds true for Mr. Beale. We talked to the giant albino but were the only ones to do any talking, and watching his blank stare for a second go-around would be bad for my blood pressure. But that still leaves the eight others, and I want to tackle them in the same order as that first night—Gustave, Romo, Erica, Vivian, Celeste, Jessica, Leo, and Oliver.

My office has a wall-mounted television that I hook up to my laptop. After sitting down on the couch and propping my bare feet on a coffee table, I press play on my computer, bringing to life once again the Adolf Hitler-decorated study of Gustave Root. Seeing him on the screen evokes a visceral flood of bad emotions, and I regret already the decision to proceed in chronological order. But Nazi-lover or not, Gustave is the spoke in the wheel connecting everyone at the party to each other. And just like that first night, starting with him again makes the most sense in my review of the evidence.

His description of events tracks how I remember it. The partygoers were mingling together after dinner in the study when Gustave announced that everyone was on their own while he talked to Jim Walker in the Billiard Room—but only after Gustave went up to his bedroom to check on his wife. Gustave took the elevator to see Vivian, came back down to the kitchen where he saw Mr. Beale and Leo Ivanov, and headed to the Billiard Room, spotting Erica Cain in the hall. The door to the Billiard Room was locked. The key wouldn't open it, and Walker failed to respond to the loud knocks. Mark Romo tried forcing it open with his shoulder to no avail. The focus then shifted to the back of the house as Oliver Twist and Romo climbed up the ladder to the balcony. Twist discovered the body, and Romo unlocked the door to Gustave on his way to the nearest liquor bottle. Gustave entered the Billiard Room, saw the red snooker ball in Walker's dead hand, and called the Governor.

Yada, yada, yada. The same script we've been working off since the night of Jim Walker's murder.

But the whole sequence of the night is off-kilter. No one on my side of the fence has been able to figure out the mystery of the locked door since the night of the murder—and that points to a sophisticated, premeditated crime. Except no one knew Walker would be alone in the Billiard Room until Gustave's announcement dispersed the party—and that signals an opportunistic decision to kill Walker made in the moment, with the murderer grabbing the Nazi dagger on the way out of the study.

This dichotomy continues to bug me when I dive into the interview of a drunk Mark Romo. I don't get far.

* * *

Marlon enters, and I'm thankful for the interruption. Watching hours of interviews a second time around isn't much in the way of fun. Procrastination feels like a more rewarding choice. He sits in a chair across from me, stares at my bare feet for a few seconds, and says, "You need a pedicure."

"My birthday's in two days if you feel that strongly about it."

"Noted. But I'm not here to talk birthday presents. I spent the morning dissecting the audio from the bug you left in the kitchen last night."

His face is inscrutable, but I sit up on the couch in a hurry all the same, my naked feet hitting the carpeted floor in excitement. This case needs a break in the worst way, and putting the murders of Jim Walker and Mark Romo to bed would be the best birthday gift of all.

Taking a laptop out of a leather satchel, he says, "Three snippets of conversation. I edited out all the extraneous noise. May be something. May be nothing."

He pushes play. The first voice I hear is Mark Romo.

"Hey, Mr. Beale! Jack Daniels—fast!"

After a pause of short duration, the bug picks up the apparent sounds of Romo's gulping down the drink, followed by a sigh of deep satisfaction. The glass bangs down on the kitchen counter. Romo barks, "Ivanov! Who killed Jim Walker?"

The tone is aggressive in a friendly sort of way—the kind you might expect from a drunk, which is no surprise. The Russian accent in response is thicker than normal.

"No idea. Who can get out of a room that is locked from the inside? That is the question."

"Is it? I wonder."

The conversation ends on that note—the exact nature of Romo's wonderings left hanging. Wonder what? Probably whatever he was going to tell me seconds before he dropped dead.

Ivanov said something similar to me about the locked door the night of the murder, and time has only confirmed the wisdom of his words. I ask, "When did this happen?"

"Sometime before dinner."

"Romo probably went straight to the kitchen after seeing me in the Billiard Room. And Ivanov made no mention of the conversation when you questioned him?"

"Not a peep."

That could just be the Russian in him—the fear that we would be quick to blame bad things on the foreigner. The exchange wasn't exactly incriminating. But it does show that Ivanov knew what to serve Romo if he was in the mood to poison him—although I don't suppose that Romo's love of whiskey was much in the way of a state secret.

"What else you got?"

Marlon returns to the laptop to press play, and I hear Gustave whisper, "You understand what to do, my friend? ... Excellent." The one-sided nature of Root's words suggests that Mr. Beale is the person on the other end of the conversation. I wait for the rest of it, but the recording stops.

"That's it? He was probably talking about seasoning the escargot."

"Just like I said. Could be something. Could be nothing."

I grunt, hoping that Marlon has saved the best for last. He punches a few keys on the computer and I hear Jessica Allen belt out a question in an entitled tone.

"Is there any whiskey in here?"

"Over there, ma'am."

The answer comes from a voice I don't recognize—likely one of Mr. Beale's kitchen helpers. Without even so much as a thank you, someone—almost certainly Allen—puts bottle to glass and lets the liquid pour. The thump of the bottle returning to the counter ends the last of Marlon's snippets. I'm underwhelmed and see my birthday hopes going up in smoke. Marlon has a question.

"Did Romo's drink have any ice in it? By the sound of it, Allen didn't drop any ice cubes into her glass. Poured it straight. Didn't hear her gulp it, either. Maybe that's the whiskey Romo was drinking when he died."

I think hard and replay the circumstances of Romo's death in my mind. Ice cubes. I strain the memory to see if it includes any ice cubes on the ground, but they're not there.

"Pretty sure there were no ice cubes."

"Then we should probably give Jessica Allen a closer look."

47

Even though Romo claimed to be sober until he saw a dead Jim Walker splayed out on the snooker table, I have my doubts. Watching the slow-witted drunk again answer our questions floods me with a sea of negative energy. His admission that he killed a kid returns me to the uneasy scene in Romo's condo when I knocked the whiskey out of his hands. I fight through the distraction to pay extra attention to the testimony, figuring that Romo's words occupy greater importance now that someone deemed him worthy of murder. But I roll snake eyes. Romo entered the Billiard Room via the ladder shortly after Oliver Twist, saw Jim Walker's dead body, and unlocked the door to get the hell out of there.

That's all I got.

I eat lunch at my desk and continue the work of going through the rest of the interviews deep into the afternoon. The returns are inauspicious in terms of fresh insights. Erica Cain—despite camping out in the hall roughly ten minutes after everyone left the study—never saw anyone entering or leaving the Billiard Room. Vivian Root admits eavesdropping to see if her husband knew about her affair with Jim Walker and even thought that he killed him at first. Celeste Wood went swimming and didn't notice anyone jumping off the balcony. Jessica Allen recognized that the murder weapon was missing from its place in the study and lied about smoking weed on the front porch. That's two points against her. But even after giving Allen a closer look like Marlon said, I can't make the pieces fit.

On to Leo Ivanov. He lied by claiming he paid his ex-lover $100,000 when he knew that Walker skimmed most of that amount for himself. But little else points in his direction, except for his presence on the same floor as the Billiard Room at the time of the murder.

And that leaves Oliver Twist. My review of the interviews up to this point fails to plow new ground—and that's bad for Twist. Why would anyone kill Mark Romo? The only conceivable motive visible to me is self-preservation. Romo knew something about Walker's death that made him a threat to the murderer. But what unique knowledge could Romo have possibly possessed? The more I wrestle with this question, the more one persistent itch keeps crawling over my skin.

Namely this: something happened when Oliver Twist and Mark Romo were alone together in the Billiard Room—the significance of which was not immediately apparent to Romo.

And more than anyone else, Twist should know how to get around a lock. That's what magicians do. Yet when I asked him for specific ideas about the problem, all he gave me was some nonsense about the power of illusion. Watching the answer again is as disagreeable in the moment as it was the night of Jim Walker's murder. When I finish watching Twist's interview, I pace around my office to burn off my rising frustration with him.

The walkabout goes on for some time as I despair at wasting my whole day traveling over tired terrain with nothing new to show for the effort. The movement doesn't do me any good, and I opt for some yoga poses instead. In the middle of a poor excuse for a downward dog—while cursing both Oliver Twist and the late Mark Romo in my heart—a new thought hits me in the head like a falling anvil. I pop up too fast and endure a bout of dizziness for the trouble but hold fast to my fresh idea.

Five minutes later, everything makes sense.

* * *

After I explain my great revelation to Scott and Marlon, I wait anxiously for their opinions. They do a lot of mulling from their side of the table—which suggests that my solution to the murders has at least some merit. Or maybe they're just humoring me because I'm the boss. Scott is the first to speak.

"Do you have any proof in support of this theory?"

"Not a single thing."

"Didn't think so."

They do some more mulling. I wait them out but remain confident in my thinking—sure enough that a tornado couldn't dislodge me from my position. Marlon says, "Evidence is going to be a bear. Impossible even."

"Agreed. Think you can find me some?"

He stands up and motions for Scott to get up and follow him out the door. I ask, "What are you going to do?"

"Re-watch the witness interviews."

"I already watched all of them today."

"Sure you did, but now we know what to look for."

* * *

Cate's working late at the office on a last-minute death penalty appeal for another midnight execution—one without a connection to me this time around. I want to wait at the courthouse to drive her home, but she sends me on my way to take care of the dogs. When I arrive alone at the house, Sweetheart and Bristol pounce on me like I've been gone away for weeks, and I return the affection right back at them, feeling better than at any point since witnessing Danny Davis' execution. Being missed—even by two German Shepherd pups—is good for the soul. It means you matter.

While the dogs run around in the yard, I give a wistful look to the garage and ponder working on the Trans Am. But my body rebels at the thought. Once back inside, the plan is to shower, sleep, and see where things stand in the morning.

* * *

The phone buzzes close to me, and my subconscious incorporates the ringing into a dream about my swimming in the ocean. But finally the noise pierces through, and I wake up in a fit. I grab the phone and see Scott's name with what little blurry vision I can muster.

"Hello?"

"Were you asleep?"

I don't answer but instead turn to see that Cate joined me in bed at some point in the last few hours. Before stumbling out of the bedroom to avoid waking her, I squint at the small clock on the cable box and realize that the time is after two in the morning.

"What do you want?"

"Thought you would like to hear the good news. We found you your proof. Watched all the witness interviews—up through Oliver Twist. That's when we found what we were looking for."

He explains the evidence and concludes, "Strong, huh?" I'm a little slow on the uptake but finally realize the significance of what he has said—and reproach myself for not paying close enough attention to what was right in front of me. Tiredness has rotted my brain. Still, the proof is not enough, and I tell him so.

"Figured you would say that. What do you propose?"

"Let me sleep on it."

Cate's back is to me when I return to bed, and I curl up right against her shapely figure. Too tired to think, I let all thoughts of the case drift away—secure in the certainty that the murderer of Jim Walker and Mark Romo is now known to me.

48

The next morning, I rise early to the sound of Cate's light snoring before heading to the back deck with coffee cup in hand. The dogs run free across the property, and I savor the sunshine while analyzing the new status quo with a clear head. Scott and Marlon didn't unearth new evidence—only spotted the damning contradiction in the testimony that I twice missed, first on the night of the murder and then yesterday in my office. Marlon's instinct to watch the interviews yet again was predictably sound. Life becomes a whole lot easier all around when you know what you're looking for.

But no jury would convict solely on our evidence—and that pickle consumes my thoughts in the peaceful serenity that is my backyard.

Cate shuffles out just as I finish my second round of coffee. She sits next to me and comments, "I hate death penalty cases." By the looks of her baggy eyes and untamed hair, she had a rough night.

"Did y'all issue a stay?"

"No."

And that's that—the finality of execution once the last appeal runs out. I get up to fetch her some coffee and keep quiet while she nurses it in measured sips. Once the caffeine restores a measure of life to her, I break the bad news.

"We need to ride in separately."

She slumps down—finally rolling her head toward me with a defeated look.

"Seriously?"

After a sad nod, I gather her empty cup for a refill. When I return from the kitchen, she says, "I'm just going to work from home today. I don't have it in me to deal with the traffic. What do you have going on anyway?"

The plan conceived in the light of morning is high-risk, high-reward—rooted in the belief that since we're unlikely to discover any other culpable evidence through the usual channels, we need to force the issue and punch the murderer in the face. But Cate doesn't need to know the dirty details, and I don't give her any, opting instead for the power of metaphor.

"I'm going to ferret out a rat."

* * *

At four in the afternoon—or tea time back in England—the gang is back together one last time in Gustave's mansion. But not a single crumpet or scone is in sight. I stand in the Billiard Room and face down all the suspects. All nine of them are present and accounted for—respectable members of society who are, on the whole, not terribly respectable. Various constituencies of the murder squad stand at various places throughout the room. Scott and J.D. to the right of me. Marlon and Sophie closer to the back.

Getting everyone here one last time was quite the chore. Celeste Wood required a personal call on my end, but at least she didn't force me to buy one of her paintings. The Cains were the hardest to cajole. Gustave—who needed no convincing—put the pressure on them, and the client is always right. Even then, they initially insisted that their new lawyer—Jack Millwood, my old boss in the district attorney's office and now one of the best criminal defense attorneys in town—attend the festivities. When I reminded them that they had the right to remain silent and could simply listen to what I had to say without uttering a word, they relented and Jack Millwood got to stay home.

A tickle of nervousness flutters inside me as I face the room—the same sensation I used to feel right before delivering a closing argument in court. The stakes are just as high. When I finish, the handcuffs are going on the murderer one way or the other, but the hope is that our killer will give us a little extra incriminating material for Barbara to use at the eventual trial. The plan has about as much chance of success as an inside straight draw, but it's the best option on the table.

I take a deep breath and get the ball rolling.

"Make no mistake—the murderer of Jim Walker and Mark Romo is now in this room. And I'm going to tell you who it is."

I scan the crowd—starting with Gustave closest to me on my left and spend a moment on their individual faces. By the looks of them, they're more nervous than I am. Except for the expressionless Mr. Beale. He stands off to my right, near the same Billiard Room door that vexed me until yesterday. I continue.

"Whether you realize it or not, each of you has been under a cloud of suspicion since the case started. Some more than others. For that reason, I think you deserve to hear the truth for yourselves—the truth that ultimately will set all but one of you free."

That's not really true. Everybody needs to be here to load more spring into the trap—to keep the murderer off guard for as long as possible. But there's more. With only a couple of exceptions, the unrepentant people gathered in front of me—murderers or not—deserve a good scorching of their egos. And I intend to give it to them.

"We knew from the night of Jim Walker's murder, of course, that someone at that party killed him—meaning one of you. The weird thing from the beginning was that all of you had a motive, all of you had access to the murder weapon, and most of you had an opportunity. Let's start with Gustave."

The only noise apart from my speaking is a slight breeze from the open windows. But after the invocation of Gustave's name, a stirring of attention and its accompanying sounds percolate toward his general direction near the door to the balcony. Unfazed, Gustave smiles as if the joke is on us. I give him a slight nod, and he returns the favor with a pronounced, prolonged bowing of his head—allowing me a full view of the top of his wild stalk of hair.

"First off, confession time. Right off the bat, Gustave rubbed me the wrong way. My grandfather fought the Nazis at the Battle of the Bulge, and seeing an Adolf Hitler painting on the wall made me disposed to disliking the painting's owner. That got things off to a bad start. The clincher was when we searched the house, and I saw the items he kept squirreled away in his closet—a framed swastika on the wall and a Hitler-signed copy of *Mein Kampf*."

The easiness of Gustave's smile eases a bit when I reveal the secrets contained in his closet—the grin remains but is more forced, strained. *Even bad taste has its limits.* Most of the suspects steal disbelieving glances at Gustave but avert their eyes so as not to stare. Except for Ivanov. His Russian face is hard and full of righteous indignation. I proceed.

"But personal dislike doesn't make a murder case. Facts do. And in my mind, a lot of the facts pointed to Gustave, too. If you pan out far enough, the killing of Jim Walker appears choreographed to be the perfect murder. A party to watch a midnight press conference in China and all the invited guests remarkably have motives to kill the deceased. Right before the killing, everyone is gathered together in the study—the same place from where the murder weapon is taken. An announcement that Walker would be alone in the Billiard Room creates the opening for anyone in the house to commit the crime. Motive, means, and opportunity for each of you—with all the circumstances arranged by Gustave himself. And on top of that litany, he had a motive as old as time. Jim Walker was sleeping with Gustave's wife."

Root's smile is long gone, and the tightening of his eyes gives off the appearance of a snake. I spare a quick peek at Vivian who watches me with somber neutrality. All the other suspects appear to be holding their breath—except for Mr. Beale. His blank stare gives way to something more malevolent. I meet his gaze head-on before resuming my story.

"Throw in the wrinkle of the locked door. Who better to have intimate knowledge of that door than the owner of the house? Add it all up, and the signs pointed straight to Gustave—but for one nagging detail. He had an airtight alibi. His movements after leaving the study with the rest of you and arriving twenty minutes later to find the Billiard Room locked are verified up and down. He first visited his wife in her third-floor bedroom—a fact that Vivian confirms. He then came down stairs to the first floor. From her hiding place in the nearby nook, Jessica Allen witnessed Gustave enter and leave the kitchen. In between, Leo Ivanov and Mr. Beale saw him in the kitchen. From there Gustave went upstairs to meet with Walker and bumped into Vivian who was lurking outside the door to the Billiard Room. Erica Cain was watching the two of them from a chair down the hall. Vivian went back upstairs, and Gustave's key couldn't unlock the door since it was latched from the other side. The murder had already taken place. Conclusion: alone among the people in the house that night, Gustave didn't have the opportunity to kill Jim Walker."

The turn of the narrative in his favor has Root smirking again. He shrugs his shoulders at me in sympathy at my dilemma. I turn to face the others.

"Because of that incontestable fact, I trusted Gustave in a way that I didn't trust the rest of you, despite my acrimony toward him. So after the murder of Mark Romo, I asked him pointblank who he believed to be the killer. He gave me a name."

I pause to let the anticipation and nervousness build among the remaining suspects. When the angst in the room reaches a desirable level, I reveal Gustave's choice.

"Aaron Cain."

49

Aaron Cain swings his head so fast in Gustave's direction that I worry it might snap off. The man of the house remains unfazed—wearing a sneer that dares Cain to make something of it. And why not? What can Aaron do to him? In Gustave Root's world, *"he who has the gold gets to make the rules."*

Receiving the message, Cain keeps his mouth shut. But harder to hide is the royal red flush lighting up his plump cheeks. Erica's manner is wariness—like a cornered viper assessing its options. Even money says she would sell her husband down the river at this precise moment if it would put her totally in the clear. But that offer isn't on the table. I continue.

"Weird thing is—Gustave wasn't the first person to suggest that Aaron killed Walker. Erica was."

I nod to Marlon standing in the back. Armed with his laptop, he presses the magic button, and Erica's voice—captured by the bug I planted in the hall—booms throughout the room.

"I want to ask you something, Aaron. Did you kill Jim? You were up there alone with him while I went to get you that Coke—the Coke you specifically asked me to fetch for you. Did you kill him?"

Cain sits there dumbfounded in tortured disbelief. At last, he feigns a pivot to look at Erica but loses his nerve a quarter of the way there. Instead, he juts his jaw out toward me in what I take to be a gesture of defiance, even though the effect is more cartoonish in quality. No problem. If he wants to lead with his chin, then I'm happy to take another swing.

"That's a strange thing for a wife to say to her husband, but she wasn't the only one to have that thought. Gustave gave me the exact same rationale for suspecting that Aaron was the killer. The reasoning makes a certain amount of sense. Aaron was the last person seen near Jim when the two walked up the staircase together to the second floor. Could be he pretended to be sick to seize the opportunity."

The accused spits out, "Outrageous! I'll sue you!"

My return smile to him is wide. Just because he has the right to remain silent doesn't mean he has to use it, which is kinda how I figured it. Another nod to Marlon, and everyone is again treated to Erica's scolding of her husband.

"You could've swallowed the roofie right after killing Jim to give yourself a perfect alibi."

That leaves a mark. I doubt he's going to sue Erica—except maybe for divorce unless she beats him to it. Out of the corner of my eye, I see Gustave wearing a grin that is full of cheerful scorn. Erica is not so sanguine. Her wariness has graduated to worry. She studies me with anxious focus, waiting for the other shoe to drop. We lock eyes for a few seconds before I shift my attention and direct the next words exclusively to her husband.

"And your motive is as strong as anyone. Blackmail. Jim Walker knew that you and Erica drugged and raped Sylvia Pinker—"

Aaron pounces, "Slander! With witnesses! That's actionable!"

"Not really. Truth is a defense."

"Lies!"

Marlon doesn't even wait for me this time, and we're treated to Erica's recorded voice one last time.

"You're the one who suggested slipping Sylvia a roofie in the first place. You've been full of bad ideas lately."

A deflated Aaron struggles to find his next breath. I stare him down to see if he wants to say anything else in his own defense. He doesn't—or no words come out of his mouth at least. I pick up the slack and address the entire room.

"Damning stuff. And I asked myself—is Aaron my murderer? Gave the question a lot of thought. But I just couldn't make myself believe it. The hang-up wasn't based on the evidence. More like character. These murders took a lot of decisiveness and nerve during moments of high stress. And I've seen how Aaron responds when the tension ratchets up. He turns into a jellyfish. Sure, he can drug a woman to make her unconscious so he can rape her, but a daring act of murder with potential witnesses all over the house? Not likely."

I pause and allow space for Cain to make a counter argument that he does possess the necessary fortitude. But he doesn't pick up the invitation—meaning it's time to move on to the next suspect.

"So, Aaron, despite a number of suggestions that you were the murderer, I concluded that the killings of Jim Walker and Mark Romo required more boldness than you could muster. But you know who doesn't lack the nerve? Your wife."

* * *

An expectant Erica seems ready for her turn. Gustave is a smirker. Aaron huffs and puffs. But Erica tries to keep most of her feelings to herself. Watching me toy with her husband allowed her time to prepare her game face, and her expression toward me now is neutral. I decide to let Aaron do my talking for me and point to Marlon in the back.

"*What about you? Did you murder Jim? You had as much opportunity as I did, hanging out there in the hall right where it happened. How come you didn't see anybody enter that room? Awfully convenient. You're ruthless enough to do it, too. And you sure as hell didn't like him blackmailing us.*"

She's smart enough to have anticipated the airing of that part of the conversation and receives the blow with practiced indifference—at least on the outside. I say, "The wife accuses the husband. The husband accuses the wife. Since they didn't know we were listening to them, the only sure bet is that they didn't conspire together. But which spouse has the better case. What do you think, Mrs. Cain?"

I wonder whether she'll consent to answering the question. Even though she is light years savvier than Aaron and knows better than to talk, silence in the wake of being accused of murder is unnatural—especially in a roomful of people expecting the denial. Self-defense in hard-wired into our DNA. She talks.

"That recording is a violation of my constitutional rights."

"Not really. You were at a party with eighty other people in the house. No reasonable expectation of privacy there. And regardless of the legalities, your husband does raise a compelling point. You were sitting right in the hall. Why didn't you see anybody enter that room?"

"Is that all you have? The speculations of a half-wit who may have committed the murder himself?"

A few seconds pass before Aaron realizes that he is the half-wit in question. He turns in pleading protest to his wife, but her withering glare puts an end to that, leaving him to cross his arms and pout at the injustice of it all. I note to Erica, "You didn't answer the question."

"The answer is obvious. The murderer had already entered and exited the Billiard Room before I sat down in the hall. And we all know whom that points to—despite your observations of my husband's character."

Erica scowls at Aaron and dares him to deny it. He just sits there and takes it, which is probably his smartest move since the beginning of the investigation. I'm far from a relationship expert but seems to me that a couple of divorce lawyers in town are about to get richer. I ask her, "You really think he has it in him to commit murder?"

"Well, I didn't do it, and I know he was getting desperate. He's never handled stress well."

We have cameras running in the room, and I would pay a hundred dollars to see Jack Millwood's reaction upon watching his otherwise sophisticated clients totally ignore his advice not to say a damn word. But if people were smarter, criminal defense lawyers would be out of work. Time to see what she says when simply throwing her husband under the bus isn't an available option.

"Speaking of desperate, you're just as guilty of rape as Aaron is, and I don't see you going to prison without putting up a fight."

Her composure takes a hit with that one. She wrestles with possible answers—the indecision dancing around different parts of her face. If Millwood were here, he would've had the good sense to march both Cains out of the room already. But he isn't, and Erica wants to stand her ground.

She says, "There was no rape. Aaron slipped Sylvia a roofie in her drink, but she saw him do it. She got mad and stormed out. I didn't know anything about it until after the fact. When she threatened to sue, we settled to avoid the publicity."

I laugh out loud and respond, "Lying to law enforcement is a crime, you know. Sylvia woke up naked in bed with no memory of the night before. Gustave told me. Jim Walker told him."

Gustave helpfully chimes in, "That's true." Client or not, Erica shoots daggers of enmity at him all the same. He smirks right back at her. She sets her mouth shut in a tight grimace, and it would require a crowbar to pry it open again. But I'm ready to move on anyway. I address the rest of the group.

"Yes, Aaron and Erica had a strong motive to kill Jim Walker and were close enough to the Billiard Room to raise eyebrows, but the evidence against them is circumstantial and not conclusive. Let's assume for now that someone else is responsible. That would mean that one of you is the killer instead. But who? If Erica is telling the truth, then no one entered the Billiard Room once she sat down in the hall—which indicates that Walker's murder happened right after everyone left the study. What were the rest of you doing during that time? I want to start with Leo."

50

Ivanov grunts—a deep, dismissive, growl-like kind of grunt. He sits there hunched over with arms crossed. The thick wildness of his beard makes reading his expression an exercise in alchemy, but gruff disdain seems to be the flavor. I proceed to educate the group as to Leo's sins.

"Speaking of motives, Ivanov had a strong one, too—although it took me some time to latch on to it. Jim Walker's talent as a lawyer was making problems go away before anyone found out about them—a skill most of you utilized at some point. In the good professor's case, he impregnated one of his students, Carliss Sherman. Not the best look in the #MeToo era. Walker arranged the abortion and the payoff to make Carliss go away."

Leo's mask holds with no visible response to the public airing of his dirty laundry. Jessica Allen is another matter. She mutters, "Gross." Ivanov doesn't move a muscle in her direction—his eyes remaining fixed in place, studying me as if I were across a chessboard from him, waiting for my next move.

"Tacky and distasteful but probably not worth killing over. The story doesn't end there, though. Leo paid $100,000 for Carliss to disappear, except she only saw $25,000 of that amount. Jim Walker pocketed the rest for himself. And Leo found out. Then we found out—after Leo lied to us about it."

Still no reaction from the Russian bear.

"The night of Jim Walker's murder, Leo said something interesting to me. When questioned about whether he had any theories as to the murderer's identity, he said, *'Ask instead who can get out of a room that is locked from the inside. Solve that riddle, and you'll find your killer.'* How true. Leo's a genius—all chess grandmasters are, especially those who are also math professors at Georgia Tech. But maybe he was taunting me about the locked door—a problem that he had solved himself when he killed Walker for cheating him. Then I learned from Jessica Allen that Leo was on the second floor at the time of the murder, just after everyone left the study—before the time Erica sat herself in the hall outside the Billiard Room."

Ivanov shifts a little in his chair but otherwise shows no indication that my words mean anything to him. I'm not surprised. Aaron Cain might be a talker, but Leo is a listener. And one always learns more by listening rather than talking.

"Leo claims that he was using a second-floor bathroom near the back staircase. Could be the truth, but nothing he could prove or I could disprove. And where does that put us?"

I look around, but no one volunteers an answer.

"A stalemate."

* * *

"What about the rest of you? Vivian was standing right outside the Billiard Room trying to eavesdrop when Erica came out into the hall. Odd behavior, certainly. Is she the killer? Or take Celeste—the weakest motive of the bunch but about the only one of you physically capable of escaping by climbing down from the balcony. And if the door to this room can only be unlocked from the inside, then the murderer had to flee the scene from the balcony. Process of elimination, right?"

While Vivian remains stoic at the mention of her name, Celeste allows herself a slight grin. She studies me with inquisitive eyes and not because of my interesting face. Persuading her to attend this gathering wasn't the easiest sell, but if she now second-guesses her decision, she doesn't show it. I shift my attention to the giant off to my right.

"And, of course, there's Mr. Beale. Real name Friedrich Bellingshausen. Someone who fled from Europe after killing a man with his bare hands."

I pause but Beale doesn't bite. Even now, the ocean blue of his irises against the otherwise bright white canvas of his face creates an otherworldly effect. Although he shows no outward reaction to my

245

statement, I swear that lurking behind his hypnotic eyes is a heartfelt desire to strangle me to death.

"Who's a better suspect than someone who has already killed before? And Mr. Beale had as good a reason for murdering Jim Walker as anyone—hatred. The two men loathed one another. Only one problem. Beale has an alibi. Celeste saw him outside—far away from the Billiard Room—walking from the garage to the kitchen shortly after the party broke up in the study. He didn't have time to commit the killing."

Gustave nods in approval but Beale remains expressionless at the good news. I go on.

"Next on the list is Jessica."

A loud snort of derision emanates from Allen on cue, followed by an exaggerated eyeroll. She really is a little snot. Once the tantrum subsides, I pick up the thread.

"Jessica's deep, dark secret is that she bullied a girl into committing suicide in middle school."

"Oh come on! Maybe I wasn't as nice as I should've been, but that girl was messed up long before she met me."

Allen's flailing rationalization of her behavior falls flat, and an awkward silence follows. Even Jessica bristles under the weight of it. I decide to let her squirm for an uncomfortable bit. God knows that I'm no saint, and I even reckon that my adult sins deserve harsher judgment than Allen's adolescent wrongs. But one thing does separate me from her. Remorse.

"Jim Walker knew Jessica's secret and what it could do to her career. He intended to squeeze more money out of her. Did she kill him because of that? On the night of Walker's murder, she lied to me about her whereabouts during the critical time. She claimed to be outside smoking weed. Later she changed her story, saying that she did her weed smoking inside the house, tucked away in the nook near the kitchen."

Upon hearing that Allen smoked marijuana inside his mansion, Gustave sends a hard stare of disapproval directly her way. But Jessica isn't in the mood.

"Don't gawk at me like that, Gustave—unless you want me to post on Instagram about that Nazi flag hanging in your closet. Would you like that? Because I'll do it! For future reference, I'll smoke in your house any damn time I want to."

Even little snots have their good points, and I silently applaud her rebuke. Gustave relents but isn't happy about it. I go on.

"But no one saw Jessica anywhere from the time everyone left the study until Jim was discovered murdered in the Billiard Room—the only person in the house without any corroboration of her where-abouts at all. She also went to the kitchen and poured out a glass of straight whiskey just before Mark Romo died from drinking a poisoned glass of straight whiskey."

Jessica pops up out of her seat like a kangaroo and screams, "You!"

"Just stating facts. What part of what I said is false?"

"People may not have seen me, but I saw them! That proves I'm telling the truth!"

"After lying initially, you mean. But I tend to agree with you, so save your indignation to use on someone who might give a damn and sit back down."

She stands there for a few seconds still steaming but finally gives up the fight and plops into her chair in a defiant gesture of pique.

"The most interesting thing Jessica shared with me, though, wasn't concerning herself but about one of you—her pick for who killed Jim Walker. Any guesses?"

When no one bothers to play along, I go ahead and announce the name.

"Oliver Twist."

Twist's immobile face nevertheless manages to drop upon hearing the news. He spins around toward Jessica and wails, "What?"

An unmoved Allen coldly replies, "Sorry not sorry."

Classic millennial.

51

"When Jessica pointed the finger at you, Oliver, I was just as surprised as you are now. But her reasoning contained a certain unassailable logic. She explained that since the door was locked no one could've killed Walker and gotten back out of the room, which means that Walker couldn't have been dead when you climbed up the ladder. Instead, he must have been alive until you killed him. That's what she told me. And give the devil her due—she had a point."

Twist searches around the room for allies but comes up empty. Jessica—now nauseatingly satisfied with herself—grins at him. I'm starting to think that she tortured animals as a kid.

"Everyone assumed that Jim Walker was dead when Gustave couldn't open the door to the Billiard Room. But maybe Walker was still alive—indeed, based on Jessica's amazing insight, he *had* to be alive. This idea gnawed at me, and I started connecting dots. Oliver slips Walker some Rohypnol to incapacitate him to make the kill easier. Oliver volunteers to climb up the ladder. Alone in the room, Oliver rushes to jam the dagger into Walker's back. Mark Romo climbs up afterward. He sees something off but doesn't realize its significance until later. When Oliver learns of Romo's suspicions, he has no choice but to kill him. A tidy story."

On the verge of tears, Twist bellows, "I didn't do it! Walker was already dead when I reached him! I swear!"

"No one's convicted you yet. A couple of problems exist with the tidy story I just laid out. First, how could you have ever counted on climbing that ladder and having the opportunity to kill Jim Walker in the first place? Second, how did you manage to get him to lock the door to the Billiard Room? Because no one else but Walker could've latched the door from the inside."

"Exactly!"

The hint of a reprieve gives a slight lift to Twist's spirits. Jessica furrows her brow in seeming contemplation of the problems with her theory. The rest of the group maintains a wary disposition, and it's hard to blame them. I've now accused each suspect—with varying degrees of intensity—of being the murderer. And by the looks of the scorecard, I don't have a provable case against anyone. I lay out my dilemma.

"All of these suspects gathered together in this room. Some wrinkle in the evidence that lands on each of you individually. But nothing I could ever make stick in a courtroom. Let me tell you, the whole investigation was frustrating as hell. Want to know how desperate I got? I concocted this theory that all of you were actually in it together—like Agatha Christie's *Murder on the Orient Express*. Well, maybe not all of you. Walker invited Celeste on his own, so I figured she was out. Vivian, too, since Gustave didn't allow her to come down for the party. But the rest of you? You could've conspired together, invented the fiction of the door to the Billiard Room being locked, and portrayed the facts in a way that made the case damn near unsolvable. The perfect crime. And when Romo got wobbly on you—which is easy to believe because he was a wobbly guy—you had to get rid of him, too."

The faces around the room don't look convinced—although some of them do throw suspicious glances around at the other suspects. The tension in the air has been taut ever since I started talking, but everyone hits a wall eventually. And that's the point of this whole exercise. Tired people make mistakes.

"But the Agatha Christie angle hit its own dead end thanks to Aaron and Erica Cain."

Both husband and wife jerk their heads up at being thrown back into the conversation—their apprehension so palpable that I can almost taste it.

"Listening to them talk to each other nixed any thought that they were part of some broader plan to kill Jim Walker. Besides, their eagerness to throw the other spouse under the bus shows the inherent problem with all conspiracies. They never work because every man and woman is always in it for themselves. No way in hell that all of you could've kept something this big on the down low for this long. So I had to let go of my *Murder on the Orient Express* theory. And that put me all the way back to square one."

* * *

"The door. Everything comes back to this door."

I stroll over and slam the door shut. The noise reverberates like an explosion—much louder than the effect I was going for. Even Beale startles a little at the unexpected sound.

"Two locks. The first in the handle that can be opened with a key from the hall. The second a one-sided deadbolt that can only be locked and unlocked on this side of this door. Gustave came up to meet with Jim and found the door locked. He knocked but Walker didn't answer. Gustave used his key in the handle, but the door—latched from the in-side—still wouldn't budge. Something was wrong. You know the rest."

They watch me as I make my way back to the front of the room—near the snooker table upon which Jim Walker took his final breaths.

"How could someone murder Jim, escape, and still latch the door from the inside? Oliver Twist is a magician. He should know how to get around locks. On the night of Walker's murder, I asked him how would one go about getting into and out of a room that is locked from the inside. He gave me what I took to be a smart-ass answer: '*Through the power of illusion, of course.*' There I was searching for a practical solution, and Oliver offers only some magician's platitude nonsense. Got our relationship off to a bad start. Then I asked him how he made Stone Mountain disappear. He gave me more of the same: '*I separated people's perceptions of what they were seeing from the reality—therein, my dear sir, lies the power of illusion.*' I watched that interview again yesterday and just got angrier, convinced that Oliver was hiding something from me."

Twist's stretched out neck visibly gulps. I feel his suffering from across the room and sympathize with it. He's not a bad man—just

250

a vain, weak, and chronically-insecure one. His biggest mistake is wanting something out of life that the world refuses to give him. He'll never be David Copperfield. I gaze at Twist with all the kindness I can spare.

"But now I know the truth, and I owe you an apology, Oliver. You were being straight with me all along. '*I separated people's perceptions of what they were seeing from the reality.*' That sentence wedged itself into my brain and stayed there. Wouldn't let me go. '*I separated people's perceptions of what they were seeing from the reality.*' And then the scales fell from my eyes."

The power of illusion. Make-believe. The key to solving the puzzle of Jim Walker's murder. After a brief pause, I let everyone else in on the secret.

"What if the door wasn't latched from the inside?"

51

Most of the audience stares back at me in confusion. All except for Ivanov—whose mind sees eight moves ahead. His eyes twinkle. He knows. I avoid peering over to my left but feel the rising nervousness from that direction anyway. Or so I imagine.

"Illusion is separating people's perception of what they're seeing from the reality. What did everyone believe that they were witnessing on the night of the murder? Someone inserted a key into a door-knob but claimed that the door still wouldn't open. Loud knocking on the door follows. No one answers. More banging. A mention is made that the door must be latched on the other side. Mark Romo comes by and puts his shoulder into the door to no effect. Concern grows that something terrible has happened to Jim. Things are now chaotic. Quick—get a ladder and enter the Billiard Room through the balcony. The now-panicked guests run off in different directions. Then the bloody discovery—Jim Walker dead with a dagger sticking out of his back. And everyone just assumes that the murderer struck long before the scene outside the locked door."

I turned to face Gustave.

"Suppose instead an alternative reality. Suppose the door to the Billiard Room was locked but only at the doorknob. Only the person holding the key would know that truth. The person with the key claims that the door is latched from the other side, and no one has any reason to believe otherwise. As the partygoers become more alarmed, the person with the key has some ideas. He sends the men to find a ladder and climb up to the room through the balcony. But that will take some time. The person with the key then instructs Erica to alert Celeste that something has happened to Jim. She runs along. And just like that, the person with the key is safely alone. When everyone else scatters to the back of the house, the person with the key remains at the locked door. But not for long. He uses the key to enter the Billiard Room and finds a disoriented Jim Walker—whom he has already drugged. He commits the murder and walks right back out to the hall, locking the doorknob on the way out. When Mark Romo opens the door to the hall after the discovery of Jim's body, the man with the key enters and feigns surprise at the death of his friend—confident that he has committed the flawless crime."

Gustave is better as a director than an actor. His crooked smile—meant to portray a lack of concern—is stressed. He even forces a fake laugh before roaring, "Preposterous!"

Still opting for the bemused persona, he shakes his head back-and-forth in an exaggerated movement. I take comfort in his theatrics. That means he's scared. Good.

"Vivian told us the night of Jim's murder that she thought you had killed him. I should have paid better attention. She also said something horrific yet illuminating: '*Gustave worships his collectibles, and I'm the finest piece in his collection.*' But Jim Walker treated your most prized possession as his own, and that wouldn't do."

"Nonsense! You think I care about monogamy? I am more than willing to share Vivian with my friends—Jim included. I told you the same the night of the murder, and I meant it."

He speaks as if Vivian is not even in the room. She doesn't appear to take any offense. The guess is that words have little impact on her after the other suffering she has been through. But her cautiously optimistic eyes latch on to me in the moment—plainly wondering if I can finish what I've started in making the case against Gustave.

"If he had asked to share her—yes. But Jim didn't ask. He and Vivian became lovers the old-fashioned way—behind your back, making you the cuckold. Gustave Root—the cuckold. And you decided to get even. Everything about this crime was planned to the last detail, including the murder weapon. The dagger with the inscription: '*Meine Ehre Heist Treue.*' Translation: 'My Honor is Loyalty.' In your distorted worldview, Jim Walker acted without honor and earned a date with your Nazi SS-dagger. Just like Himmler intended when he ordered them made."

The "*cuckold*" bit was intended to drag a razor blade across Root's preening ego. It worked. No longer pretending to laugh the whole thing off, he shakes with a wrath that strikes me as powerfully authentic. I keep up the attack.

"You drugged Aaron, sent him upstairs to lie down right next to the Billiard Room, and then told Erica she could work in the hall—right where you wanted her to be. You needed at least one witness to back up your magic trick about the door being locked from the inside. You also set up both Cains as alternative suspects to keep everyone off your scent—and fed them to me with a silver spoon, even telling all about Sylvia Pinker. Brilliant in its way—like a grandmaster moving pieces around a chessboard. And with Aaron drugged with a roofie, Jessica Allen predictably off stoned somewhere, and everyone else headed to the back of the house following your instructions, you had the stage all to yourself. The plan worked, too—until Mark Romo realized that when he ran out of the Billiard Room that night he only unlocked the doorknob, not the dead bolt. He stupidly told you, and you had him poisoned. Isn't that right, Beale?"

I throw a look over at the giant and detect an ever so slight flare-up of his nostrils. Nothing more. On the night of Romo's murder, our bug in the kitchen caught Gustave saying, "*You understand what to do, my friend? ... Excellent.*" The working theory is that Root ordered Beale to poison Romo. But good luck ever proving that.

Gustave moves one step closer to me. I hold my ground. He sticks an angry finger in my direction and spits out, "I don't care how close you are to the Governor. There will be hell to pay for this grotesque charade. You've flailed around this room accusing everyone of murder and all but admitting that you have no idea what happened. You have no evidence of anything! I will personally see to it that you are destroyed."

"Nah. You'll be in prison. I have an unimpeachable witness—you."

* * *

I signal again to Marlon in the back. The sound of his fingers dancing on the laptop keyboard echoes in the silence. When the last button is pushed, the television screen above the fireplace comes alive with a paused picture of Gustave sitting in the ad hoc witness chair on the night of Jim Walker's murder. A confused Root turns to face the screen, and the video of him speaking begins to play.

"Strange that the first thing I noticed upon entering the room was Jim's Rolex—the light hit the gold in a way that created this noticeable glare, and he clutched a red snooker ball in his watch hand."

Just like that, the video clip ends. Gustave's manner transforms from confusion to smugness. He bursts out laughing—a throaty laugh, full of relief. When he finally recovers his wits, he sneers, "That's it? Your grand proof? What a fraud you are!"

He chuckles again for effect. I glance at Oliver Twist and wonder if he has put two and two together yet. Marlon catches my eye, and I give him one final nod. Within seconds, Twist becomes the next face on the television. Root spins back around to the television and says, "What's this?" Twist starts talking on the screen.

"Gustave called down from upstairs and explained the situation. I volunteered to climb into the Billiard Room from the outside balcony. Mr. Beale retrieved the ladder, and I ascended it with great haste. When I entered the room, Mr. Walker was face down on the snooker table with a shiny object of steel protruding out of him. I lifted up his left hand to check his pulse—the way you're supposed to do—and heard nothing. Everything was deathly quiet. The only sound was the thud of a red snooker ball he was holding as it fell onto to the green felt. The impact startled me. I dropped Mr. Walker's hand back down to the table immediately and stepped away. Mark Romo had joined me by that point, and I announced that Mr. Walker was dead. Romo shrieked like a hyena and ran out the door to the hall."

Gustave scratches his head. He faces me again and barks, "So what?"

I study him—wondering if he's playing dumb or really doesn't see it. The guess is the latter.

"Don't you get it? The red snooker ball wasn't in Walker's hand when Romo opened the door to let you in. And yet you told us that Jim was clutching it when you entered. He wasn't. But how could you have known that the red ball was ever in his hand? Only if you were in the room before Oliver Twist climbed up that ladder—when you killed Jim Walker. Credit where credit is due. The red ball was a nice decorative touch. I figure that you staged the display yourself—a little directorial flourish to complete your masterpiece. When you get to prison, you can tell the skinheads all about it. You'd fit right in—although you'll probably have to shave off that trademark hair of yours."

He swivels back to stare at the now-black television screen—his mouth ajar in distorted disbelief, his eyes wide with shock as if he has seen a ghost. He even flashes a desperate glance toward the door to the Billiard Room, but that's a non-starter. I have that direction blocked—with Scott and J.D. providing an extra barrier near the door for good measure.

The whole plan for today rests on what happens next. The red snooker ball is strong evidence but not enough for a slam-dunk conviction, even in Barbara's capable hands. The hope is that a flustered Root will try to talk himself out of trouble and further give the game away. He yells instead.

"Mr. Beale—attack!"

53

With remarkable swiftness for a man his age, Root snatches a snooker cue stick off the wall and swings the heavy end on a direct arc toward my head. Surprise gets the better of me. I do manage to fling up an arm in self-preservation at the last second, deflecting the impact of the strike some but not enough. I fall to the floor—the taste of blood bitter in my mouth—and hazily watch Gustave sprint to the balcony.

The next moments are a blur. Getting handcuffs on an unwilling person is harder than it looks on television. And Mr. Beale is big enough to count as two people. Scott and J.D. struggle to subdue a wild Beale, but the effort doesn't take—despite Scott's repeated punches to the giant's kidneys, blows that would disable just about any other man. J.D.'s head snaps back and smacks hard on the Billiard Room door. He collapses to the ground.

Sophie rushes over with a taser to save the day. The device discharges, and the electrical current shoots straight in Beale's back—to absolutely no effect whatsoever. When Sophie gets closer, Beale unleashes a backwards mule kick that catches her flush in the stomach and sends her flying into the snooker table with a resounding clash. She joins J.D. and me on the floor.

Beale mashes both of his hands against Scott's face—his stringy fingers suctioned with such tightness on the target that Scott's brains might very well ooze out. The giant palms cover both nose and mouth to make breathing impossible. I try to get up to help before my head disabuses me of the notion.

Pulling a gun on an unarmed suspect is usually bad policy but not now. Scott manages to remove his pistol and tries to point it at his attacker's stomach. But he never makes it. His arm goes limp, and the unfired gun bounces to the ground. Sore head or not, I manage to crawl to it. I force myself up on my knees and try to take aim at Beale's skinny legs—afraid to go much higher lest I accidently kill someone else.

Nothing happens when I squeeze the trigger.

After checking to make sure the safety is off, I repeat the action with the same result. Only then do I remember that the pistol is biometric and requires Scott's fingerprints on the handle to shoot. Since the gun is useless as a firing device, I sling it like a frisbee straight at Beale's groin and land a direct blow.

If Beale feels anything, he doesn't show it. Maybe he's a eunuch, too. Fed up with this nonsense, I remove my own revolver—ready to shoot any part of Beale's body that I can hit. But before firing, I spy Marlon grab the giant battle axe off its place on the wall and wield it high in the air. With furious energy, he brings the axe straight down on one of the arms holding Scott's head in place.

One clean cut above the wrist later, Beale's dislodged hand tumbles through the air almost in slow motion before landing on the floor with a dull splat. That, at least, finally gets his attention. He stares down at the severed hand and then at Marlon in stunned astonishment. Beale's working arm still holds Scott hostage and shows no sign of loosening its grip. Marlon raises the axe again on high and brings it down full of fire and brimstone. A split second before impact, Beale releases his hold and withdraws his remaining hand out of the danger zone. The axe slices through clean air before crashing into the floor. Scott slumps down the wall.

Beale stands there with a forlorn expression, staring down at the lost hand. Standing up, I level my revolver straight into his chest and warn, "Be extremely careful, big fella." I don't care if he's literally unarmed. Another aggressive move on his part and he eats a bullet. Instead, he bends over to pick up his hand and heads over to sit down on the snooker table. The room is eerily quiet but not for long. Beale flashes a look of hatred toward Marlon and snarls, *"Fick dich selbst."*

Marlon looks at me and asks, "Did he say what I think he said?"

Some curses transcend all known language barriers—and I remember enough German to know that Beale's suggestion to Marlon is anatomically impossible. Scott mumbles from the floor, "I knew that son of a bitch could talk."

I call for an ambulance. Marlon ties a tourniquet around the stump of Beale's wrist. Beale doesn't resist the administration of the first aid, but a now-recovered Sophie keeps her pistol trained on him just in case. The rest of the guests—no longer murder suspects—remain frozen in their chairs with war-torn expressions. All except for one.

From the outside balcony, Jessica Allen screams her head off.

* * *

Being the closest, I sprint to the balcony, gun out—hoping that my legs hold. When I reach her, she glances up at me and points down to the ground below before rushing back inside.

I came over here today seeking to flush out more evidence against Gustave. Mission accomplished—from a certain point of view. Fleeing from the cops is what prosecutors call, "Consciousness of guilt." And a jury always eats up that kind of soft confession. But this case will never reach trial.

Grace is hard to give in the midst of the battle, and Gustave worked overtime to make it a difficult sell. Looking at him now, I reflect on the tension between mercy and justice—the mercy I'm required to give as a Christ-follower, the justice I'm paid to pursue in the realm of men. Before me lies a certain rough justice, and it's hard to quarrel with the results. But I don't have to feel good about my role as executioner. First Danny Davis getting the needle in his arm, now this.

Face down on the concrete, the distorted body is bent in every direction—an unnatural sight that gave Jessica a damn good reason to beat a hasty retreat. The head took the worst of it—the blood from his cracked skull now trickling like a slow creek into the blue water of the adjacent pool. No way he could ever make that leap—panic overcame reason. Gustave had a plan for everything except for what to do if he got caught.

Scott joins me on the balcony—his face still red with the imprint of Mr. Beale's hands. He scowls down at the dead man and pronounces his own judgment.

"Good. Now he and Hitler can talk about art together in Hell."

I reckon they can. He heads back into the Billiard Room and takes out his handcuffs. I follow him—closing the door behind me. We walk over to Beale, who is sadly staring at his severed appendage—holding it tight with his one good hand. Sophie's gun remains leveled at him—just in case he wants to lose the use of more body parts. I check around and find J.D. recovering his wits in a corner of the room. Looks like we're all going to live.

Scott stands before the sitting giant for a few contemplative seconds before turning toward me with disgusted exasperation. I ask, "What?"

"How the hell am I supposed to cuff him?"

* * *

Hours later, I check on Vivian sitting alone in the study. Gustave's body has been carted away to Alona Mendoza, and Beale is off somewhere getting his hand re-attached to his arm. Hopefully, the guards assigned to watch him have tranquilizer guns with them—the same type that zookeepers use to put elephants to sleep.

If Vivian has displayed a discernable emotion since learning of her husband's death, I've yet to pick up on it. The lid on that box is sealed good and tight. She sits there in the same chair from which Gustave unknowingly implicated himself in Jim Walker's murder.

I try to think of something to say, but she beats me to it and asks, "Is all of this now mine?" Her arms make a circle of the entire room.

"Did he have a will? Any children?"

"Gustave never thought he would die and believed that a will might encourage someone to kill him. As for children—no. No family at all. Except me."

"Well, I'm no probate lawyer, but based on what I remember from taking the bar exam, I would think that everything your husband owned is now yours."

After a contemplative nod, Vivian stands up and retrieves one of Gustave's many daggers from its honored place on a shelf. My eyes narrow and try to work out the possibilities behind her action—hoping like hell she's not intent on hurting herself or me. But I may as well be invisible to her. Weapon grasped tightly in her hand, she marches straight to the Adolph Hitler painting and plunges the dagger right into its heart. Vigorous slashing follows, and it doesn't take long for her to reduce the painting to figurative rubble.

Gustave always did keep his blades extra sharp.

When finished, she stands back and admires her handiwork—as if she had just created a great work of art herself. Only then does Vivian—real name Madeline Moses—turn to look at me.

A smile as wide as a kid on Christmas fills her beautiful face.

EPILOGUE

"You looked good on television."

Cate's talking about my press conference this afternoon. Gustave's leap of death last night cost me another chunk of precious sleep, but the Governor's insistence that I get in front of the public to tout the successful close of a high-profile investigation clinched my cranky mood. He explained that doing so would buy the murder squad some political goodwill to cash in down the road. Figuring that Minton knows best about such matters, I played my part by answering questions and trying to appear appropriately serious. But speaking to the media always makes me twitchy.

"No talk about work."

"Look who's grumpy—can't even pay a man a compliment."

I grunt and take another bite of pizza. As birthday dinners go, tonight's not the most glamorous. No matter. The thought of going out to eat had all the attraction of a root canal. So when Cate asked me what I wanted to do to commemorate the special occasion, I opted for takeout pepperoni pizza—complete with extra pepperoni and cheese to mark the celebration. Not a traditional choice, but it'll do. Besides, finally being free to spend a night at home with my wife feels like a decadent luxury after recent events.

"You ready to open your gift?"

A large, thin rectangular present sits propped against a nearby wall. An excited Cate jumps up and brings it over to me. The look of expectation of her face is so joyous that I am compelled to give her a kiss. She orders me to open the package. I obediently tear off the wrapping paper and stare in amazement once all is revealed.

"You didn't!"

"I did!"

An old saying contends that God and your parents give you the face you're born with, but after age forty you have the face you deserve. The truth of the proverb is not for me to say, but either way the face now before me is mine and mine alone. I study myself as reflected in Celeste Wood's brushstrokes and agree that I possess an interesting face. A lot of years and heartbreak went into the carving of it, but the hint of hope that the portrait conveys gives me confidence about the days ahead—especially with Cate by my side.

"Like it?"

"I love it. But giving me a painting of myself is a weird gift. I'd much rather have a painting of you—preferably a nude."

"Hold that thought."

That gets my attention, and Cate shoots me a little wink as a down payment. I laugh and ask, "Where on earth am I supposed to put it?"

"We'll think of something. Now for your other present."

She grabs my hand and leads me back to our bedroom, pushing me down on the bed. After explaining that she needs to run to the closet for a quick costume change, she orders, "Don't fall asleep!"

"Yes, ma'am."

I make myself comfortable, pleased with this turn of events, wondering what type of lingerie she procured for the celebration. I don't have to wait long.

Cate emerges, and my mouth drops to the floor. I never expected this.

Forget the lingerie. My wife sports something better—her old cheerleading uniform from high school. When we first started dating, I joked with her about dressing up in the outfit for me sometime—never imagining that the fantasy would become a reality.

The clothes are a smidge tight. In a good way. But not being suicidal, I keep that observation to myself. Instead, I say, "Nice pom-poms."

She sticks her tongue out at me and says, "Behave—or I won't do my cheer for you." I decide to behave. When satisfied that I'm on my best behavior, Cate begins a series of cheerleading movements and belts out in a cheerleader's voice—

Has working too hard got you down?
Let me turn that frown around.
I am here to restore your pluck.
Cause I am in the mood to f—

She completes the cheer, and I gasp, "I must be dreaming."
"You want to pinch me to find out?"
That and a lot of other things. Cate performs a few other maneuvers to demonstrate that she still possesses her cheerleading form of decades ago. I watch her and conclude that being forty isn't all that bad.

The End

ACKNOWLEDGEMENTS

My journey as an author would be much more difficult without the help and support of my Dream Team—Nancy Boren, Browning Jeffries, Joanna Apolinsky, and Tom Lacy. The willingness of these talented individuals to sacrifice their free time to read through my rough drafts continues to humble me, and their efforts improve the final product in too many ways to list. I appreciate every one of them from the bottom of my heart.

The dedication of this book reads: "To My Son James—The Best Buddy A Guy Could Ever Have." Holding my son in my arms for the first time changed my life for the better forever. Being around James enriches me every day, and I am so proud of the young man he is becoming. Maybe one day he will make this book into a movie! I love you, James!

As always, the biggest thank you goes to my wife, Carla. Without her love and support, my writing career wouldn't be possible.

Finally, many thanks to my team at Bond Publishing for their encouragement and support—especially Emily.

All mistakes are mine alone.

ABOUT THE AUTHOR

Lance McMillian is a recovering lawyer who gave up the courtroom for the classroom. For over a decade, he has taught Constitutional Law and Torts to future lawyers at Atlanta's John Marshall Law School. Lance is married to Justice Carla Wong McMillian of the Georgia Supreme Court. *To Kill A Lawyer* is the third book in the best-selling Atlanta Murder Squad series.

Lance loves to hear from his readers. You can connect with him via email (lancemcmillian@icloud.com), Twitter (@LanceMcMillian), or Facebook (fb.me/LanceBooks).

If you enjoyed this novel, help other readers discover it by leaving a rating or review on your favorite retailer or Goodreads. Even a very brief review can make a huge difference.

To receive updates on Lance's next book, sign up at
https://bit.ly/2ZIfY6L

Made in the USA
Monee, IL
10 September 2021